MEMORY

MEMORY

CHRISTOPH MARZI

For those who are with us as dreams
C.M.

ORCHARD BOOKS
338 Euston Road, London NW1 3BH
Orchard Books Australia
Level 17/207 Kent Street, Sydney, NSW 2000

First published in Germany in 2011 by Arena Verlag GmbH,
Würzburg under the original title *Memory. Stadt der Träume*
English translation first published in the UK in 2013 by Orchard Books

Published by arrangement with Rights People, London

ISBN (UK edition) 978 1 40832 650 3
ISBN (Australia edition) 978 1 40832 832 3

A CIP catalogue record for this book is available
from the British Library.

1 3 5 7 9 8 6 4 2

Printed in Great Britain

Orchard Books is a division of Hachette Children's Books,
an Hachette UK company.

www.hachette.co.uk

I see thee still! Thou art not dead
Though dust is mingling with thy form
The broken sunbeam hath not shed
The final rainbow on the storm.

– OLD INSCRIPTION AT
HIGHGATE CEMETERY

PROLOGUE

The nameless girl lost her history in the hour before midnight. But that dark, glassy night seemed to be the start of everything. Silence lay like a mist over a landscape that appeared to consist of nothing but shadows and silhouettes. One feeble street light illuminated that forsaken corner which was no place for a girl at that time of night.

She was sitting on a park bench next to the high, blackened iron gate, as motionless as a mannequin. Silvery moonlight, as cold and cutting as the last trace of a memory, flooded the gravestones beyond the paths; a cool wind hustled the brown leaves along the ground and into the entrances to the mausoleums.

Once upon a time, the dead tended to sing at moments like this. The songs they sang were, of course, about life, shimmering-golden and elusive, like a ray of sunshine that ends in a rainbow. And so it was no surprise that the boy, who seemed just as much out of place here as the girl, began to hum a tune. A hesitant introduction to 'Heart of Gold', perhaps.

He suddenly stood still and stopped humming. Nothing but night and silence.

And the girl.

'Hello?' The boy spoke quietly as he cautiously groped his way towards the figure on the bench. He knew that you had to be careful at this hour. You never knew what might happen if you came here at night. The world of the graveyard was just as treacherous as the world beyond the walls.

Quietly he repeated it. 'Hello?'

The girl didn't move.

The stone angels – none weeping – regarded her with cold stares, unmoving.

The mousy-grey boy looked at the girl. In the night, here in the graveyard, he was barely there. Like a poem whose meaning is only clear to one who listens closely. Brown eyes, as big as moons, scrutinised the figure on the bench.

'Are you OK?' He approached her cautiously. His dark brown, curly hair was gleaming in the nocturnal mist. 'What are you doing here?' She had to be about his age, he guessed; perhaps a little bit older. But not old enough to be hanging around here at this time of night. 'Are you asleep?'

Again, no answer. Not surprisingly.

'I know, it was a dumb question,' the boy said, shaking his head.

He took a further step towards her. A breath of cold air caressed him like a whisper. She was still sitting silently and bolt upright on the bench. Once the boy was just a metre or so away from her, he could see that she had her eyes shut. She was breathing peacefully, thank God.

'You're asleep.' He shook his head. 'I don't believe it.' His voice was as thin as the mist. The approaching winter was already in the air. In the night and the early hours of the morning, autumn was giving the world a taste of the months to come.

Slowly, warily, the boy took the last few paces towards the girl and stopped in front of her. He was streaked by light from the street. 'It's cold out here,' he said.

Again, there was no reply.

He looked her up and down. She looked like a normal girl. Or, rather, like a normal *pretty* girl. A normal, pretty girl, sleeping bolt upright on the park bench by the huge gate. At that time of night. She was wearing a coat with a fur collar, a long striped scarf, jeans and black boots.

The boy pondered. The gate that led out into

Swains Lane had been locked for hours – the graveyard was only open to visitors until 4pm. That meant she couldn't possibly have come in through that gate.

And she didn't live in one of the graves around there. She certainly didn't look as if she did, and in any case he'd never seen her here before. Could she be a guest? Someone who'd been invited to the party? No, they'd have told him. Gaskell would have mentioned her, no two ways about it.

So who was she? Who on earth would hang out in a graveyard late on a cold autumn night – and why?

'Hello?' he said once more.

She didn't stir. Her face was covered with tiny freckles. Her smooth, shoulder-length hair shone red like flaming poppies under the streetlight.

'You have to wake up, or you'll freeze to death.'

No, she definitely didn't live here. Her clothes were too new for that. Maybe she was one of those curious people who sometimes hung around graveyards at night, hoping to uncover secrets in the shadows. But she didn't look like one of those types either.

Maybe I should fetch help? the boy wondered, thinking about Gaskell and his illustrious mob partying. Or maybe not. He didn't want to scare her.

And Gaskell and the others might be a bit, let's say, surprised if he arrived with a strange girl.

'You don't need to be afraid,' he said, remembering the dangers that his new friends had often warned him about. Strange creatures who lurked in the night. 'I'm not afraid either.' As he knew, telling a lie out loud could work wonders.

Now of all moments, he remembered Gaskell's stories.

'You are only you, aren't you?' he said. 'Not someone else?'

Again, she made no reply, but carried on sleeping. Well, that answered that one.

'Just you, just a girl, nothing else.' He said it like a mantra that would protect him from horrible surprises if he only believed it hard enough.

Boldly, as if sleepwalking, the boy stretched his hand out towards her. He had to; there was no other way to find out. He touched her cheek with his finger, and it immediately seemed to sink into her warm skin. It was like sticking his finger into a wall of fog, and he jerked his hand away.

But he did at least now know what she was.

Shocked, he whispered, 'But why aren't you cold?' She was like Gaskell, yet completely different. No: she was just *completely* different. She was as warm as if her heart were still beating.

But the two things didn't add up. Who, or what, on earth was she?

The mousy-grey boy reached out his hand to touch her once more.

But just before his fingers could sink into her skin again, she opened her eyes. He could see in the glow of the street light that they were hazel brown and full of fear; as deep as the night and just as beautiful. Shocked, she blinked quickly then screamed loudly – a scream of astonishment and anger combined.

With the boy still staring transfixed at her beautiful eyes, she jumped up, glided past him and, limping slightly, headed off into the shadows beyond the street lights.

'Hey!' was all he managed to say.

Then the bell, together with his racing heart, struck the hour of midnight – to herald the birth of another new story in the old graveyard.

CHAPTER 1

Just hours before, nobody had had the faintest inkling of what would happen that night. Least of all the boy himself.

London was golden and bright, like the autumn that had settled over the city, casting everything in the rusty colours and smoky smells of October. *Autumnland*, Miss Rathbone had called it. In the parks of Kentish Town the trees were losing their leaves, and it looked as if the streets were moving with each gust of wind.

Seventeen-year-old Jude Finney, who didn't look in the slightest bit mousy or grey by daylight – unlike in the moonlight – and who didn't go around humming tunes either, liked autumn just as much as spring. The world was filled with a mysterious magic that wasn't there in summer or winter. He liked it when the air smelled of brown colours and charcoal and roasting chestnuts, and when memories of summer faded away into the morning mist. When it seemed as if the sunshine couldn't decide whether to warm you or leave you to shiver. It somehow all made him feel as if he could breathe more easily and think more clearly.

And the city seemed to move much more slowly than normal.

Now, though, dirty windows lay between him and the air and the life outside. On the desk in front of him lay a weedy pile of blank pages waiting to be filled with his profound thoughts. He had two hours to do this. And while his classmates were busily writing their clever essays on the topic of *The World in Which We Live*, Jude was staring out of the window, thinking about the party that Gaskell had invited him to that night. Jude knew for a fact that it was going to be a fun night, as all Gaskell's neighbours were coming to sing in the moonlight.

However, Mr Ackroyd, head of English at that venerable institution Kentish School, managed to cast a dark cloud over everything that morning. He had stuck a green index card onto the whiteboard. *A Level – General Certificate of Education* was printed on it. Underneath, he had scrawled unnecessarily: *Impromptu Assessment*.

Jude sighed. His brown hair stood out stubbornly – just like the rest of him. As soon as he set foot in school, he felt like an alien. He straightened his black-rimmed glasses and looked once more at the page in front of him. Apart from the circular school stamp in the right-hand corner and the pre-printed lines, it was still as white as snow.

'What I'm expecting from you,' Mr Ackroyd had declared nasally at the start of the lesson, 'is, like everything else in life, essentially quite straightforward. Show me that you can think critically. *The World in Which We Live*. Write down your thoughts, and make me proud to call yourselves my class. Be creative!'

Jude rolled his eyes. He was tired and sleepy, and this boring topic was only making it worse. What could he write about? The wealth of experiences that he'd had in the last few weeks were presumably not what Mr Ackroyd had in mind. He stared at the empty page, and the empty page stared back at him. Jude yawned.

It was just yesterday that everyone had been speculating as to whether Mr Ackroyd was going to set the test this week or next. They'd all agreed that it probably wouldn't be until next week. But this had turned out to be mere wishful thinking.

Jude rubbed his eyes. He fiddled around with his glasses for a while before putting them back on.

He could write about Gaskell and all the other

inhabitants of Highgate Cemetery, and about Miss Rathbone. But he feared that was rather too far removed from what might be expected in an A-level assessment – albeit an *impromptu* one. Mr Ackroyd never called it a 'surprise assessment'; he loved bandying around poncey words.

But as this was the most interesting part of *The World in Which He Lived*, Jude carried on sitting there like a stuffed turkey, just waiting for the time to pass.

Only the clattering of the heating pipes and the occasional moans and groans of the other students broke the brooding silence that lay like a carpet across the classroom. Mr Ackroyd was sitting at the front desk, making notes.

Jude tried out several positions that allowed him to inconspicuously prop his head up in order to prevent it from crashing loudly onto the desk, should he happen to drop off. His thoughts turned to his father and their house in Twisden Road. To the smell of microwave meals. The silence that awaited him there. He looked down again at the empty page in front of him, relishing the whiteness unspoilt even by one stray letter.

The World in Which We Live.

He laid the palm of his hand on the blank page.

The white emptiness was somehow beguiling, rather like Neil Hannon tracks on a Divine Comedy album. Sometimes that's how he felt – like a blank sheet of paper. He almost felt as if he could dive into the silent whiteness that was like a faint rustling in his ears coming from some unknown source.

Jude turned his head sideways and saw Melanie Briggs diligently scribbling away, frowning as she did so. As if it were excessively arduous, pouring out the triviality of her life onto paper – undoubtedly something involving substantial amounts of make-up and boys on motorbikes. Just behind her was Herbert Sorkin, who was laboriously forcing out sentences that were presumably just as profound as the chants that he bellowed when Manchester United were on TV.

'You're not writing anything.'

Jude looked up. Mr Ackroyd had appeared behind him. *Crept up* behind him would be more accurate. He must have noticed the empty sheets.

'I've finished.' Jude looked innocent as he held up the pages.

'Impressive.' Mr Ackroyd's expression betrayed no emotion as he looked down at Jude. 'Very impressive.' The corners of his mouth twitched downwards disapprovingly. 'You've not put anything down on paper.'

'It's all there,' Jude replied.

The other students cast furtive glances his way. The room crackled with secret anticipation. At last: one of those rare moments when something was going to happen during an impromptu assessment.

'So you're striking another of your attitudes, are you?' Another one of those patronising expressions that made Mr Ackroyd look even more stupid in Jude's eyes. He certainly wasn't going to impress Jude that way. 'And you can put a stop to that facetious behaviour.' Mr Ackroyd liked students who did exactly as he asked, and Jude Finney wasn't among them.

'I don't see what your problem is.'

One thing could be said for Mr Ackroyd: he never lost it. He never even raised his voice. That wasn't his way. 'This,' he said, tight-lipped, 'is an important assessment. The result will make up part of your final mark.' He tried to keep his voice as low as possible in order not to disturb the rest of the class unnecessarily, but loud enough for them all to hear what he was saying.

'I know.'

'Then you need to make more of an effort.'

'I've been thinking.' Jude was quite serious. 'And I wrote down my thoughts.'

Little red veins stood out on Mr Ackroyd's cheeks. 'But you haven't written anything down.' He emphasised each word.

'An empty page can say something too. You just have to look at it for long enough.'

'I advise you not to make fun of me.'

Jude looked at him earnestly. 'I'm not making fun of you,' he said calmly. Something about the look in his eyes seemed to convince the teacher that he was telling the truth. Jude really did not intend to make fun of his teacher.

'Hmm.' Mr Ackroyd seemed to be thinking again. 'Well, I refuse to accept blank pages for any reason whatsoever.' He sighed. 'Is that clear enough, Jude Finney? No blank pages!'

'But—'

Mr Ackroyd interrupted him. 'The essay topic,' he said through gritted teeth, 'is *The World in Which We Live*.' He glared at the boy. 'We talked about it in the lesson.' He now turned to the rest of the class, who were silently taking in the whole performance. 'I want you to deal critically with a serious topic. Nothing more, nothing less.' He turned his attention to Jude once more.

'But that's what I did.' The boy looked down at his piece of paper. He hadn't expected Mr Ackroyd to understand. Just like the other students – or so he deduced from the looks they were giving him. But they were glad of the diversion. Jude ought to have known. That was precisely the problem with school. Nobody understood you. And Mr Ackroyd, an English teacher, someone who claimed to understand the thoughts of all the greatest writers and poets, ought to be better able to grasp unusual ideas.

The World in Which We Live.

Oh, great.

'You will write something!' Mr Ackroyd commanded. 'Do you hear me, Jude Finney?'

Jude stared at the blank sheet. *The dead are far more alive than my English teacher*, he thought. 'OK,' he said. He adopted a thoughtful countenance and looked down again.

He was of course well aware that he couldn't write weird-sounding sentences like *I know a vixen who's almost forgotten how to be a vixen*, or *Last week, I met a boxer with a lion on his grave.*

'OK,' he muttered, his voice quieter this time and noticeably irritated.

Unimpressed, Mr Ackroyd remained where he was for a moment longer. Then he started making his way down the aisles to make sure that Jude was the only *singular* and *obstreperous* student.

Jude gazed longingly outside at the endless greenery of Hampstead Heath. If only he were there. His classmates were presumably all thinking about exam results, new clothes, smartphones, money.

The World in Which We Live.

'Just write something. Anything,' Mike whispered from the desk next to him. Mike spent his whole life outside school on Facebook, chatting with other reptile fans about the lifestyles and illnesses of caymans, snakes and lizards. And despite this unusual hobby, his life was still more normal than Jude's had been recently.

'Yeah, yeah,' Jude merely mumbled. Then he drew a question mark in the middle of the page. Not a particularly big one: just a question mark.

Mike saw it and rolled his eyes before turning back to his own work.

Jude looked at his question mark and couldn't help grinning with satisfaction. Yes, that was it. Better than a blank sheet, and better than any number of words.

?

Nothing else.

?

Perfect.

He stood up and, followed by the others' curious

gazes, went to the front. Mr Ackroyd's eyes narrowed as he approached the desk. Jude handed the sheet to him.

The teacher took the sheet and looked at the question mark. 'We need to talk.' That was all he said. 'In my office, later.' With a curt nod, he sent Jude back to his place. And as Jude sat down again, Mr Ackroyd pulled out a biro and covered the almost empty page with comments.

Jude looked out of the window again at the park, where the bare trees were reaching up into the autumn sky.

Jude was well aware of the curious looks that followed him as he trailed out of the classroom behind Mr Ackroyd. Jude wasn't particularly disliked, not least as there was nothing particularly dislikeable about him. But nor was he a student who would be particularly missed if he suddenly wasn't there. He was all right, and he thought his classmates were all right. No more, no less.

As he followed his English teacher down the corridors and into the stairwell, Jude was aware of the strange sound that Mr Ackroyd's rubber-soled shoes made, and the barely audible noise of his own red and green tartan Converses. Mr Ackroyd, who didn't say a single word, was evidently relishing his own silence, which lent the situation an air of drama.

The English department staff room smelled of warm photocopiers and coffee. Miss Reng, who taught the lower years, was sitting at her desk. Irritated, she looked up from her marking as they came in. A steaming cup of coffee was on the desk beside her.

'I don't understand you,' Mr Ackroyd began in a tone that Jude found suspiciously amiable. 'You're articulate and intelligent.' He was holding Jude's work. 'And then you come out with something like this.' He leant on his desk and sighed again. 'No, I just don't understand you.'

'I mostly don't understand myself either,' Jude replied. He had been parked in the swivel chair in front of the desk like a defendant.

'You surely want to pass your A Levels.'

Jude nodded.

'And you're aware that the impromptu assessment result counts towards your final mark.'

'Yes, Mr Ackroyd.'

'So why did you hand in a blank page?'

'It isn't blank.'

'It's as good as blank.'

'The question mark means something.'

Mr Ackroyd was starting to lose patience. 'So what's it supposed to mean?'

Jude wondered whether he should explain, but decided against it. He had a feeling that any explanation would land him in even more trouble.

'Everyone else' – Mr Ackroyd tapped the pile of assessment papers on the desk in front of him – 'made an effort and wrote long essays on this topic.' He paused. '*The World in Which We Live*.' Another pause. 'That's the world in which you live, Jude. Don't you ever think about it? About yourself? Your life? Your future?'

Jude shook his head.

'I think I need a word with your father.'

Jude was aware of his fingers tightening around the arms of the chair. 'He isn't here.'

'What do you mean, he isn't here?'

'He's away for two days.'

'Oh yes?'

Jude nodded. 'Yes. Honest. He's in charge of some kind of project.'

'*Some kind of* project?' Mr Ackroyd gazed at him suspiciously.

'Yes, for the Environment Agency. Something to do with a pond.' That was true: his father was a hydrologist for the Environment Agency in Southwark.

'Aha. An expert in water.'

'He's involved somehow with regenerating the Rhodes Lodge Lake in Manchester.' This was what interested Jude's father: the chemical and biological make-up of waters; the forms and shapes that rivers could take in different landscapes.

'When's he coming back?'

'On Friday. But I don't imagine he'll be back until late.'

Mr Ackroyd thought for a moment. 'Right. Then I'd like to speak to him when he gets back home.'

'I'll let him know.'

'I'll write to him too,' said the teacher. 'Just to be on the safe side.'

Jude nodded.

'You may go now.' And with this, Jude was dismissed and returned to lessons.

Four o'clock found Jude wandering homewards. Twisden Road was an ordinary street of the type that might be found in any English suburb. To either side of the road were small Victorian terraced houses, all looking alike with their tiny front yards and letter boxes. On the corner of York Rise and Chetwynd Road was a corner shop that stocked pretty much everything – without the fifteen-minute Tesco queues. Jude called in and bought a few groceries on his way home.

He didn't find it hard to cast all thoughts about school from his mind. The day was so wonderfully golden, pure autumn-land, and he thought about the party to come. Gaskell was counting on him bringing his guitar. He decided to have a lie-down as soon as he got home in order to be fit for the night.

Moments later, he was standing outside number 288, Twisden Road. The letter box was rusty, and the blue paint was peeling off the front door. He fumbled around in his pocket for the key, opened the door and went in.

'Anyone there?' he asked into the silence, as if to make sure that his father really was away. He lugged the shopping bags into the kitchen and put the milk and other perishables in the fridge. Then he switched on the TV next to the microwave, sat down, ate two slices of cheese on toast and watched a repeat of *Primeval*. Then he fell asleep.

When he woke up with his head resting on his arms, it was already five o'clock. He lolled about, thinking wearily about the homework that was due the following day. He sighed. Then he went into the bathroom, put his music on very loud and sang along as he showered. Finally he wandered aimlessly around the house.

His father's study was, as always, tidy. On his desk were neat heaps of carefully filed documents. The pictures on the wall were all landscapes of rivers, mostly views of the Thames.

Nowhere was there a picture of Jude's mother. How he wished he could have seen her face, even just once. He wondered whether he looked like her. That was one of the many question marks etched in dark ink onto the white pages of his life. In fact, it was the very biggest. His father never spoke about Jude's mother. And Jude had stopped asking questions that were never answered.

He left his father's study and went into his own room on the top floor. The pitched roof made the room feel like a cosy cave. Clothes, books, CD cases and all sorts of other stuff lay strewn between the wardrobe and the bed. The walls were decorated with posters of Lou Reed, Scouting for Girls, Quentin Gaskell and Thea Gilmore.

Jude felt good here. This was his little empire. But...

'*Will you* ever *learn to tidy up after yourself?*'

Even when George Finney wasn't there, his voice echoed through the house.

'I—'

'How do you ever hope to achieve anything? For crying out loud: when are you finally going to get a grip?'

Jude knew that his father didn't really expect an answer. He just wanted him to listen. Whenever it fell quiet in his son's room, George Finney would smell a rat. Sometimes he burst in without knocking. So far as he was concerned, there were two possibilities: either Jude was doing something that had nothing at all to do with school, or he was lying on his bed, possibly even asleep. At any rate, he wasn't *doing his job*.

'School is your job,' George Finney never tired of preaching.

Jude would then trot out some spurious excuse. 'I was about to start my homework.' 'We had a test, and I'm completely exhausted.' Or: 'I've already finished.' Though this latter excuse didn't cut any ice so far as his father was concerned. In his view, you had never finished with the truly important things, and anyone who neglected his duties would find his pocket money docked.

They were always arguing, as was presumably quite normal. George Finney was only relaxed when he was cooking – particularly Indian food, his speciality. Then he seemed to be completely in his element, like a totally different person.

'We don't talk enough,' he had said to Jude in one of these strange moments.

'You're often away.' Jude loved the aromas of tandoori, garam masala, curry and cumin powder.

'That's the way it is when you're grown up.' There had been a trace of regret in his father's voice, but he hadn't elaborated on it. There were some things that his son knew nothing about, and which his father wanted to keep to himself.

When they ate together in the little kitchen, the relationship between father and son was almost harmonious. Then it was as if dhal makhani and chana masala, George Finney's favourite dishes, exerted some secret magic that brought them together. And which made the unanswered questions that stood between them seem unimportant.

'India,' Jude's father said at one of these strange moments, 'is like a fairy tale.' Jude knew that his father had worked for a long time in India. But that was before he was born. When his father was in the right kind of mood, he would talk about India's sacred rivers, the mysterious rites, the exotic animals and the exuberant life in the over-populated cities.

Jude looked out of the window. Evening was slowly drawing in.

At last.

When his father was away, Jude spent most of his spare time playing the guitar. Or he would sleep or read comics, waiting for the day to end. And he would think a lot – about himself, about the world, about the graveyard and the things that he knew nothing about and was so desperate to find out about, and which had been so neatly symbolised by that question mark.

In short: leaving aside the business with Gaskell and co., Jude Finney was a perfectly normal teenager.

More than thirty years ago, Quentin Gaskell had landed a legendary chart-topper with 'My Perfect Little Daylight'. And Jude was invited to one of his no less legendary parties this very evening.

Just before eight, he got ready for Highgate Cemetery. When his father was away – as he was today – his nocturnal escapades presented no problem. But when his father was at home, as was unfortunately more often the case, Jude used Miss Rathbone as his excuse; Miss Rathbone was, so to speak, his alibi. She too, of course, was invited to the party along with everyone else. But Miss Rathbone was a whole other story…

Jude picked up his guitar case, slung it over his shoulder and set off.

Kentish Town was quiet in the evenings. It was far removed from the bright lights of central London, and life had a different rhythm here. He went on foot to Swains Lane and as he passed Miss Rathbone's house, he noticed that all the lights were off. She must already be in Egyptian Avenue, where Gaskell had his abode.

By now, Jude could have made his way into the graveyard – he knew a way through a hole in the wall – and to Gaskell's grave with his eyes shut. The other partygoers were already inside. As soon as he arrived, Jude unpacked his guitar and played songs by Neil Hannon, Justin Sullivan and The Beatles, accompanied by Miss Rathbone's fabulous foxy voice which beguiled everyone. Even Quentin Gaskell was enchanted, nodding his head in time to the rhythm. Then they brought out the CD collection and an old CD player, and the walls shook to the sound of the rock and roll era's 'Greatest Hits'.

At some point, Jude became desperate for a pee and went outside. He found himself a place where the gardeners kept their tools, well away from the avenue.

Just as he was ambling back to the party, he saw the girl on the bench by the northern gate.

And that was the moment when the story with the girl began...

'Don't run away!' he called after her as the girl disappeared into the shadows. He made no attempt to follow her. He knew there was no point. He was still wondering why on earth she had felt so incredibly warm.

The girl stopped. She had run all the way along a row of graves and statuary and had reached the hedge by the wall further back.

She turned slowly to look at him. 'Who are you?' she asked.

'I'm Jude,' he said. 'And who are you?'

She didn't reply. She blinked, and pale moonlight shimmered in her eyes.

'What are you doing here?'

'I could ask you the same.' Her voice was mysterious, like an unfinished melody. Its rhythm was that of leaves rustling in the wind. She came closer and looked at him cautiously. 'I don't know how I got here.' She looked around, evidently unsettled by what she saw. 'Where am I, anyway?'

In a place that, only six months ago, I'd never have believed even existed, thought Jude. *Or at any rate not like this. No, definitely not like this. Not so alive and so mysterious and so full of the stories that its inhabitants were so keen to tell.*

'You're in Highgate Cemetery,' he said. He was standing stock-still on the path.

'In the graveyard?'

'Looks that way to me.'

She came towards him, slowly. She moved like a marionette, awkwardly and carefully. 'What am I doing here?' She had a faint trace of a limp.

He shrugged. 'No idea.' How should he know?

'And what are you doing here?'

Jude decided to come straight out with the truth. 'I was at a party,' he said. 'Or rather, I was just going back to the party.' She really didn't need to know about the pee.

'A party? In the graveyard?' She looked at him sceptically.

Jude didn't see why she needed to look like that. 'You've still not told me who *you* are and what you're doing here.'

She took a deep breath. 'I...I don't know.' She swayed slightly, as if she were dizzy.

'So you've forgotten your name.'

She nodded.

'And you've got no idea how you came to be sitting on that bench.'

She nodded again.

'Maybe I can help you,' he said.

'How?' She emerged from the gravestones and stood on the path. Jude could see her face better in the glow of the street lamps. He was still transfixed by her hazel eyes.

'I know some people here,' he said.

'The people at the party?'

'Yes.'

'And you really think they can help me?'

'Maybe. They're nice. They'll definitely try.'

'Who are they?'

'They live here.'

She was now standing right in front of him. 'Can I trust you?' The light was caught in her hair. She looked like a normal girl. She could easily have been a girl from his school.

'I'm a completely normal boy,' he said, as if that were reason enough for her to trust him.

'Great. And I'm just a girl.' Her tone was slightly mocking.

'I really am harmless.'

'That's what everyone says.'

'I'm not everyone.'

'Some comfort.'

'You're like them,' Jude suddenly said.

'Like who? Your party friends?'

He nodded. And now Jude knew that the moment had come to tell her about the ghosts.

Sometimes strange things happen to you that nobody can really explain. The business with the ghosts had begun six months ago with Miss Rathbone and an accident in Hampstead. Until then Jude had been firmly convinced that he was a completely ordinary boy. He did find some things strange and slightly troubling – but he was no less ordinary for that.

Whatever the case, what was done couldn't be undone.

It was springtime, and Jude was passing a crossroads where there had just been an accident. Before that, he'd been over in Hampstead. He, Benny Andrews and Joolz Ellison had spent the whole afternoon rehearsing New Model Army ballads at Parliament Hill Fields.

On the way back to Hampstead Heath station, he chanced upon the accident. A businessman had been hit by a motorbike on the corner of Parliament Hill and Nassington Road. The motorcyclist seemed to have been injured too. Jude hadn't actually witnessed the accident, but he had heard the noise of a squealing engine and a loud crunching sound in the distance. Other passers-by were also hurrying over to the scene, and he saw that a police car was already in the middle of the road, with two policemen bustling to and fro.

The motorbike was lying in front of a red Mini with a badly dented side, and a crowd of curious onlookers had gathered around the Mini and the motorbike.

The businessman in the blue pinstriped suit, however, lay all alone on the other side of the road, where nobody seemed to really notice him. Jude hadn't seen how the man had ended up there, yet he stopped immediately, put his guitar case down and knelt down by the man, who was still young and seemed flustered but unhurt.

'Don't move,' Jude said.

The young man looked at him. 'I was run over,' he said. He shook his head as if he couldn't get his mind round it.

'I can hear the ambulance.' The Royal Free Hospital wasn't far from Hampstead Heath station. 'Help's coming soon.'

'I'm so cold.' The sun was shining onto the man's face. It was a warm spring day.

Jude loosened the man's tie. 'Just lie still.' He was regretting never having done a first-aid course. But in TV programmes like *ER* or *House*, they always told injured people to lie still. It seemed to Jude to be good advice; at any rate, it couldn't do any harm.

'I can't feel my legs,' the man said. His eyes were wide with fear.

Jude touched his hand. It was freezing cold.

'It's my girlfriend's birthday today.' The young man sounded desperate now. 'She's called Amy.'

Jude took a long look at him. 'You'll see her later. You'll see.'

'I don't know. I was run over.'

'Just lie still.'

'I didn't see the stupid motorbike coming.' The man was coughing, shivering.

On the other side of the road, a crowd appeared to be gathering around the motorcyclist.

'Excuse me?' Jude called over to the policemen.

One of them looked across at him. 'What is it?'

'Can't you see?' The policeman's gormlessness was infuriating. There was something strange about the whole business. The sun was high in the sky; Jude felt hot.

'Go home!' the policeman merely called to him before turning and being swallowed up by the crowd.

An ambulance came along with lights flashing and sirens wailing. Paramedics jumped out; everything was chaos.

'Is he crazy?' Jude cursed. Hadn't the policeman seen that there was another casualty? What was going on?

Suddenly the man groaned loudly. He was staring at the other side of the road, and his eyes were wide with horror.

'Hey!' Jude called across the road once more, but nobody paid any attention. He turned back to the man – but the man had vanished.

Jude almost yelled with shock. He had only looked away for a fraction of a second. He could have sworn that the man had been lying there before; now he was gone. Just like that. He looked across the road again and saw the motorcyclist, who was now standing at the edge of the crowd being interrogated by the policeman.

Jude was baffled. What on earth was going on here? The motorcyclist was evidently unhurt and the man who had just been lying there on the ground talking about his girlfriend had vanished into thin air. He shook his head in disbelief.

All of a sudden, as though out of thin air, an elderly woman was standing next to him. 'He's fine,' she said. Jude stared at her in astonishment. She looked somehow grey and very dusty, with straw-coloured strands in her hair. 'Look!'

Dazed, Jude followed her outstretched finger and and saw the paramedics carrying someone to the ambulance on a stretcher. It was the man who had just been lying on the ground in front of him. And as a completely baffled part of him was still wondering how on earth the man in the suit had got there, another part of him, deep inside, was already getting a vague sense of what had happened. Even if he didn't really want to believe it because it was so completely crazy.

'I'm Ayelet Rathbone,' the woman said. She was still standing beside him.

'Er...Jude Finney. What happened?' Jude asked. His voice was catching in his throat, and he could see the air shimmering before his eyes.

'You just saw a ghost,' the stranger said. She reminded Jude of a vixen, and he wondered whether he had misheard her. She didn't repeat herself, but stood beside him expectantly, waiting until Jude had finally got his mind around the fact that he had seen the ghost of a man whose living body was just now being stretchered into an ambulance.

'The others couldn't see it,' Miss Rathbone explained. 'Just you.'

Jude gasped. No. This was impossible. It couldn't be real. He looked down at the pavement, taking in all the tiny details – the bumps and discolorations – that he didn't normally notice. He bent down and touched his guitar, as if to reassure himself that this at least was real.

'So he was lying on the other side of the road the whole time?' His voice didn't sound like his own. It seemed to be coming from far away.

'Yes. It was just his dream of life that was hurled across here.'

Jude stood up again. 'And he's still alive.'

Miss Rathbone nodded. 'He's very lucky.' She looked satisfied. 'He doesn't have to dream about life any more, because he survived.'

Jude felt his legs starting to tremble.

'You *did* see him,' the woman said insistently. 'And that *is* real.'

'But...' His head was full of questions, but he found the lady so completely beyond the pale that he couldn't manage to formulate even one.

'Do you know what this means?'

Jude shook his head. But he knew full well that this stranger was telling the truth. It was quite clear. It was in her gleaming eyes, dark and wild, like those of a vixen blinking cautiously into the daylight.

'You can see them,' he heard this Miss Rathbone saying. And at that moment, Jude's life changed forever.

'You mean you can see ghosts?' the girl asked. She seemed both amused and unsettled.

'Yes.' Jude still marvelled at the naturalness with which he said it.

Silence.

'You believe in ghosts?' She shook her head in disbelief.

'It's not that I believe in them,' Jude tried to explain. 'It's just that I can see them. And I can speak to them.'

She mulled this over. 'And you think I'm one of them? A ghost?'

'I don't know.'

This time she laughed, but she didn't sound either amused or relieved. 'So aren't I alive any more?' She paused. 'I feel alive.'

'So do they all.' Jude cursed himself for saying that. It wasn't very nice of him, even if it was true.

'Stop taking the mickey,' she snapped.

'I'm not.'

Angrily she kicked a stone into the undergrowth. 'So why can I do that, then?'

'Why shouldn't you be able to do that?'

'Because I'm a ghost?'

'Ghosts can do that stuff.'

She glared at him and put her hands on her hips.

He shrugged. 'We ought to go and find the others.'

'You mean the other ghosts?' Her eyes blazed again.

'It's complicated,' he replied, shrugging again. It was in fact quite simple.

Fear and anger were doing battle in her expression. Neither one had the upper hand. 'You're serious. You're really trying to tell me that I'm a ghost.'

'Yes...no. On the one hand, yes...but on the other hand, you feel warm.'

'What's that supposed to mean?' She put her head slightly on one side so that her hair dangled in front of her face.

'I didn't know whether you were, well, um, dead. You were sitting there on the bench and...' He grimaced and then spat it out. 'I touched you. Very briefly.'

She stared at him. 'Yes, and gave me one heck of a fright.'

'I'm sorry.'

'It's fine.' She seemed to have calmed down slightly.

Jude didn't know how to explain it to her. 'You felt warm. The others feel cold.'

'The ghosts?'

He nodded. 'They're cold. Like fog, only more alive.'

'Right.'

Jude wasn't sure whether she was taking him seriously. 'Look, I know how this must all sound to you.'

'Oh yeah?' she retorted. 'Are you sure about that?'

He nodded. 'Between us we could find out what's happened. But if not, then the least I can do is take you to the nearest bus stop.'

She sighed resignedly. 'And then what?' She suddenly looked terribly sad and scared. 'I've no idea where I belong. For God's sake, I don't even know my name.'

Jude took a step towards her. This time she didn't run away. 'Can I show you something?'

As he took her hand, she put her head on one side again. Then she saw it. Her hand seemed literally to sink into his. It looked as if her hand turned transparent the moment it touched Jude's. But all the same, her hand was still lying in his – just indistinct and foggy. And he could feel it, albeit only just.

She whipped her hand away as if she had burnt it. 'What's all that about?' she said briskly yet anxiously, as if what she had just seen were his fault. 'God, that was really weird.' Her eyes filled with tears. She suddenly looked upset and completely rattled.

'Just come with me,' Jude said without touching her again. Silently, she followed him. That was at least a start.

The silent magic of the graveyard night enveloped them. Jude took a narrow, winding path that led up a wooded hill. After a while the weather-beaten gravestones jutting up out of the darkness like crooked teeth gave way to magnificent mausoleums with statues reminiscent of Egypt, including gods with feline faces and owl-like heads on muscular bodies.

'Nearly there,' Jude said every time he changed direction.

The nameless girl, sensing the peace and isolation of the place, imbibed its aura. 'It's fabulous,' she whispered.

The lofty monuments cast long shadows in the

moonlight. Several of them were crowned with mute, oversized heads depicting the dead, some of whom Jude had already met. Immortalised in speckled basalt were the faces of aristocrats with bushy whiskers and high collars – presumably the height of fashion a century ago – their severe expressions chiselled in grey stone, as cantankerous as their ghosts who rarely left their graves.

Leaves were whirling around their feet, rustling and scurrying like the creatures that dwelt in them.

'You said there was a party going on here.'

'Over there.' Jude gesticulated to her to follow him.

There were headless angels on high plinths, and mighty lion sculptures pawing lambs to the ground. There were eagles, fiercely spreading their stone wings; pale marble maidens in dying poses were draped across graves. Jude knew most of the people who lived here. They weren't all as chatty as Gaskell, but he got along perfectly well with the majority of them.

They passed a crescent-shaped group of elegant graves with a large cedar tree in front of it. 'This is it,' he said. 'Egyptian Avenue.'

'Looks like some venerable old town.'

'Yes, and lots of people live here.'

Twisting passageways and steps and squares led off the avenue. Proud sphinxes kept watch over family graves decorated with columns.

'Like palaces in a country where the sun never rises,' the girl marvelled.

Then they heard it. The silence was penetrated by a melody that became louder and louder as they neared the Victorian graves. Someone was playing the guitar; countless voices were singing along. Jude knew that song. It was 'Yesterday Man'. The party was still in full flow.

CHAPTER 2

The graves looked like Egyptian burial sites, commanding reverence and respect. The age that they harked back to had left its traces in the furrowed stone, as though determined not to be forgotten. The moonlight was caught by the mixture of moss, wildly proliferating ivy, and other plants that seemed to be pulling the walls back down into the earth.

The final bars of 'Yesterday Man' were dying away in the entrance to one particular tomb, which enveloped them like a yawning chasm as Jude shut the cast-iron gate behind them. The start of 'Hang on Sloopy' greeted them from the damp, musty darkness. It had to be: it was Gaskell's party, after all.

Despite the darkness, the girl followed the mousy-grey boy sure-footedly down the steps. The music showed them the way. 'Hang on Sloopy' seemed somehow inappropriate for a place like this – but then again, maybe not. Halfway down, they spotted a glimmer of light filled with dancing shadows and merry voices.

Just a few more steps to go.

'We're there,' Jude announced.

The girl followed him into the tomb. Although the place seemed strange to her – scary, even – she felt reassured by the way her companion was so at ease, as if completely at home in this weird world.

'Don't worry – they'll be nice to you,' he said, as if he could sense her apprehensiveness.

'But they don't know me.'

'Doesn't matter. They're an accepting bunch.' *Well, most of them are*, he thought.

The atmosphere was the same merry one as when Jude had gone out half an hour before for his breather. The illustrious company mostly consisted of the inhabitants of neighbouring graves and tombs. Alongside them were a couple of others from the other part of the graveyard (the part on the other side of Swains Lane, where everything was a bit more modern and well-kept and *different* from here).

Although the wind was chilly outside, it wasn't cold in the tomb. On the contrary, it felt cosy and rather more reminiscent of a Victorian salon than a place intended for eternal rest. The space was filled with old furniture, the walls decorated with posters and wall hangings. Candlelight cast a warm glow on the ceiling. On the coffin was a portable hi-fi, the source of the music.

The twenty or so guests who had gathered in the tomb included a whole variety of people. One of them, Sir Harvey Humblethwaite, was dancing with Tilda Murray. Both had perfected their hip-thrusts – rather surprising in the case of Sir Harvey, who had been run through by a Turkish scimitar during the Battle of Gallipoli in the First World War, but less so in the case of Tilda Murray, a 1960s flower child who never stopped telling everyone how cigarettes and drugs had brought her there. A slightly squiffy Nettie Palliser, a former writer whose books had fallen into obscurity when she died, was chatting with Alfred Lamert, one of Charles Dickens's younger brothers, while Miss Rathbone had spent a solid hour locked in conversation with Carl Mayer about the silent film era in Berlin.

'Are they all ghosts?' the girl asked hesitantly.

Jude nodded.

The other guests – a taciturn man wearing a shabby, threadbare admiral's uniform, two women in long old-fashioned dresses, a man who looked like a black and white caricature of a professor from an adventure film, and a collection of other people whose clothes offered a comprehensive overview of the various fashions of the last hundred years – paused only briefly as Jude entered the tomb with the girl.

'And you really think one of them can help me?'

Jude nodded. 'Hang on, and I'll introduce you to a couple of them.'

Gaskell, however, got in there first. As he would. 'I see you've brought your girlfriend, Jude.' Gaskell pushed his way through the dancers and came over to them. He was twitching his head around like a bird – it was one of his quirks – and throwing back his sparse blond hair. 'And at such a late hour and quite out of the blue. What a surprise!' The rock star was wearing a dark blue shiny suit and a brightly coloured shirt with a psychedelic pattern. A deep red silk scarf was wound around his neck. Gaskell was thin and wiry and skipped about charmingly, as though on stage.

'She isn't my girlfriend.'

'Ah. So you've just met her?'

Jude nodded.

Gaskell bowed to the girl, looking like a cross between a gentleman and a crow. 'She's frightfully pretty.'

Jude cleared his throat. 'Look at her more closely.' He cleared his throat again.

The girl looked down, embarrassed, but then immediately looked up at Gaskell expectantly.

Gaskell, however, had no intention of responding to Jude's demonstrative throat-clearing. Instead, he said in his typical way, 'I could have sworn you'd gone out for a pee?' His deep blue, keen eyes twinkled at Jude through his spectacles.

Jude pulled a face, nodded and cleared his throat a third time.

'Yes, I know, you cleared your throat,' said Gaskell. 'I heard you.'

'He found me.' The unknown girl spoke for the first time.

Quentin Gaskell raised his eyebrows. 'Here in the graveyard, perchance?'

'Over by the north gate.' Jude explained how and where he had taken the girl in tow.

Music was still playing in the background. The party guests were still dancing wildly.

'You went over to the north gate for a pee?'

'People live here – I didn't want to...'

Gaskell nodded in time to the music.

'I don't know how I got here,' said the girl.

'What's your name, my pretty one?'

She suddenly seemed despairing. She shook her head.

'OK.' More throat-clearing, this time from Gaskell. 'So you have no idea who you are.' The former rock star looked at her thoughtfully. He reached out his hand, touched her gently on the arm and immediately withdrew his hand. 'You're one of us – but you don't know who you are?' He looked at her for a long moment. 'But you feel warm.' He pointed to her leg. 'And you're limping. I'm sorry, but I couldn't help noticing, even though it's not much of a limp.' He looked around. 'None of us limps. None of us has bad eyesight, not even those who in their heyday were as blind as a bat.'

'You're wearing glasses,' she countered.

'Well spotted, little one.' Gaskell tapped his index finger on the old-fashioned frame. 'Pure vanity,' he said. 'I don't need glasses. But they suit me. Yes, very clever, little one.' He cleared his throat demonstratively and winked at Jude.

Jude replied with a grimace.

Gaskell continued, undeterred. 'When you're dead,' he told the girl, 'you lose all the afflictions that bothered you while you were alive.'

'Do you mean—' She broke off.

'No.' Gaskell shook his head and scratched his chin. 'I don't know what it means. Normally we remember the life we led. We remember our death.' Gaskell sighed. Then he made a dismissive hand gesture. 'Well, those of us who didn't want to die.' He laughed. 'The dead, you see, dream of life. Incessantly. It's what gives us the strength to keep on living. So to speak.' He looked around and raised his glass.

The others instinctively raised theirs too.

Gaskell smiled impishly. 'I do apologise – we're celebrating my deathday today.' He twitched his head slightly once again. 'All very stupid.' He touched his chest. 'A heart attack saw me off. Just like that.' He laughed, but he sounded embarrassed rather than cheerful as he had intended. 'How banal can you get? Someone who had the kind of glamorous life I'd had – after all, I was a rock star – surely deserved a spectacular death.' He bent down to her and whispered conspiratorially, 'You know, little one. Drugs, alcohol and stuff...' He grinned.

'You were a rock star?'

A woman emerged from the throng. 'Not *were*,' she said. 'Gaskell *is* a rock star.'

They both laughed.

'Rock 'n' roll never dies,' said the woman, who looked like a real lady. 'Any more than Gaskell does.'

'I died as a rock star, and was reborn as a legend,' he replied modestly.

'That's Miss Rathbone,' said Jude.

She came over to the girl. 'Ayelet Rathbone.'

'Are you...?'

'Dead?' Miss Rathbone ran her long fingers through her thick hair. She was holding a glass of red wine in her other hand.

The girl nodded.

'No, I just live near the graveyard.'

The girl stared at her in astonishment, and Jude understood exactly how confusing this must all be for her. He decided to tell her the rest of his story later on – how Miss Rathbone had first taken him to the graveyard.

'You've lost your story,' Gaskell said pleasantly. 'So we'll call you Story.' He smiled charmingly. 'Everyone needs a name.'

'Here's to you finding your story.' Miss Rathbone raised her glass.

And the girl, who was now called Story, didn't contradict her. She was secretly glad to have a name. Story was at any rate better than *the girl* and much, much better than *nobody*. She stood there, astonished and slightly embarrassed, deep in the tomb, which didn't look at all the way one might expect a vintage grave to look.

'Where are we?' she asked.

'This is Gaskell's grave – his home, that is,' said Miss Rathbone. 'Most of the guests are dead, apart from Mr Bronowski.' She pointed to a man wearing dungarees and a thick pullover. 'He's one of the staff.'

'And he's a crow,' Gaskell added.

Story didn't ask what he meant. 'So the others are all ghosts?'

Gaskell grinned. 'Well worked out, little one.'

'And what, mysterious Story, are you?' asked Miss Rathbone. 'Are you a ghost too?'

Story looked down and shrugged helplessly.

Yes, Jude thought, *and no. She's different.*

'You're limping. Just a bit, but you're limping,' Miss Rathbone observed, then added, 'And you've forgotten who you are.'

'That's unusual. Ghosts mostly don't do that,' Gaskell pointed out.

'Can you help me?' Story asked hesitantly.

Gaskell laughed cheerfully. 'I brought the house down twice at Carnegie Hall, and Miss Vixen here has visited more than a few foreign countries,' he assured her. He winked at her, a gesture of warmth and confidence. 'Of course we'll try to help you to find yourself, dear Story – for who else is going to do so? But let me speak with Miss Rathbone and the professor first. Then we'll meet again,' he declared mysteriously.

And after he'd gesticulated to the pair of them to

make themselves comfortable, he and Miss Rathbone huddled in a corner, discussing what to do.

'What do you think they're talking about?'

'You,' Jude replied.

He and Story were sitting on a sofa, watching what was going on. The unconventional location aside, Jude felt almost as if he were at an ordinary party. A guitar was next to the sofa; Jude stroked the strings. It was the same guitar that he'd been playing only an hour ago – 'Green and Grey', 'Dear Prudence' and 'I've Been to a Marvellous Party' – with Quentin Gaskell and Miss Rathbone singing a duet.

The other guests were now bawling The Who's 'My Generation'. Gaskell and Miss Rathbone were standing at the other end of the tomb, locked in conversation with a man.

Story sighed. 'You *look* like a normal boy.'

'I *am* normal,' Jude said, almost as if he were trying to defend himself.

'But what am I?' she asked, looking at him imploringly. 'Your friends obviously don't believe that I'm one of them. A ghost, I mean.'

'I don't know.' Jude looked across at Gaskell and Miss Rathbone. 'I think that's what they're just talking about.' At any rate, their conversation with the professor was evidently about something very serious. Gaskell didn't nod in time to the music even once – he looked completely focused, and his little eyes were twinkling behind his glasses. The professor, a crooked old man with the crumpled face of someone very learned, was emphasising his words by raising his index finger as he kept looking across at the sofa. Then he gesticulated with his hands once more, making strange shapes in the air. This and his facial expressions made him appear somewhat eccentric.

Story smiled and touched Jude's hand. Once again, her skin looked transparent and fuzzy where it touched his. She quickly withdrew her hand. 'What's happening to me?' Her eyes were wide with fear. 'Do you think I'm dead, Jude?' He could tell that she was scaring herself with the sound of these words.

'Listen,' he said. 'I don't know, but I'm sure that my friends will have some ideas and that they'll be able to help you. I'll carry on with my story in the meantime. I'll tell you how Miss Rathbone brought me here.' Maybe that would take her mind off it.

'The world in which we live,' Miss Rathbone said that spring day as the injured businessman was bundled into the ambulance on the other side of the road, 'is like autumn-land: orange and brown and October-golden. There, where the shadows are long and dark, life flourishes even in death.' She smiled mysteriously.

Not that Jude understood a word of it. All he knew was that he had just seen a ghost. A real ghost!

'Jude Finney, if you want to know what this is all about, then come and see me.' Miss Rathbone told him her address, also writing it down on a Tesco receipt. She handed him the crumpled slip of paper, then disappeared down the road before he could ask her anything else.

Flummoxed, Jude stood there for a while. Then he stuffed the receipt into his pocket and went home. That whole afternoon and evening, and then wide awake in bed, he mulled over the mysterious things that the strange woman had said. Who was she? How could she see ghosts – just as he could? The whole thing was crazy. Ghosts? Here in London? These anxious questions weighed upon him as he finally fell asleep – but there was no dream in sight: just dull fear in the pale glow of the street lights.

The following day, he couldn't wait for the end of school. Exhausted, he sat hunched in his seat, desperate for the bell to ring, as sundry teachers rambled on. When the bell finally did ring, after what seemed like an eternity, Jude headed straight for the Highgate address scrawled on the crumpled receipt.

Swains Lane was a narrow road that snaked its way between the two parts of the graveyard. It was bordered by large green trees that rustled in the mild spring air, and Jude felt as if he were in the middle of a forest, even though every now and then parked cars blocked the pavement. He could just hear the dull roar of the city far away.

He suddenly wondered what he was doing there.

The house with the address that Miss Rathbone had given him looked like one of those spooky pictures in the books that languished more or less forgotten on the obscure shelves of public libraries. Ivy was proliferating wildly across the red brick façade, and the narrow tower with the pointed roof arose from the greenery like a bony index finger. The old doorbell emitted a sickly rattle, far removed from the melodious sound it must have made once upon a time.

Jude waited patiently. He could hear footsteps approaching.

'Well, look at that. You came,' said the lady, her eyes sparkling in the gloom of the entrance hall. 'I'm not surprised to see you here. You have that curiosity in your eyes that most people don't have.'

'Hello,' Jude said hesitantly.

'Hello, mousy-grey boy,' she said kindly. 'Would you like a cup of tea?'

Mousy-grey boy? he thought. But he merely nodded, even though he didn't actually want a cup of tea.

She ushered him in. 'No need to be afraid,' she continued. 'Not of me.' Which immediately made him wonder who or what he *should* be afraid of. But he didn't ask. Perhaps because he was afraid of what the answer might be. 'I'm sure you've got all sorts of questions – you look as if you haven't slept a wink. Don't worry – it's quite normal.'

'Why can I see ghosts?' The really big question came tumbling out.

'That,' she said, 'is a very difficult question.' Smiling, she shut the door behind her. 'Or rather, the answer is difficult.'

'But do you know the answer?'

'Come on.' She led him down the high, bright hallway. 'All in good time.' She spoke gently to him, like a song on a scratched record.

Jude followed her up a narrow, creaking staircase. 'Are you a ghost too?'

'No.'

Miss Rathbone wasn't really old, but she wasn't young either. Her eyes in particular looked timeless; they reminded Jude of the actresses in the old films that were sometimes shown on BBC Two. Her movements were lithe, like those of a wild animal in the undergrowth.

On the narrow stairs were pots of all sizes, filled with an endless variety of green plants – wild, exuberant creations with large, serrated leaves. Some were creeping up the stairs; others were scaling the walls. At the top, Miss Rathbone and Jude went down a corridor, which enabled Jude to peep into some of the rooms.

There was something cave-like about the house. Plants and pots in every conceivable shape and size were everywhere. Just like the outside walls, the inside walls were covered with ivy and tendrils of other plants, which also framed the windows. As he passed, Jude spotted stone figures in some of the rooms; they looked like Buddhas with foxes' heads. There were fountains with water gently splashing into stone cups, in some of which fish and little turtles were swimming. The whole house breathed *life*. Even the wooden floorboards looked almost like actual branches. Here and there were mats made of some material that Jude didn't recognise.

‘That’s rice straw,’ Miss Rathbone said. ‘Tatami.’

Jude couldn’t see any furniture anywhere. Instead, the corners of the rooms were filled with colourful cushions, some of them piled up like mountains, others pushed together like little nests. Every room was painted a different colour: a variety of shades from orange to yellow to bright red – mixed with a soft green. And the rooms were divided by strangely patterned screens, the windows dressed with paper blinds which let muted daylight stream into the house, while oddly shaped lampshades dangled from the ceilings or were perched precariously on slender wooden poles in the rooms.

‘Hayashi lamps give off a light that’s good for the soul,’ Miss Rathbone explained.

‘Is this all Japanese design then?’ Jude asked.

She nodded. ‘What do you think to it?’

‘Looks a bit like something from a fairy tale,’ he said.

‘Precisely. My dwelling is a cross between a cave, a forest and a temple.’

Jude was curiously struck by the way she said ‘dwelling’ rather than ‘house’.

Then she led him into a room where they sat down on a row of large cushions. As Jude thought how sitting cross-legged might take some getting used to, Miss Rathbone offered him tea from a dark-coloured teapot.

'Tea is like life,' she said, handing him a small bowl.

Jude sipped the hot drink. He could taste a whole host of unknown spices and aromas that magicked a smile of pleasure onto his face.

'To answer your question, my boy,' she said, 'anyone who dies but doesn't want to turns into a ghost. The dream of life doesn't simply let him or her go.'

'But that means there must be loads of ghosts?'

'You bet!' She sniffed her tea and shut her eyes for a moment. 'Ghosts are nothing more than the dreams of the dead. They dream about life, and these dreams help them not to be forgotten.'

Jude paused only briefly. 'Why can I see them when other people can't?'

Miss Rathbone gave him a long look. She sipped her tea, breathing calmly, and silence fell across the room with its cushions and books and plants, and tea in its shallow bowls. 'You, mousy-grey boy, are something special,' she finally said. 'If you weren't, you wouldn't see them.' She took another sip of tea. 'Yes, you're something special, Jude Finney.'

'I don't believe that. Why would I be?'

'You have a gift that most people don't possess.' She put her head on one side. 'I've never met anyone who does have it – until now.'

'You can see them too, can't you?'

She smiled kindly. 'But I'm not human, my mousy-grey boy.'

Jude swallowed. Had he heard right?

'If you didn't possess this gift, you wouldn't have seen that poor man in the road, never mind been able to speak to him.'

'But he wasn't dead.'

'No – he was in the twilight zone. He was determined to cling to life and just sneaked a quick peek at the world that had nearly become his.'

Jude nodded, although he was really none the wiser. In fact, he was completely baffled. Moreover, he was wondering what Miss Rathbone was if she was claiming to be neither human nor a ghost.

Miss Rathbone, however, seemed very full of beans. 'You need to meet the others,' she said merrily, getting up from her cushion. 'Come on!' She led him to one of the numerous windows which, from the outside, looked like narrowed eyes. As she raised the blind, Jude looked out onto the street and across at the wall with the cemetery behind it.

'It doesn't look like a graveyard,' Jude murmured.

'More like a forest.'

'It is a forest. A forest with graves in it.'

Then they went across to the other side of the road, and Jude met Quentin Gaskell for the first time.

He was sitting on a gravestone in the sunshine, looking anything other than dead. He wasn't at all how Jude had imagined a ghost to look. The man who was sitting there reading a book (*The Napoleon of Notting Hill* by G. K. Chesterton) looked as if he were enjoying the close of that spring day. He was wearing old-fashioned dark-rimmed glasses – his trademark, as Jude discovered later – and looked up as Miss Rathbone and her young companion came along the path.

'My dear lady vixen!' he greeted her, laughing.

'Gaskell, this is Jude Finney.'

'He's alive and can see me?'

She nodded.

'Hey, Jude,' he said cheerfully, pausing only for a fraction of a surprised second. Every syllable was curiously shortened. 'It's your first time here, is it?'

'Yes,' Jude replied politely.

'And you can really see me?'

'Yes.'

Gaskell looked at Miss Rathbone and nodded again. 'I'm Quentin Gaskell. And you must be the mysterious boy who Ayelet picked up in the street yesterday.' He laughed and snapped his book shut. 'Right. Then I'll explain a couple of things. From now on, you'll be coming here as often as you can, I expect – Miss Rathbone can show you a way in when the gates are locked.' He chortled. 'Highgate Cemetery is old, a quiet old place. But if you're not careful, it can be a dangerous place too...' He paused meaningfully, but didn't take this any further. 'Otherwise, there are loads of nice people living here. All of them dead, of course. Ghosts, you'd call them. Ha! Many of them don't say much – most of them are rather solitary – but there are some chatty ones, like me. Or the admiral; a couple of others too. You can talk to us any time you like.' He took a step towards the boy. 'Tell me, Jude Finney, you don't by any chance play an instrument, do you?'

'Yes, I do. Guitar.'

Gaskell clapped delightedly. 'Perfect.'

'Acoustic.'

'Even better. Now, our Miss Rathbone believes,' Gaskell continued, 'that hanging out with me will do a boy of your age a power of good.' He chuckled merrily. 'How splendidly mistaken!'

Miss Rathbone was grinning from ear to ear.

At this point, of course, Jude didn't know that

Quentin Gaskell had been a famous rock star during his lifetime. He was responsible for much-quoted lines such as 'Why buy drugs when you can become a rock star and get them for free?' and 'Equal rights are fine by me – I'll have any groupie who wants me.' Jude read all that stuff later on in old copies of *Rolling Stone* or *NME*. He also went on to buy Gaskell's autobiography *Me!* from a second-hand bookshop – Gaskell had published it at the end of the 1980s but now, twenty years on, it was out of print because nobody was interested any more in the torrid past of an old glam rocker.

But the Quentin Gaskell whom Jude came to know bore barely any resemblance to the singer he read about from back then, with his make-up and drainpipe trousers and platform shoes. Now he was a friendly, eccentric elderly man.

'You're welcome to visit as often as you like,' Gaskell said.

And from then onwards, Jude Finney made his way to Highgate Cemetery pretty much every day. He did his homework in the shadow of the huge gravestones, even calling on famous names for help. Michael Faraday helped him with maths; the author Radclyffe Hall, for her part, told him how wrong the teachers were who tried to interpret her poetry. And one hot summer's day, Tom Sayers showed him how to fell your opponent with a single blow in the way that they did a hundred years ago.

That summer turned Jude's life completely on its head. He came to know the ghosts' habits. Some of them told him their life stories. On sunny days, he would lie on the grassy hill, warmed by the sun, wondering whether his father would miss him if he weren't there any more. Or whether he would be as indifferent to Jude's absence as he was to the disappearance of the woman who was Jude's mother.

His classmates didn't notice any difference in him, and just as before, Jude rehearsed with his band.

'Those riffs are improving,' Gaskell said to him one day. Jude often brought his guitar with him, and Gaskell would teach him new techniques. 'You've got talent, Jude, but you mustn't hide from life by coming here.'

'I'm not hiding.'

'You prefer being with ghosts to being with people of your own age,' Gaskell reminded him.

'I've got friends.' Which was true.

'But you're here every afternoon.'

'I like the peace and quiet.'

'Peace and quiet – at your age?' Gaskell looked at him sceptically. 'This is no place for the living. You should be hanging out in bars and coffee shops and clubs. Places where' – he leant over conspiratorially – 'you meet pretty girls.' He gave Jude a dig in the ribs, his touch as cold as a breath of wind.

'The main thing is not being at home,' Jude said softly.

Quentin turned serious. 'It can't be easy for your father either, being a single parent with an exhausting job.'

Gaskell's words did make Jude think. And he began to see his father through new eyes.

'And that,' said Jude, 'is how I ended up in Highgate more than six months ago.'

'So you like it here,' said Story. The girl had listened intently as Jude recounted his tale. The fact that she had no story herself seemed to make her all the more interested in his.

Jude nodded.

'What about your life?' she asked. 'I mean your real life, away from here?'

Jude shrugged. 'I live with my father in Kentish Town.'

'What about your mother?'

'I haven't got a mother.'

'No mother?'

He shook his head. 'No, I never had one.'

Story gave him a sidelong glance. 'Come on, everyone has a mother to start with.'

'I didn't.'

'Are you an orphan?'

He laughed, but didn't sound very happy. 'A foundling, more like. I turned up on my father's doorstep one day.'

Story shook her head incredulously. 'No! You were seriously left on a doorstep?'

'One spring day, my father found me on the steps.' He paused, searching for the words that sounded meaningful enough for the way he felt.

'You don't have to tell me.' Story looked at him. 'Unless you want to, that is.'

Jude thought about the story, one of the earliest his father had told him – years ago, when he had still been small and his father had taken the time to read to him and tell him stories.

'I was in a holdall – an old, stained, brown leather holdall, to be precise – covered with stickers from exotic places. The bag was kitted out with cushions and a warm blanket.'

'How old were you?'

'Almost a year.'

'How did your father know that?'

'There was a note in the bag with my date of birth on it.'

On the note, which was now rather battered and lived in Jude's bedroom chest of drawers, it said in a dainty female hand: *This is Jude. He's our son. You know why you've got him. He can't stay with me*. No signature. Just this brief message.

And thus his mother had vanished from his life. At any rate, Jude assumed that it was his mother who had left him on the doorstep in a holdall.

'What did your father do?'

'He kept me and brought me up.'

George Finney, who had become a father overnight, had been living in Bedford then, close to the station in a largely Pakistani and Indian area full of exotic colours, scents and aromas.

'What did he tell you about your mother?'

'Nothing.'

That wasn't entirely true. George Finney had told his son a couple of things about his mother over the years – that he'd met her while travelling, by a fabulously beautiful river in the light of the sinking sun. But he'd never said where exactly it was – just that it had been in some distant, exotic land, and that he had truly loved this woman, Jude's mother. Jude came to realise by his father's wistful tone that he wasn't deliberately leaving so many gaps in his story. It was more that he didn't know the answers himself. Or that he remembered it differently from how it had happened in reality.

Memories – Jude had worked this out at a young age – were a tricky business.

'She decided to get on with her life without us,' George Finney always said. 'Let's leave it at that.'

And Jude, who knew his father's musical tastes, would sometimes imagine as he grew up that his parents had been listening to John Lennon when they fell in love with one another. And he began to fill in the gaps in his father's story. In his imagination, his mother became an exotic beauty whom George Finney had met on one of his trips to India – in those days, his father had been part of several projects in India and Pakistan in his capacity as a hydrologist (Jude thought this sounded rather better than 'water scientist'). But even though his mother carried on living in his imagination, that changed nothing about his motherless childhood in real life.

'Apart from the old holdall and the note, she didn't leave a trace of herself,' Jude said.

He suddenly fell silent. David Bowie's 'Let's Dance' boomed around the tomb.

'You're sad,' Story observed.

'It's just...' He paused. 'I mean, it's really weird that I'm at a party telling you all this stuff that I've never told anyone before...I don't even know you.'

She looked at him. 'I'd love to tell you about myself,' she said, 'but there's nothing to tell.'

'I know. It must be far worse for you than for me. I just don't remember my mother, but you can't remember anything about your life.'

She looked at him silently, waiting for him to continue.

'When I started seeing ghosts, you know, I had a feeling that it was something to do with my mother.' He looked at the partying crowd. 'Weird. And now we're sitting here in this strange place, both of us with our strange stories. I'm sure there's some reason for this, even if we don't know what it is yet. I think everything happens for a reason.'

'I know what you mean.'

'How do you feel?' he asked.

'Lonely, somehow. Empty. Lost.' She suddenly laughed out loud. 'For God's sake, I look like a ghost, but I'm not a ghost. I didn't even believe in ghosts until today. And now here I am. At this party. Among strangers.' Another laugh. 'Among ghosts.'

'They're nice ghosts.'

'Yeah,' she breathed softly.

Miss Rathbone detached herself from Gaskell and came across to the sofa. 'Story, you can come with me,' she declared in a tone that brooked no objections. 'I live just opposite. You can rest there, and we'll worry about everything else tomorrow.'

'Do ghosts sleep?' asked Story.

Miss Rathbone smiled indulgently. 'For one thing, we don't know that you're a ghost. For another, yes, ghosts do sleep. That's what they mostly do, regardless of what they did when they were alive. They're just a bit...restricted, let's say.'

'What does that mean?'

'They can't be everywhere.'

'Why not?'

'They're bound to their bodies.'

Story winced. Jude knew what she was thinking at that moment. Until then, he had suppressed the thought: the thought of the girl's corpse. If indeed she was dead. If so, there had to be a body somewhere – a lifeless body that looked like she did.

Miss Rathbone put a consoling hand on Story's shoulder, and Jude noticed that her hand didn't sink in, as it would have done with a real ghost. Instead, Story's skin just yielded slightly. 'Don't be afraid.

We've consulted at length with the professor, and he thinks you're not dead yet.'

Story frowned. 'You mean...?'

'Precisely,' said Miss Rathbone. 'We think you're close to death – but still alive.'

Shocked, the girl gasped for breath. 'What does that mean?'

Miss Rathbone shrugged. 'I have no idea what it means. It is as it is. It's a beastly mystery, and we need to find the solution. Ghosts aren't normally far from their bodies, you know.' She carefully avoided using the word *corpse*. 'When someone dies, their ghost carries on living where their body is buried.'

Story nodded numbly.

'But how did she get here?' Jude wondered how Story had come to be sitting on the park bench by the north gate. If her grave was somewhere in that area, then there must have been a burial. But there hadn't been any new arrivals recently. Miss Rathbone and the others would have heard about it.

No. This didn't add up.

It was Story who asked the crucial question. 'So what now?'

Despite the uncertainty, Miss Rathbone was in good spirits. 'Gaskell's asking around. Someone's bound to have seen something. This is a graveyard –

nothing happens unobserved. The dead are as nosy as anything.'

'So do you think I can leave the graveyard?'

The vixen nodded. 'I'm quite sure of it, little one. Even Gaskell's been to visit me.'

'He likes ginger tea,' Jude remarked.

'With lemon,' she added.

'Nowhere's too far for that, so far as he's concerned.'

'And no weather's too bad.'

Story looked at them both, baffled. 'But what if I go too far?' she said anxiously.

'I don't know.' Miss Rathbone stroked her hand. 'But it's not far to my house.'

'What about me?' asked Jude slightly indignantly.

'You presumably want to be with her?' Miss Rathbone could sometimes be rather too direct.

'No, um...I...' he stammered awkwardly. Then he said simply, 'yes' before adding defensively, 'After all, I found her.'

'You stumbled upon her, I know. But you have school tomorrow morning.' Miss Rathbone winked at him. 'You need your sleep and to have your wits about you if you want to help Story.'

'Can't I stay with you tonight?'

'No, you go home.' Miss Rathbone looked at

Story, then at the boy. 'For goodness' sake, you'll be in trouble if your father can't find you tomorrow morning. Neither of us wants that.'

'He's not there.'

She looked at him and raised an eyebrow.

'Working away, the usual stuff. He's in Manchester, inspecting ponds. In any case, I've got to get up in five hours.' He well knew he was trying to get round her. 'If I don't have to go home but spend the night round the corner instead, I'll be asleep sooner. And I'll wake up earlier tomorrow. And be more productive.'

Story smiled. Jude wondered where she went to school and what kind of life she led – or had led before she got here.

'Very well,' Miss Rathbone finally conceded. 'But on condition that you promise to be at school on time. Agreed?'

Jude grinned. 'Agreed.'

And so they left the party. The rest of the night was already history.

CHAPTER 3

The next morning Jude was rudely awoken by the sound of a huge, old-fashioned alarm clock. Half blind with tiredness, he flailed around in the direction of the ear-splitting *ring-a-ding-ding*, finally managing to silence the irritating, clunky contraption with one blow. Only then did he realise that he wasn't at home, but had stayed the night at Miss Rathbone's house.

He blinked and saw Story lying opposite him on a tatami. She was still asleep, curled up like a cat, a multi-coloured woollen blanket pulled up to her chin. The blanket rose and fell gently in time with her breathing, and her eyelids flickered like silk scarves in a gentle breeze. She didn't seem to have heard the alarm clock. And she didn't look remotely like a ghost.

Jude wondered what she had been dreaming about. She looked peaceful, like someone who felt comfortable and safe. The sun had already risen, and as the thin rays of autumn-coloured light fell through the half-closed blinds into the room they caught the girl's hair, a symphony of coppery red and brown. A fountain was splashing in the corner, and the air was filled with the scent of orange and red, of flowery joss sticks. Jude, who had slept in his clothes, sat up slowly and stretched. Then he sat still for a moment, watching the girl.

Story. He let the name run around his head until it had almost turned into a song. For a ghost, she was having a blessed sleep. She was breathing peacefully, and there was nothing to suggest that she wasn't human. Only the bright glow of her hair in the sunshine made her seem in any way different. She was decidedly pretty, and Jude wondered once more about her normal life.

She was *shimmering*, albeit only slightly.

Jude sighed softly, then stood up, gathered his stuff together, put his jacket on, grabbed his guitar and took one last look at the sleeping girl before he crept quietly out of the house. He knew that Miss Rathbone wouldn't be up until midday. She loved nights, and liked to sleep during the day.

He walked down the slowly awakening streets of Highgate back to Twisden Road. There he had a quick wash, then grabbed his school bag – hoping that it contained everything he needed – and sprinted off. He arrived at school just in time for the first lesson. At his desk, he holed himself up behind his bag, trying desperately to stay awake.

The day passed uneventfully. Just another ordinary, boring school day. At least Jude was spared an encounter with Mr Ackroyd. Once school was finally over, he made a beeline straight for Swains Lane and Miss Rathbone's house.

Story was awake, as was Miss Rathbone.

'Where've you been?' she greeted him.

'At school.'

'Ah, yes.' As if she'd forgotten.

Story was sitting on the floor, watching water splashing into a basalt basin. When Jude came in to the room, she looked up and smiled. 'We've just eaten,' she said.

Jude knew that ghosts could eat, so he wasn't surprised.

'Gaskell's expecting us – he's got news,' Miss Rathbone said. She swirled through the room, picked up her cardigan and brightly coloured shawl and put them on. Swiftly she set her sunglasses on her nose, making her suddenly look like an eccentric diva. 'What are you two waiting for?'

With that, they set off once more for the graveyard opposite.

'How was school?' Story asked as they walked.

'Boring.'

'I don't know which school I go to. I do know that we had to write an essay on *Social Media Networks: Blessing or Curse?*, but I've no idea when that was.'

Sounds like an A-level topic, Jude thought. So that must mean she was in fact the same age as he was... 'Maybe that's a clue,' he said. 'We did an assessed essay yesterday that counts towards our final A-level mark. Maybe you're in the same school year as me.'

'Then we'd be the same age.'

Bingo! 'Yes, presumably.'

Miss Rathbone turned to them and scrutinised Story silently. Jude had no desire to know what her eyes were saying behind her sunglasses. He felt somehow caught out.

'Maybe it will help us to work out which school you're at,' he said. 'I could Google the essay topic.' That would at least be a start.

'Good idea,' said Miss Rathbone, hurrying onwards. Jude and Story hastened after her.

At the lower end of the graveyard wall was a hole with blackberries running riot in it – Jude's usual way in once the gates were locked. They pushed their way through and into the western part of the graveyard.

There, it was quiet, the graves slumbering in the shadow of the mighty trees. Autumn had generously scattered bright leaves across the graveyard; they went rustling across the ground with each breath of wind. The leaves covered the graves and piled themselves up in the gaps between them and around the edges of the mausoleums, while the weak light of the late afternoon sun stroked the heads of the stone angels and animals, giving the gravestones an unreal air.

Miss Rathbone followed a well-trodden path that led upwards between hedges and undergrowth. Highgate Cemetery was hilly, cut off from the city: a world of its own, a thicket of woods, graves and hidden corners.

Gaskell was waiting for them. He was standing almost motionless in a clearing which offered a good view of Egyptian Avenue.

'You look as if you've made a discovery,' said Miss Rathbone, who had evidently heard from him. Maybe Gaskell had sent a fox to call her?

'You know Mr Monkford, who lives over there by the monument with the lions?'

'Mr Monkford the bookseller?' Jude asked. He was a neighbour of the dead boxer who had explained the knack of fist-fighting to him (for a presentation that Jude had to give in History).

'That's the one.'

Mr Monkford had died in 1892, against his will obviously, otherwise he wouldn't have ended up as a ghost in Highgate. The former bookseller didn't say much, and was rather reminiscent of grouchy Mr Scrooge since he spent most of his time complaining, and he had no patience with visitors. Jude avoided him wherever possible.

'He was sitting on the wall last night.'

'Mr Monkford?'

'Who else?'

Miss Rathbone seemed surprised. 'Why on earth was he sitting on the wall?'

'He was enjoying the night.'

'Since when has that old grump enjoyed the night?'

'He was looking for peace and quiet, and then he saw something.'

'You're making it sound exciting.'

'A story – whatever it's about – is only as good as the way it's told,' Gaskell replied. 'Just like a good rock song.'

'Yes, yes. But did he give you any useful information?' Miss Rathbone asked impatiently.

Gaskell pointed to Story. 'Yes. And it was to do with her.'

They all stared at him.

'Well I never,' said Miss Rathbone ironically. 'Could you please now spit it out?'

Gaskell looked innocent, and Story grinned. Jude stole a glance at her.

'Mr Monkford ought to tell you the story himself,' said Gaskell. 'After all, it's his story, and he has the right to tell us himself.' Stories were something special; everyone at the graveyard knew and respected this fact.

'So what are we waiting for?' said Miss Rathbone.

They set off for Mr Monkford's grave, Gaskell leading the way.

Again it seemed to Jude as if the graveyard were endless, and he often felt as if he were on a film set. There were trees everywhere: tall ashes, dark firs, huge maples, ancient oaks and sweeping chestnuts. The dying sun's rays that pierced the leafy canopy bathed the whole place in a magical light, while the remaining birds were singing their songs into the silence. Ravens were perched on the gravestones over by the big satyr fountain, and every now and then Jude thought he could make out a fox scurrying through the undergrowth.

'Who's the man we're looking for?' asked Story.

'A dead bookseller.' That's all Jude knew about

Mr Monkford.

'Do you know him?'

'Yes, but I normally steer clear of him.'

'Is he dangerous?' she asked nervously.

Jude shook his head. 'No, just weird. A loner.'

Miss Rathbone and Gaskell stopped. Mr Jonathan Hamish Heathcliff Monkford lived in one of the smaller graves, which looked rather more homely than the colossal vaults. The gravestone was covered with a thick layer of moss, and tendrils of ivy curled around the inscription bearing the dead man's name and dates.

Gaskell took a step forwards and knocked on the gravestone. 'Mr Monkford!' he cried. 'We're here!'

Miss Rathbone stood still in the sunlight. Story moved closer to Jude. He could almost smell her presence.

They waited. But when the dead man didn't emerge, Miss Rathbone said impatiently, 'Come on, Mr Monkford!'

The autumn leaves by the grave started to rustle, then a figure materialised in the sunlight. He was almost transparent, wearing a brown suit that looked threadbare and shabby with a grubby scarf knotted around his neck. He had a scrawny, long-nosed face.

Mr Monkford nodded at the little company then

stared at Story. 'She's the one, no doubt about it,' he said. 'She's the girl they carried off.' He nodded again.

Story stared at him. 'I've never seen you before.'

The man looked like a chipmunk – all the more so thanks to his thick sideburns – and his little eyes were small and watchful in his pale face. He still wore the gloomy expression that he would have had when he was still alive and selling books, counting his coins and totting up his balance sheets late at night by the dim light of a flickering candle.

'You're staring at my scarf, girl,' he grumbled. 'It's bad manners.'

Baffled, Story looked at him. Then she looked across at Miss Rathbone for help.

'He was murdered,' Miss Rathbone whispered to her. 'And he's still fed up about it.'

'I heard that,' snapped the little old man.

'I didn't mean to be rude.'

'If you want to tell a story, my dear, then do at least tell it properly,' the former bookseller retorted.

'Thanks – I'll bear that in mind. Perhaps you'd rather tell it yourself?'

The bookseller sighed. 'It was my former business partner, Roderick Garlick. Yes, he murdered me. Why? Pure greed, that's why. He buried me in a field, in the park over there, then reported me as missing. And so he collared our whole business for himself.' Mr Monkford rubbed his hands gleefully. 'But then someone found me and moved me to Highgate. And that scoundrel Roderick was caught and hanged.' He snorted contemptuously. 'I'm just glad he isn't here. They buried him somewhere else.'

'That's sad,' said Story.

'Yes, it is, but what's happened to you is at least as sad as that, my girl. We – Roderick and I, that is – wanted to expand the business. We wanted to open a branch in Massachusetts. Create a booming import and export business.' It was almost unbelievable the way his eyes still lit up at the thought of all the money they could have been raking in.

'Mr Monkford,' Miss Rathbone interrupted, 'we all love to hear your tales but that's not why we're here.' She gave him a stern look. 'Gaskell said you knew who this girl was.' She gesticulated at Story.

'I said I'd seen her. Not that I know who she is.'

'Go on,' said Gaskell.

They all stood around the gravestone, listening intently as the bookseller told them what had happened.

'I was sitting on the wall because I wanted to enjoy the night-time peace and quiet.'

Miss Rathbone couldn't disguise her impatience any longer. 'So?'

'There wasn't much going on.' As he spoke, Mr Monkford strolled round and round the gravestone. 'That crazy Dorothy Gissing was ghosting around over by the pond, moaning and groaning as always.'

'That's Dorothy Gissing from Spitalfields, who goes out looking for her children every night,' Gaskell put in. 'They died when their house fell in on them. Dorothy died shortly afterwards of a broken heart, and was buried here – but her children were buried elsewhere. Such a run of bad luck. Since then, she's spent every night wandering around, looking for her children.'

Story looked concerned. All these stories presumably reminded her of her own missing story.

Mr Monkford finally returned to his tale. 'Otherwise it was quiet, apart from the noise made by certain people who seem to believe that parties are necessary.' He narrowed his eyes and glared sideways at Gaskell, clearly doing his utmost to look resentful. 'That kind of noise in the middle of the night – it really is a disgrace,' he said emphatically.

Gaskell took silent note.

'And there were two stone angels roaming around behind the hill.'

Jude pricked up his ears. He knew that everyone needed to beware of the angels. He secretly hoped never to meet one.

'So I sat myself on the wall and watched all the goings-on outside the graveyard. Several cars drove down Swains Lane, and a couple walked past, having some silly argument. That dead duck from the pond waddled down to the pavement, turned round and waddled back to the fountain in Waterlow Park. And that was that.'

Gaskell leant casually on the gravestone, shifting his weight from one leg to the other. Every now and then, he straightened his glasses on his nose.

'But then,' said Mr Monkford, 'I saw *her*.' He nodded at Story, who was looking tense.

'What was I doing?' she asked.

'You were walking purposefully down Swains Lane,' Mr Monkford remembered. 'You were coming from Pond Square, and you kept looking around you. It looked as if someone might be following you, but I couldn't see anyone.'

'Who would want to follow me?'

Mr Monkford waved his hands around in the air. 'Just listen, girl, I've not finished my story yet.' He snorted before continuing. 'Then it all happened very quickly.'

They all listened intently. The shadows on the ground and on the stone sculptures were becoming gradually longer.

'Two men suddenly jumped out of a car parked inconspicuously at the side of the road. At any rate, I hadn't noticed it before. The men grabbed you and dragged you into the car. You tried desperately to defend yourself, and even managed to get free for a moment, but they overpowered you again.'

Jude couldn't contain his impatience any longer. 'What did these men look like?'

'Dangerous.'

'Could you be more precise?' Miss Rathbone knew that the details might be crucial.

'They were wearing dark suits. I couldn't see their faces.'

'But you managed to recognise this girl.'

Mr Monkford made a dismissive hand gesture. 'That's different,' he growled. 'I could see her face. But the men looked as if they didn't *have* any faces.'

Jude swallowed. Mr Monkford's story had seemed so promising – and now this. Story looked disappointed too.

'No faces, you say?' Miss Rathbone's eyes were suddenly bright.

'No faces,' replied the bookseller.

'Do you think it was *them*?' Miss Rathbone said, turning to Gaskell.

Gaskell shrugged and gave a barely audible sigh. 'Let's hear the rest of Mr Monkford's story first.'

Miss Rathbone turned back to the bookseller. 'What about the car?'

'It was black, even the windows,' replied Mr Monkford.

'Great,' Story muttered under her breath. 'I was abducted by Torchwood.'

Jude looked at her in surprise. 'You remember a TV series, but you don't remember your own name?'

She nodded, puzzled. 'Yes. Weird, eh?' She turned pale. 'I remember the episode with the alien who looked like a pelican.' Lost in thought, she touched her lips. 'I was eating something while I was watching it.' She thought hard. 'Cheese on toast. With pickle.' She gazed at Jude. 'Why can I remember that, and nothing else?'

'We'll find out why,' Miss Rathbone promised.

Story shut her eyes briefly and took a deep breath. 'Yes,' she whispered, so quietly that only Jude heard her.

Miss Rathbone turned back to the old bookseller. 'What kind of car was it?'

Mr Monkford did know the answer to that one.

'A 1947 Rolls-Royce Silver Wraith.'

Gaskell suddenly straightened up and shook his head. 'A hearse?'

Mr Monkford nodded. 'Yes. An ancient hearse. But it didn't look ancient. Quite the reverse.'

Gaskell leant on the gravestone once more. He raised his eyebrows and looked at Miss Rathbone. 'A Silver Wraith. Now I really *am* stumped.'

Mr Monkford resumed his story. 'Hmm,' he said, turning to Story. 'As I was saying, you defended yourself.'

Story's eyes widened with horror. 'What did they do to me?'

'You wriggled and kicked, and one of the men held a cloth in front of your nose and mouth. You immediately stopped kicking, and they injected you with something.' He scratched his whiskers. 'Once you'd stopped moving completely, they put you in the boot.'

Jude found 'boot' a rather strange way to describe the back of a hearse, but no better word sprang to mind.

'Then?' Gaskell was looking worried.

The whole scene sounded to Jude as if it were from some grisly crime film. He could imagine the doors of the Silver Wraith slamming, the tyres squealing, the engine roaring, and the car disappearing into the night. With two faceless men who had abducted a young girl.

'What happened then?' asked Miss Rathbone.

'They drove off.'

'Did you see the numberplate?' Jude asked hopefully.

Mr Monkford shook his head sadly. 'I'm afraid not. But there was something written on the window.'

A clue!

'*Lightwood and Son.*'

'So why am I here now?' Story had a feeling that there was more to come.

Mr Monkford blinked in the sunlight. 'I was just about to jump off the wall,' he continued, 'when I saw you lying in the middle of the road. You were just a shadow of a ghost, wispy and transparent. A poor newborn creature.'

Story put her hand to her mouth.

'Then a gust of wind carried you off into the graveyard, where you disappeared into the darkness.'

'Didn't you follow her?' Jude said indignantly.

But Mr Monkford looked at him uncomprehendingly. 'Why would I have followed her?'

'To find out who she was,' said Jude.

'I didn't care who she was,' the bookseller replied frankly. 'I was tired and wanted to go home.'

'Why didn't you help me?' asked Story. Despair was threatening to overwhelm her.

'What could I have done? Chased the car? It sped off, and I can't stray far from the graveyard.' Mr Monkford pointed gloomily at the grave beneath his feet. 'The fine figure of the man that I was many years ago is here under the earth, and that means I'm bound to this place whether I like it or not.'

'OK. So what now? How does this help us?' Jude asked.

'We know that she was abducted by faceless men in a Silver Wraith.' Gaskell made it sound as if this were an everyday occurrence.

'What did the men do to me?'

'They put you in a state in which you're neither dead nor completely alive,' replied Miss Rathbone.

Story was struggling not to cry. Her lips were trembling and she was breathing quickly.

'They gave you something that almost killed you.'

Jude would have given anything to help her. But all he could do was stand there, as helpless as everyone else. 'Maybe it's like with the injured businessman,' he said, desperately casting around for an explanation. 'The one I told you about.'

'I'm still not really dead.' Story was clinging to this fact like a shipwrecked person clinging to a life belt. 'I'm not dead, not yet...'

Gaskell shook his head. 'You're *in-between*.'

Story cleared her throat and wiped her eyes defiantly. 'So am I going to die soon?' she asked. 'What will happen when I die?'

Jude suddenly realised that they presumably didn't have much time left to solve the mystery and save Story. Her body was somewhere else, and it was fighting for life. 'We need to find your real self as quickly as possible,' he said nervously. He suddenly had the feeling that they shouldn't be wasting a single second longer. 'That's what matters.' He looked pleadingly at the others. 'Miss Rathbone. Gaskell!'

The two of them gazed thoughtfully across the rows of old graves. Now and then there came the soft thud of a horse chestnut hitting the ground.

'Let me tell you another story first,' said Miss Rathbone. She took off her sunglasses, and Jude shivered when he saw the look in her eyes. He could tell that Story felt the same. A cloud pushed its way in front of the sun, briefly casting everything into gloom. For Jude, it was a graphic reminder of the winter that was lurking in the autumn leaves, just waiting to emerge from its hiding place.

Then the old vixen began her tale, and they listened to the echo of highly ominous events which, as she told them, had happened long, long ago.

'Up in the Staffordshire hills, there was once a village,' Miss Rathbone said. 'Its name was Lud-upon-Trent.'

The very name conjured up images that weren't exactly black and white, but were as colourless as the landscape first thing in the morning when the dense fog that lies over the valleys lifts only gradually.

'That's where it happened, long ago.'

Jude and Story had sat themselves down on a cracked gravestone made of stained marble. Gaskell was standing next to Miss Rathbone, and Mr Monkford had already excused himself. 'I need some rest after all that nocturnal excitement,' he had said. And with that, he had returned to his grave – though not without wishing them good luck in their search.

A warm wind bearing a hint of fresh coolness was wafting among the graves as Jude and Story listened intently to Miss Rathbone's words. That was what you did when someone was sharing a dusty old story with you in a graveyard. Stories, Jude knew, were valuable because they helped you to understand the world. They distracted you from the truly dreadful things and sometimes, in the best-case scenario, allowed hope to flourish once more.

Miss Rathbone, having made sure that her listeners were paying attention, relished spinning her yarn. 'It was only a little village,' she said, 'with houses that had once been huts. A place like the one where Robin Hood and Friar Tuck hid when fleeing from the sheriff's men.'

Jude could picture the place exactly as Miss Rathbone's husky voice conjured it up: a small village, surrounded by green hills, with a narrow river snaking its way through them. He could imagine the clouds that touched the hills in the distance; he could feel the wind blowing through the fields, and could even hear the trees creaking. The village itself was a collection of little houses with pointy roofs and crooked chimneys puffing smoke up into the air, the streets made of cobblestones, possibly left over from Roman times. In the village square was a fountain, equally old. On the outskirts of Lud-upon-Trent was a graveyard, surrounded by a rough stone wall. On the weather-beaten graves were crooked crosses, their names and dates rendered illegible.

'The dead lived there peacefully and quietly,' said Miss Rathbone. 'Until something happened one summer's day, something that nobody – and I mean nobody – had ever guessed would happen.'

Story was sitting close to Jude, and he could not only feel her presence but smell her too – an earthy orangey-brown aroma of leaves. He had sat next to many ghosts but he'd never been able to smell them.

'What happened?' Story asked anxiously.

'They disappeared.' Miss Rathbone looked thoughtful. 'One day they had simply vanished.' The clouds dissipated and the sun's rays stroked Miss Rathbone's face like a promise. 'The fox that took care of the graveyard turned up there one morning and found the whole place completely deserted.'

Gaskell, fiddling with his spectacles, looked peevish.

'What do you mean?' Jude frowned.

'The ghosts had gone. They'd simply disappeared.'

Gaskell nodded meaningfully. 'And ghosts don't just vanish into thin air, you know.'

'The fox – Mr Fosbrooke was his name – searched the whole graveyard.'

Miss Rathbone and her foxes, Jude thought, secretly wondering when Story would start asking him to explain all this business about foxes.

But Miss Rathbone had settled into her story-telling stride. 'He bumped into the ghost of a witch who didn't even have a proper grave.'

Jude nodded knowingly. In the olden days,

witches had been buried deep in the earth in unmarked graves. No gravestone was allowed to reveal that the evil, guilty sinner had once walked the earth, and no Christian soul was to mourn for her.

'She was still a very young ghost,' Miss Rathbone continued. 'She'd spent her whole time hiding in her hole – that was all she was allowed to do. She'd been buried in the earth following her agonising death.'

'So did she see what happened?' Jude asked.

'Hang on a moment, not so fast,' Miss Rathbone replied. 'After he found her, the old fox immediately summoned a council meeting.' As she talked, she paced up and down in front of the gravestone occupied by Jude and Story. The soles of her boots scrunched on the gravel. 'All the foxes in Staffordshire appeared, including those who guarded the graveyards miles away on the other side of Wolverhampton. They all came to Lud-upon-Trent to decide what to do.'

'And the witch told them a very strange story,' Gaskell added.

'To put it mildly,' replied Miss Rathbone.

Gaskell looked at her in thoughtful silence.

'This,' she continued, 'was what had apparently happened: some strange men had appeared in the graveyard during the night. They were carrying lanterns with peculiar lights in them.' Miss Rathbone paused meaningfully before carrying on. 'The witch said that the strange lights looked like darkness in the form of a flame.'

The idea made Jude shiver. 'Sounds weird,' he whispered to Story, who was listening intently, her eyes wide.

Miss Rathbone nodded. 'The men lit their way with this darkness that burned like light in the lanterns. So said the witch.'

Jude imagined a row of shrouded figures holding up dark lanterns. He could almost see the curious ghosts before him; ghosts peeping out of their graves, wondering who their strange visitors were.

'The ghosts were friendly, as is their wont. Their spokesman, a former priest, addressed the strangers, but they didn't reply. Whilst most of the ghosts went up to see the strangers, the little witch hid underneath a gravestone.' Miss Rathbone stopped. 'The witch was young, and hadn't been dead for long, you see, so she was very wary of everything that went on in the graveyard.

'Even though she didn't know these men, she remembered the people who had tortured her and tried to drown her in the Trent. Like the hypocritical priests who had caused her so much suffering, these men were wearing rough habits which soaked up the moonlight, with hoods that hid them completely. The young witch was very frightened. She could still barely shut her eyes to sleep as she could always hear the hungry flames crackling (she had miserably survived the attempt to drown her in the river – but only in order to be burnt at the stake once her torturers had decided to convict her for witchcraft).

'And at once, her worst suspicions were confirmed.' Miss Rathbone lowered her voice to a sombre murmur. 'The strangers took their hoods off and the young witch saw what they had been hiding.'

'They had no faces,' Gaskell declared.

Miss Rathbone looked thoughtfully up at the sun, letting the silence play its own part in the story. After waiting for a moment, she continued, 'It's said that people go mad when they see a creature without a face.'

'What do you mean?' Jude asked.

'They had no faces. As simple as that.'

'That's why they couldn't speak,' Story said fearfully. 'They had no mouths.'

Miss Rathbone merely nodded. 'The witch couldn't understand how they could communicate with one another.'

'How many of them were there?'

'Countless,' said Gaskell. He looked worried.

'Did they have eyes?'

'No.'

'So how could they see?'

'There are other senses that even the dead don't know about,' Miss Rathbone replied mysteriously.

'What happened next?' Story couldn't contain her impatience any longer.

'They spread across the graveyard like a disease.' Miss Rathbone gazed across the graves, as if afraid that the faceless creatures might be about to appear at Highgate Cemetery. 'The ghosts who lived in Lud-upon-Trent had no idea who they were dealing with. Some of them just wanted to greet the newcomers, but...' She paused. 'But then came the first screams.'

Jude preferred not to imagine the sound of panicking ghosts.

'The ghosts of the dead who were still resting in their graves that night were awoken by the screams of their friends and neighbours, and also came creeping out of their homes.'

Jude pictured the scene and shuddered.

'The Faceless Ones wandered around the graveyard, their lanterns raised.'

Jude's left hand was resting on the gravestone. Story moved slightly closer to him and put her hand on his. He could feel her trembling and noticed that her slender hand didn't sink into his. It barely touched his, but just lay there gently. Jude dared not move.

Miss Rathbone, who hadn't missed the gentle movement, continued unperturbed. 'Every ghost who encountered the glow of the light that was darkness became part of it.'

The ghosts, she told them, could only stand and screech in despair as they disintegrated one by one. Jude tried to imagine it, but failed. He could picture the lantern, but not the light that was darkness.

'They were sucked into the light that was deep as an abyss. Panic broke out in the graveyard. The inhabitants didn't have the slightest chance of escaping,' whispered Gaskell, who was peering through his thick spectacle lenses like a hawk. 'As you know, we all have to stay close to our remains.'

Miss Rathbone nodded. 'The Faceless Ones with the lanterns made their leisurely way through the graves. They went down into the graves, illuminating everything with their dark lanterns, and any ghost who was caught in the glow disappeared into it.'

'They were captured by the lanterns,' whispered Story.

'How's that possible?'

'It's just a story that people have been telling for

years.' Gaskell straightened his glasses and frowned glumly.

But Jude knew that there was always some truth to the stories that people had been telling for years.

Miss Rathbone picked up the thread of her ancient story once more. 'The foxes believed that the young witch had gone mad. Nobody had ever mentioned faceless creatures before.' She took a deep breath, then added quietly, 'Not in this country, at any rate.'

'So how can anyone be sure that it actually happened?' asked Story.

'We don't know,' replied Miss Rathbone.

'Though Lud-upon-Trent has at any rate been cursed since then,' said Gaskell.

'By the next day, the ghosts had gone,' continued Miss Rathbone. 'There wasn't a single one left in the graveyard.'

'What about the witch?'

'She cowered in her hole and waited until it was all over.'

Jude imagined her hearing the others' cries and being unable to do anything.

'They didn't see her grave because there wasn't a grave to see.'

Jude shuddered again. 'Why didn't anyone help them?' he asked.

Gaskell twitched his head nervously. 'Who do you think could have helped them? Humans can't hear ghosts' screams. Animals? They are terrified of ghosts too.'

'Mr Fosbrooke wasn't at the graveyard that night. He was out,' Miss Rathbone said.

'Where was he?' Jude asked.

'Sometimes,' Miss Rathbone replied enigmatically, 'foxes have to do foxy things.' Her voice took on a wistful note. She quickly brushed it aside with a hand gesture. 'Something unimaginable and unprecedented happened in Staffordshire. Something that robbed the village by the River Trent of all its ghosts.'

'What happened next?' asked Story. Her hand was still resting on Jude's.

Someone cleared their throat. Gaskell. 'The same thing that always happens when the spirits of the dead are no longer there.' Gaskell looked like a scarecrow – albeit an elegant one.

Miss Rathbone gazed at the graves again. 'The people of Lud-upon-Trent were plagued by strange dreams.' She sighed. 'And they increasingly felt that something was missing. Something they couldn't do without.' She looked earnestly at Jude and Story. 'The spirits of the dead are much more than you'd think at first glance,' she said. Her voice dropped to a mysterious whisper. 'They're memories. If they're gone, people lack something highly important.'

'Can they tell?'

She shook her head. 'No. They're not conscious of it.' She blinked in the sunlight.

'And if the spirits of the dead disappear,' Gaskell put in, 'the people change who were once close to them. And things change too. They become somehow...false. People have bad luck instead of good luck. Misfortune keeps striking them. They have bad dreams, and when they walk down their village streets and alleyways, everything suddenly seems empty and colourless. It's just a vague feeling. A feeling of emptiness and loss.'

'And people change,' Miss Rathbone continued. 'They become grumpy. They stay at home, avoiding other people; when they do see one another, they exchange mistrustful looks because they secretly suspect one another of being to blame for their problems.'

'What then?' Story was hanging on Miss Rathbone's every word.

'Then the same happens as happened in Lud-upon-Trent.' The vixen looked at the girl.

'The inhabitants of Lud-upon-Trent became *spooky*,' Gaskell added.

'Nobody felt welcome any more in this weird place where everyone had changed overnight,' Miss Rathbone continued. 'Merchants, travellers, entertainers and other itinerants started to avoid Lud-upon-Trent. Eventually, all the young people left the village. The old people died one after another, and they were buried in the graveyard. But they didn't become good ghosts.' Miss Rathbone raised a warning finger. 'If humans cling to a life that they in fact loathe and detest, and then die anyway, they become malign, mistrustful ghosts.'

Jude swallowed.

'In short, Lud-upon-Trent became a ghost town,' Miss Rathbone concluded. 'Figuratively speaking, that is.'

Jude tried to imagine a village with nobody at the windows, no voices, no laughter. Where bare branches waved in an icy wind, with nobody there to enjoy anything.

'What about the faceless creatures?' Story asked.

'They were never seen again.'

'What did they do with the ghosts in the lanterns?' She evidently found it hard to get the words out.

Miss Rathbone shrugged. 'Nobody knows what happened to the ghosts in the lanterns. It might all just be a story to warn us to beware of strangers.'

'But what if the faceless creatures do exist?' It was Story who asked the question they were all desperate to ask. 'If Mr Monkford really did see the Faceless Ones, then surely that means...' She trembled. Gingerly she moved her hand away from Jude's and touched the grey gravestone.

Miss Rathbone looked silently up at one of the trees. Its branches glowed in the autumn light.

'How am I mixed up with these Faceless Ones?' the girl asked anxiously.

Miss Rathbone shrugged. 'That, child, is the question we need to answer. As soon as possible.'

That was the moment when Story began to cry. She had been fighting back the tears for so long that she had no choice.

Jude Finney had absolutely no experience of taking weeping girls into his arms, least of all weeping girls who might possibly be ghosts. Indeed, he had very little experience of taking *any* kind of girl into his arms, even ones who were neither weeping nor ghosts. On the couple of occasions when he'd dared to put his arm round a girl, he'd felt clumsy and shy. But in the golden light of that autumn day, he dared to do it again. He put his arm round the girl next to him and, although she was a ghost – or a kind of in-betweener, neither human nor ghost – she didn't shrug him off.

Jude held her cautiously. She was there, and her presence was like a scent that he couldn't quite catch, tender and gentle and unreal. For one exquisite moment they sat there, Story willingly caught in his embrace.

Then he felt her sobbing cease. 'I'm fine,' she said suddenly, extracting herself and moving away from him.

'OK,' Jude murmured quickly. He folded his hands irresolutely in his lap. Realising that he had done so, and that he looked ridiculous, he propped himself up on the gravestone instead. The moment had passed.

Story stood up and took several paces along the gravel path before stopping with her back to the others. A breath of wind touched her hair, and her body was moving in time to some melody that only she could hear.

'I'm sorry, I...' Her gaze was fixed on a group of weather-beaten stone crosses standing in the shadows.

'No problem,' said Jude, trying his best to sound chilled out.

Story turned to look at him, her eyes bright with tears. 'I don't even know who I am, and...' She came back and stopped before him. 'I'm sorry, I feel in such a mess.'

'That's understandable.'

She smiled. 'Thanks anyway,' she said, looking into his eyes so deeply that he felt as if he were sinking into hers.

Gaskell cleared his throat noisily. He was still leaning on the gravestone, evidently enjoying Jude's embarrassment.

'There is someone who might be able to help you,' Miss Rathbone suddenly declared.

Story stared at her. 'Really?'

'Jude would have to go with you because I can't, I'm afraid.'

'So can I leave the graveyard?'

'We'll soon find out, child, but I think you can.' Miss Rathbone narrowed her eyes thoughtfully. 'You were able to get to my house, so you should be able to go a bit further. We'll have to try. The person in question doesn't live around here.' She looked at Jude. 'You need to see her today. It'd be best to go by Tube.'

'You must be joking,' said Gaskell indignantly. 'You're surely not sending her to the Loveless One?'

Miss Rathbone glared at him. 'Do you have any better ideas?' she replied tartly.

Gaskell straightened his spectacles. 'No.'

'Well, there you go then.' She turned to Jude and

Story. 'She's called Lady Lovelace. Loreena Lovelace.'

'Loveless Lovelace,' Gaskell put in. 'The Loveless One.'

Sounds very promising! thought Jude. One look at Story told him that she felt the same.

'Who is she?' Story asked.

Miss Rathbone sat herself on a large stone cross. 'She's a statue over in Abney Park Cemetery,' she said, dangling her feet. 'Yes, a statue. Made of stone. Or with a stone heart, at any rate.'

Jude and Story exchanged quizzical looks.

'*Terra incognita*,' Gaskell muttered. It sounded to Jude like a warning. He couldn't make out at first whether Gaskell meant the graveyard or the Loveless One.

'Why do we need to see her?' Story asked. 'Her name doesn't make her sound like someone you'd ask for advice.'

'That's right,' said Jude. 'She sounds more like someone to steer very clear of.'

'The problem is that you would both have to go and see her completely on your own.' Gaskell sighed. 'And anyway, what do we actually know about the Loveless One?'

'That she helps people who are in dead-end situations.'

'Says who?'

Miss Rathbone rolled her eyes. 'For goodness' sake, Quentin, you know the stories.'

'That's what bothers me.'

'But,' Miss Rathbone countered, 'she knows things that nobody else knows.'

Gaskell dug the point of his boot into the gravel. 'Maybe she does.'

'She's a kind of oracle. A little...dangerous, perhaps.'

Jude raised his arms. 'Hang on a moment,' he said loudly. 'Hold your horses. Objection! This doesn't sound very...'

'...reliable,' said Story. They both nodded.

It was Gaskell of all people who asked, 'In what way?'

Jude stared at him. Typical Gaskell. Always unsettling people. 'Well, is she dangerous or not?'

'That depends,' said Miss Rathbone.

Jude sighed. 'On what?'

'On whether the stories are true.' Gaskell's head was twitching nervously.

'The Loveless One doesn't like foxes,' said Miss Rathbone. 'That's why I can't come with you.'

Jude looked at her in astonishment. So that was why!

'I don't understand,' said Story. 'How does that affect you?'

Miss Rathbone smiled kindly at her, as if at a dim child.

'Ayelet *is* a vixen,' Gaskell explained.

'I beg your pardon?'

'I'm a *kitsune*,' Miss Rathbone said, as if this were the most normal thing in the world. 'I was a fox that could turn itself into a woman.' She pulled a face. 'And now I'm a woman who, unfortunately enough, only rarely turns into a fox.' That was a part of the story that Jude had never heard either.

'So that's why people call you "the vixen"?' Story couldn't help smiling.

'Yes.'

'I thought it was because you were so cunning.'

Miss Rathbone theatrically brushed a strand of fox-coloured hair away from her forehead. 'Oh, yes, I'm certainly that.'

Gaskell nodded. 'I'll vouch for that.'

'Be that as it may: I am a kitsune.'

'She guards this graveyard,' Gaskell told Story.

'That's what kitsunes do,' Miss Rathbone explained. 'Every graveyard has foxes to make sure that everything is in order. And every graveyard has a kitsune. A good fox to take care of everything. Male or female.'

'That's what she is,' said Gaskell.

'Hmm.'

'You're magic.'

Miss Rathbone smiled, flattered.

'Some foxes become capable of taking on human form once they reach a certain age,' said Gaskell.

'How old are you, then?' Story asked Miss Rathbone.

The vixen raised her finger in mock admonition. 'Never ask a lady her age. I'm older than you think, and look younger than I am. I hope.' She grinned broadly and suddenly looked more fox-like than human. Once you knew that she was a kitsune, it was obvious to look at her. It was there in her hair, her narrow eyes, her mouth, in every secretive movement, in all her little gestures.

'But what about the Loveless One?' Jude asked, gripped once more by a sense of vague impatience.

Miss Rathbone crossed her legs. 'A long, long time ago, Lady Lovelace fell in love with a kitsune.'

Story was listening, transfixed, and Jude wondered whether she had enjoyed books and stories this much in her forgotten life.

'She first met the man at one of the societies in Victorian London, and immediately fell head over heels in love with him. From then on she kept seeing him, just in snatched moments; she yearned for these encounters but he never really let her into his life.' Miss Rathbone was particularly skilled in adjusting her voice to convey the gaslit London of times past. Effortlessly she conjured up for her listeners elegant men in top hats and fine ladies in exquisite dresses. 'He took her for walks in Kensington Gardens, and they visited the Crystal Palace together.' She paused to look at her listeners. 'But after each of their meetings, he disappeared back into a life that remained a mystery to Lady Lovelace.' Miss Rathbone winked at Jude. 'However, the lady was, like most women, cunning.'

'Hear, hear,' Gaskell remarked.

'One night,' continued Miss Rathbone, ignoring him, 'she followed him through the streets to see where he lived. She wanted to find out the thing that gives all women sleepless nights: whether he was serious about her.' Miss Rathbone's voice took on a nocturnal tone. 'And so she followed him to the graveyard. He went straight through the gates and vanished into the shadows.'

Story was completely captivated. Her eyes were glowing. *Oh yes*, Jude thought, *she likes a good story*.

'And so Lady Lovelace made her way across the

graveyard to find him.'

'Abney Park Cemetery,' Gaskell added ominously.

Story, who evidently also knew how to tell a story, whispered, 'And she finally found him.'

Miss Rathbone smiled. 'He was sitting on a gravestone in the moonlight in his human form. Lady Lovelace went up and revealed herself to him. And then she asked him the crucial question.'

'And he told her who he really was?'

'Yes.'

Story nodded, satisfied yet afraid, for she sensed that the vixen's husky voice was going to send the story suddenly in a different direction.

'Then,' Miss Rathbone continued quickly, 'everything happened in the way that Fate had planned for them.'

Jude had guessed it. Something bad.

'They hadn't noticed the stone angel approaching them.'

'What about the kitsune?'

'Lady Lovelace had never seen a stone angel before. Not one that moved, at any rate. The kitsune, however, knew how dangerous these creatures are.'

Story was chewing her lip nervously. 'He left her in the lurch.'

Miss Rathbone nodded. 'The stone angel came

closer, and the kitsune took to his heels and fled.'

'The bastard,' whispered Story.

'Lady Lovelace watched the supposed gentleman to whom she had lost her young heart disappear into the dense undergrowth in his foxy form. He abandoned her to her fate.'

Jude had never seen a stone angel, but he could well imagine what a dreadful sight it must be. Until now he had only heard stories about them; they were said to roam around at night in Highgate as well on occasion.

'Bitter despair turned her love into hate.' Miss Rathbone staged a pause. 'That was precisely why the stone angel left her alone. But from then on, her life was no longer a life. Love turned to hate is like wine turned to vinegar.' The vixen's eyes glittered dully. 'The remains of a tired life, now bitter hatred, carried on living in Lady Lovelace. And so she became a creature that was half stone angel, half human, not really living and not really dead. She became cold, grey stone that was filled with life.'

'And so the Loveless One was born,' Gaskell said simply.

'Poor thing,' Story blurted.

'There's nothing worse than a woman whose love turns to hate,' said Gaskell.

Miss Rathbone didn't gainsay him. 'From then on, the Loveless One assumed control of the graveyard. Abney Park Cemetery became her empire. It wasn't long before she'd driven out all the graveyard foxes. She wanted nothing more to do with creatures that were fickle, unprincipled and cowardly. With the help of the stone angels, she made sure that no fox ever set foot again in her graveyard.' She pulled a face. 'The cowardly kitsune never returned either.'

'What became of him?'

'Nobody knows.'

'What about Lady Lovelace?'

'That was the end of her. From then on, she was the Loveless One. She still lives in Abney Park Cemetery,' said Gaskell. 'She's said to be wise.'

'Who by?'

'People.'

'She belongs to both worlds,' said Miss Rathbone, 'and over the years she has accumulated knowledge about the essence of things denied to ghosts, humans and kitsunes alike.'

'Or so it's said,' remarked Gaskell.

'She's an oracle,' Miss Rathbone said, ignoring him. 'But' – and here she returned to the problem at hand – 'she hates all kitsunes.'

'So that's why you can't come with us,' said Jude.

'She might help you.'

'Lots of ghosts ask her for advice...so it's said.'

Again, that blasted 'so it's said', thought Jude. 'But if ghosts can't leave their graveyards, how do you know what goes on in Abney Park?'

'That's the point,' said Gaskell, evidently assuming the role of the sceptic. 'Nobody actually knows. It's just what's said. By everyone.'

'The ghosts of the various graveyards are in contact with one another,' said the vixen. 'They find out what's going on in each other's graveyards via the kitsunes of the Magnificent Seven. We meet once a month.'

'The Magnificent Seven are London's big old graveyards,' Jude told Story.

She nodded.

'And as Abney Park Cemetery doesn't have a kitsune, it's *terra incognita*,' said Gaskell. 'Unknown ground.'

Jude was starting to find his friends' vague chatter somewhat irritating. He wanted to do something, not just sit around. 'So you don't know whether or not she might be dangerous. What if she tries to harm us?'

'Why should she try to harm you? You're just two friends needing advice.'

'So what are we supposed to ask her?'

‘Ask her what happened to Story. Maybe she’s heard of the Faceless Ones. Maybe she can tell you what to do next.’

Jude was still not convinced. ‘And what are you going to do in the meantime?’

‘I’m going to see what I can find out about the Silver Wraith.’ Miss Rathbone winked at Jude and Story. ‘I’ve got my contacts,’ she whispered mysteriously. They couldn’t get another word out of her.

For several minutes, they were silent in the sparkling sunlight, all of them entertaining their own particular fears. Their thoughts were as autumnal as the air. Highgate Cemetery lay peacefully and expectantly before them. As a gentle wind swept the bright leaves across the grey gravestones, Jude screwed up his courage. He took Story’s hand and set off with her, heading for a new, strange tale with an uncertain ending.

CHAPTER 4

Autumn days, like life itself, can sometimes be unpredictable. And seldom had an autumn day been as unpredictable as this one. The sun was casting the streets and old houses of Highgate in a magical, sand-coloured glow – which couldn't have been any more deceptive if it had tried.

Jude was filled with an unfamilar sense of excitement, as if he were in the middle of an adventure whose ending was completely unknown.

'What are you thinking about?' Story asked.

'Nothing special.' About the results of that stupid test that Mr Ackroyd must long since have marked; about the other kids at school who were at that moment doing all the normal stuff that teenagers do; about his father, who would be standing in some puddle somewhere, analysing the water and not giving his son a single thought; about the near-empty fridge that Jude absolutely had to restock before his father got home; about the homework he hadn't done.

'Tell me.'

He told her. 'Sounds crazy, doesn't it?'

'Sounds like normal life.' She sighed heavily. 'I'd be glad if I could remember anything about school. Or about anything at all.'

They left the graveyard, crossed Swains Lane with its long shadows cast by the low sun, and walked through Waterlow Park, which was almost deserted. They passed the hideous radio masts and the tennis courts, and followed the path that led between high horse chestnuts and oaks to Highgate High Street.

'Do you think I can go wherever I like?' Story asked anxiously. Jude could tell that she was afraid, but she was trying not to show it.

'Yes,' Jude replied – though it was a lie. Or, rather, a promise, an attempt to convince her that everything would still turn out fine. 'Don't worry – you can do it, Story. I'll help you. Nothing's going to happen to you.'

'Are you sure?' She cautiously put one foot in front of the other.

'Yes.' You could get used to telling lies. 'Yes, I'm sure.'

Miss Rathbone had at any rate been sure about it, so Jude had decided to take a leaf out of her book and be as certain as she was. Unfortunately, though, the vixen wasn't with them; she had remained at the graveyard. She and Gaskell were planning to try to find further witnesses to what had happened on the night that Story had appeared at Highgate Cemetery. The business with the Faceless Ones had evidently disturbed her much more than she was willing to let on.

This was in fact deeply disturbing. If the Faceless Ones really were responsible for Story's plight, then Jude didn't like to think about what it meant for Highgate.

'OK?' Jude asked, partly to cheer Story up and partly to take his mind off his own dark thoughts.

Story, who seemed at the moment to be immune to all attempts to cheer her up, did say yes – but Jude could tell how tense each footstep was making her. How long would she be able to carry on setting one foot in front of the other? This question was written all over her face.

Neither of them knew exactly how it would feel when she was suddenly prevented from continuing.

'What if I can't do it?'

'Don't worry – you *can* do it.'

'Will I just dissolve into thin air?'

'You went to Miss Rathbone's, and nothing happened to you.'

'That was just across the road, not far from the graveyard.'

'All the same.'

'Will it hurt?'

'No, definitely not!' He tried to inject as much confidence as possible into these words.

Story, however, was finding every step difficult. She couldn't be careful enough. 'I keep thinking every step is going to be my last one,' she whispered.

When they finally emerged on Highgate High Street by Lauderdale House Arts Centre, their anxiety still hadn't lessened. It was as if they themselves couldn't believe that they had got this far without any problems.

'Look, we're already quite a long way from the graveyard.'

'Yes, maybe you're right.' She allowed herself a hesitant laugh.

'Of course I'm right.' Jude sounded satisfied.

The heavy traffic in Highgate High Street brought Jude back to reality. Back to the world beyond the old graveyard. The world where crowds of people scurried along the pavements and delivery lorries stopped to let men in high-visibility jackets unload crates and parcels and cart them into shops. The world where run-of-the-mill teenagers sloped around on street corners, looking either apathetic or challenging, some of them with fags hanging out of their mouths. This world was so goddamn ordinary, like a kitschy painting in lurid hues that a gallery would have to hide away to stop it being laughed at.

They passed the Whittington Stone pub and followed the road down to Archway station. There they took the escalator down into the depths of the Underground, with its stale, dry air and strong smell of oil and gloom. Jude didn't particularly like the Underground. It was narrow and crowded, and the train tunnels always seemed to him like coffins, only longer and even more lifeless.

'We're fine,' he said as they waited on the platform.

'Mmm.' Story's grin lit up her face as it always did, making her look like a completely different person.

At the same time, Jude noticed that the other people on the platform were looking askance at him and he was suddenly aware of the dour expressions of the hordes of commuters and other people who normally filled up the Underground. People didn't normally look at one another; today, though, they were eyeing him suspiciously. Mothers with children glanced at him, and their expressions seemed to whisper: *don't look at him, or he'll come this way.*

Jude knew those kinds of looks. They were like the ones that passengers gave to the homeless people shivering in old newspapers at the entrance to the Underground. Or the looks that girls gave the boys in the playground who were even greyer and more mousy than Jude. Yes, he knew those concerned, patronising glances, but he couldn't understand why they were now being directed at *him*.

'They're giving you those looks,' said Story, answering his silent question, 'because you're talking to yourself.'

For a moment he didn't see what she meant, so accustomed had he become to her presence.

'None of them can see me,' Story explained. She laughed loudly and waved her hand around in front of the face of the man next to her.

He didn't react. The corner of his mouth twitched slightly, as if he had felt something that he couldn't quite explain.

Damn. 'You're right.' Jude allowed himself a smile. He must look pretty weird: a gawky youth talking animatedly to someone who wasn't there. The other people could hear Jude, but couldn't hear Story. They were witnesses to a one-sided conversation. But hey, this was London, a city whose streets were filled with mad people and freaks alongside the normal-seeming ones. Everyone was used to people who talked to themselves or sang loudly into space. All the passengers on the platform quickly turned their attention to other things, soon forgetting about the strange youth.

The train arrived and Jude and Story got in. The passengers moved out of the girl's way; they seemed instinctively to make space for her.

'I've never been to town with a ghost,' Jude teased his companion.

'You're not now, either. I'm not a real ghost. Had you forgotten?'

'No, of course not.' Jude glanced at Story. Here, in the middle of the city, she looked to him just like everyone else. Like a pretty girl whom he'd never have spoken to at school because boys would have been flocking around her.

'People really are weird,' said Story. 'None of these people knows that there are such things as ghosts.' She looked at him. 'They're only real for you.'

'Crazy, eh?'

A woman in a green hat, who was standing next to Jude, jumped.

'I didn't mean you,' Jude said politely.

'Who are you talking to?' the woman asked, blinking in confusion.

'Rupert,' said Jude.

'Rupert?' Story asked curiously.

The woman didn't respond.

'A white bear with a red jumper and yellow trousers,' Jude explained.

When he turned back to the woman, she had moved away from the weird boy and was looking studiedly in the opposite direction.

Story giggled. 'Rupert!'

'Yes – do you know him?'

'I...um, yes. From the TV.' Story stopped abruptly. 'No,' she muttered, confused. Then, again, 'Yes.' She took a deep breath. 'That's pretty weird, you know? I can kind of remember that bear. From the TV. I've seen him, but...'

'Maybe your memory's finally starting to come back?'

'No.' She shook her head, disappointed. 'It was just...Oh, never mind.'

'Your memory will come back one day. Believe me.'

'You're an optimist.'

'Aren't you?'

'No.'

The woman in the green hat had meanwhile inched her way to the end of the carriage, and was casting concerned glances in the direction of the boy who was talking to himself. Her left eye was twitching nervously.

'If you follow her down there,' Story said, 'I bet she moves away again.'

'Do you reckon?'

'Are you going to give it a go?'

'Better not.'

The train hurtled down the tunnel. Outside, red lights shot past. The passengers swayed to the rhythm of the train.

'Can you tell the difference between people and ghosts?' Story suddenly asked.

'You mean by looking at them?'

She nodded and gesticulated around the carriage. 'Yes. Can you tell me which of them are dead and which are alive?'

Jude looked at her and said firmly, '*You're* alive, at any rate.'

Story swallowed. 'Are you sure?'

He looked around, taking in all the busy people who played their roles day in, day out, tackling the journey between home and work with sour faces. The same thing day after day. Dulled by the tribulations of life, they no longer enjoyed ordinary things: an early-morning dewdrop caught on a spider's web; the light that gleams in puddles in spring before the city fully awakens; the songs sung by young buskers in the street.

'You're more alive than anyone here,' Jude said. He ignored the looks that these very same people were giving him. Let them think he was mad. What did it matter?

Story smiled quietly to herself.

'Do you feel like a ghost?' Jude asked.

The man behind Jude turned his head away, as if he hadn't heard anything.

'What's a ghost supposed to feel like?' Story retorted.

'I don't know.'

'Neither do I.'

The people around Jude and Story were trying inconspicuously to back as far away from them as they could.

'Gaskell is mostly cheerful,' Jude said, unperturbed. 'The others are too.' Jude did in fact mostly know only the cheerful ghosts, although he also knew one or two curmudgeonly ones such as Mr Monkford. But those ones mostly avoided hanging around with the others.

'That's right,' agreed Story. 'They didn't look as if they were sorry about being ghosts.'

'Life isn't over once you're a ghost.'

'Do you really believe that?'

He nodded.

The other passengers now seemed to have decided to treat him as if he weren't there at all. They all stood at a distance from him, staring at the floor, peeping furtively at him out of the corners of their eyes.

'How do you feel?' Jude asked.

'Supercalifragilisticexpialidocious.'

Jude knew exactly what Story meant. 'Do you know the film?'

She frowned. 'Yes,' she said. 'I remember it.'

'Like you remembered Rupert Bear.'

'Funny, eh?'

'What else can you remember?'

Story shrugged her shoulders. 'Stories that someone read to me. Yes, I remember those. But I don't know who it was.' She bit her lip. 'I don't know where the room was that I heard the stories in.' She rubbed her eyes, exhausted. 'I can't even remember what the storyteller's voice sounded like.'

'You like stories.'

She stared at him as if he'd uncovered her secret. 'I don't know, maybe I do. What makes you think that?'

The next station was announced.

'It was the way you were listening to Miss Rathbone.'

She regarded the dark carriage window thoughtfully. 'It's strange when you can't see your own reflection,' she said.

'In a bad way?'

She shook her head. 'Not bad, just weird.' She put her head on one side. 'And I don't even know whether I normally like looking at myself in mirrors.'

He shrugged. 'You don't need to.'

She blushed. A genuine blush. 'What does my hair look like?'

'Pretty.'

She pulled a face. 'Typical boy reply.'

'I'm a typical boy.'

'No you're not.'

'Oh yeah?'

'Jude, do I look vain?'

This question surprised him. 'I don't know...um...I don't think so.'

'Do I look weird?'

'No, it's just...'

'What?'

'You just look kind of different from the girls at my school.'

'What do the girls at your school look like?'

'They're all conceited and up themselves. Well, not all of them – but lots of them are.'

'So I don't look like that.'

'No.'

'So what do I look like?'

'Like someone who enjoys life.'

She laughed. 'And yet I'm a ghost.'

'Not a proper one,' he replied quickly.

She turned serious again.

'You look like a girl who knows the meaning of life.'

'What's that supposed to mean?'

'Precisely that.'

The train stopped at King's Cross. Jude and Story were swept along with the crowd heading for the exit. They switched platforms, went up one flight of steps, down another, and got onto the Piccadilly line which would take them to Manor House.

This train was even more crowded than the previous one. Once again, Jude noticed that people avoided Story, just as if they could feel her presence. They instinctively changed direction, enabling Story to pass undisturbed.

'Jude Finney,' Story said, once they were standing in the carriage, 'you're a strange boy.'

'The ghosts in Highgate are nicer than people. At

least they know how to live, even though they're already dead.'

'You like them, don't you?'

'I feel at home there. No idea why. Just the way it is.' He thought of his father, who was due home the following day. And about how life at home would change. Their house would feel smaller, and his room would feel like a prison. Jude didn't know why; that was just the way it was. When his father was around, he often felt as if he couldn't breathe for lack of oxygen, and this feeling sounded much like the noise of the television that George Finney fell asleep in front of at 9pm.

'You're thinking about depressing stuff again, aren't you?'

He nodded. 'About my ordinary life,' he said.

'At least you know who you are,' said Story. 'That's a bonus. I'd love to know who I am.'

'You're Story,' said Jude.

'But that's not my real name. It sounds lovely, like a song that a stranger has written for me. But it's not my name. I'm not Story – you know that. I want to know who I really am.'

He nodded. 'We'll find out,' he promised.

'Do you really think so?'

'Miss Rathbone and Gaskell will help us.'

'They're really nice.'

'Yes.' Once you'd got used to it, it was perfectly easy to ignore the other passengers' dirty looks.

'What does your father say about you hanging around with Miss Rathbone?'

'I'm in my school reading-aloud group. It's kids who read to elderly people in their spare time.'

'Really?'

'Well, I did only join when I needed a reason to visit Miss Rathbone.'

'You read to her?'

He shook his head. 'No, but she told the school that she wanted a kid to come and read to her. So I can go there any time I like without anyone bothering. I officially do her shopping too.'

'So your father thinks you're a public-spirited type who reads to old folks?'

He nodded. 'What's wrong with that?'

'You really are cunning.'

'So should I have told him the truth? That I spend all my time at Highgate Cemetery, hanging out with the spirits of the dead?'

'Maybe.' Story's eyes glinted mischievously as the train pulled into Manor House tube station. 'We're there.'

As they emerged into the fresh air and daylight

once more, Jude breathed out, relieved to have escaped from the stuffy tunnels of the London Underground. They now had another couple of miles to walk.

It was rush hour. The roads were full of stationary traffic and grumpy drivers. Some of them were making angry hand gestures, their faces contorted into impatient or irritated grimaces. As in the Underground, everyone on the pavement avoided Story. They seemed to feel her presence like a vague sensation that touched them briefly then floated off in the October wind.

Jude gave her a sidelong glance. He was surprised again by how full of life she looked. He'd never in a million years have taken her for a ghost – or whatever she was.

'Do you play the guitar?' she suddenly asked.

He looked surprised.

'You had a guitar with you at the party yesterday.'

'Oh yeah, right. But I don't play particularly well.'

'What sort of stuff?'

'Anything and everything.'

'I like Fran Healey,' said Story.

'You remember the music you liked?'

'Yes, but that just suddenly occurred to me. I don't know why.'

Thoughtfully, Jude looked straight ahead. The

street they were on in Stoke Newington was bordered by trendy cafés, boutiques and market stalls; everything was loud and bustling. A road where you could reach out and touch real life. Nobody here guessed that there was such a thing as ghosts. People could only see what they wanted to see. Sometimes Jude wished he could laugh out loud at the thought of everything they couldn't see.

He turned back to Story. If only he could give her back her memory. 'Do you remember any other stuff?' Maybe other fragments of memories would resurface if she concentrated hard enough. 'Where do you go when you're not at school? Do you go to particular pubs or clubs?'

But again her hazel eyes remained blank as she searched desperately for images of a life that seemed to have disappeared just like that.

'Do you think she can help me?' she asked as the graveyard walls loomed up in the distance.

'*The Loveless One*.' The name made Jude uncomfortable. He didn't know himself whether it referred to some magical creature or a curse.

'Don't say that name,' she said quickly. 'It sounds horrible. Maybe she really likes it when other people's hearts end up just as broken as hers was.'

'Miss Rathbone thinks she'll be able to help you.'

The sun was slowly sinking. The treetops, roofs and pylons on the horizon were already an unreal shade of orangey red. The shadows were long and pointed, hinting at how cold it would be before long.

'Jude?'

'Yes?'

'Can we stop talking for a bit?'

'Fine,' he said. And it was fine, for now at any rate.

By the time they reached Abney Park, the sun was ominously low. Before long, it would be dusk. Jude had no desire to go stumbling around a strange graveyard in the dark. Particularly not *this* strange graveyard – one that even ghosts described as *terra incognita* and seemed to find as scary as humans normally find ghosts.

'Right then, let's get it over and done with,' he said, largely to boost his own courage.

'OK,' muttered Story, no less apprehensive.

They entered the graveyard via an imposing Egyptian-style gate. With its stone columns on either side, it reminded Jude of the set of an old epic film. Above the entrance, it said in hieroglyphics:

'Very inviting,' Story murmured. She pulled up her jacket collar.

Jude was surprised. 'Are you cold?'

'Yes.'

He stared at her. 'That's weird.'

'Why? Aren't ghosts normally cold?'

'I don't know, to be honest, but I don't think so.'

'Then I'm the only ghost who feels the cold.' She had a good sense of humour – something else he liked about her. She stopped and turned to him. 'Does that mean anything?'

'What – you being cold?'

She nodded.

'I don't know.' Jude had also felt the sudden chill in the air as they had entered the graveyard. But he didn't want to worry her any more than necessary.

'What's the matter?' asked Story.

'Nothing.'

'You look as if you'd seen a ghost.'

He forced himself to laugh.

'Dumb joke,' she added.

Jude, meanwhile, was scrutinising the graveyard. Abney Park was a beautiful graveyard, one of the Magnificent Seven, but he'd never been there before.

In fact, he had had nothing at all to do with any graveyards before he'd met Miss Rathbone. As he had no mother – or, rather, no mother whom he'd ever known – he didn't have any maternal grandparents either. His father's parents were long dead, but Jude couldn't remember their funerals. It was too long ago. Why would he have had any reason to hang around graveyards? And why on earth did he have the ability to see ghosts? Sometimes, during the long nights in Twisden Road, he lay awake wondering just that.

He sighed. So here he was. And he *did* feel cold; it was as if he'd somehow strayed into a completely unknown realm.

'Something about this place is different from Highgate,' Story said.

Jude knew exactly what she meant, even before she'd said it.

The Magnificent Seven were established during the nineteenth century to solve the problem of London's dead. The paupers' graves and the graveyards of the city's countless small parish churches were hopelessly overcrowded. What could they do with all the bodies? To try to solve the problem, Parliament decreed that seven cemeteries be established outside central London. And so the Magnificent Seven were born. These were parks with broad paths, suitable even for royal burials; modern resting places with newfangled hoists to convey the coffins into the depths. Then there were giant catacombs and vaults, crematoria and chapels, awe-inspiring sculptures in the form of life-loathing mythical creatures who watched over the dead. Everywhere a hotchpotch of pseudo Ancient Greek, Egyptian Renaissance and neogothic architecture. These new cemeteries were carefully embedded in beautiful scenery, more reminiscent of a park than a graveyard. Places where London's upper crust could combine a weekend stroll with remembering their dear departed.

'A Victorian Valhalla,' Miss Rathbone had called this graveyard culture.

Over the years, nature had gradually reclaimed what had once been hers. Undergrowth and creepers proliferated, covering the grey stone, the entrances to the vaults, the crooked crosses. Or that was the case in Highgate, at any rate.

'Something's not right,' Jude murmured. The Egyptian gate had meanwhile closed behind them. He wasn't sure whether it was only the cold that was bothering him.

'What do you mean?'

'It's just a feeling,' he replied. 'But there's

something...wrong here.' He could tell that she felt it too but that she couldn't quite put it into words either.

'What should we do now?'

'Carry on. But we need to be careful.'

Story nodded. 'Highgate's different,' she said, more to herself than to him.

'Yes, you feel safe there,' Jude replied. All he had was a vague feeling that something was wrong about this place; it was as if someone were eavesdropping on them, hiding in the shadows that stretched in all directions.

The clouds were gathering in the evening sky, which was now the colour of rusty iron.

'The further we go, the colder it gets,' said Story.

Jude sensed it as well. It really did feel as if the temperature was dropping with every step they took. He wanted to say something reassuring, but had no choice but to agree with her. 'Yes, I think you're right.'

'How can it?' she asked.

'I don't know.'

'But you can feel it too?'

'Yes.'

All the same, they carried on walking. Apart from the traffic outside the graveyard walls, their footsteps were the only sound. There wasn't a bird to be seen or heard. No twittering, no stirrings in the undergrowth, nothing at all, however hard they listened.

Total silence.

But it was a strange silence that seemed out of place. It felt wrong. Graveyards were silent, but not *that* silent. Nothing suggested that they were welcome there. The whole place was dark and as cold as the moss on the stone crosses. It was plain forbidding.

'Do you think we'll be able to find her?'

'Lady Lovelace?' Jude gazed at the apparently endless rows of graves ahead of them. 'I certainly hope so.'

'Do you think the stories are true?' asked Story.

Jude shrugged. He didn't really want to talk about it. Not now.

'I reckon there's a grain of truth in most stories,' Story persisted.

'Let's hope they're just stories,' Jude replied. He remembered the Faceless Ones. 'Come on!'

Following Miss Rathbone's instructions, he strode purposefully down the broad path. The Magnificent Seven were all built along similar lines. A main route led to the chapel, which tended to be in the centre of the graveyard. From there the paths fanned out, shimmering like the rays of a strange sun illuminating death and transience.

But unlike at Highgate Cemetery, where Jude had immediately felt at home, his feeling of discomfiture increased the further they walked – along with the cold. It was a feeling of being in the gathering dusk in a rambling park in which nothing was as it first appeared.

As the vixen had said, the broad path led northwards to a gothic chapel with bell towers pointing up into the dark sky like needles. The windows tapered upwards, flashing like the eyes of an animal waiting to pounce in the dark. The gravestones and stone crosses that lined the paths were very similar to the ones at Highgate Cemetery, but less monumental – more simple, though no less elegant. The symmetrical, streamlined paths seemed to Jude to be so clean and well-tended that they looked somehow fake. In Highgate the greenery spread willy-nilly, and even the huge buildings in the so-called Circle of Lebanon were covered with undergrowth. But here...

No, Jude didn't like it.

'There's evil afoot,' he murmured, wondering why he should suddenly have thought of this quotation. It came from a cheap Hammer Horror film starring Christopher Lee or Peter Cushing (or, more probably, both of them). Jude had seen it as a child, and it had left him so scared of nocturnal noises that he'd felt as if his heart was going to stop.

'That's from the film with the grave-robbers,' said Story.

Jude was startled. 'How do you know stuff like that? When you've forgotten the really important things?' He too remembered the grave-robbers, even though he had only seen the film that one time.

'I couldn't remember the film either – it suddenly just popped into my head.'

'What's the difference?'

'The difference,' she said, 'is that I only just remembered it now. I hadn't remembered it before. Simple.'

'You mean you suddenly remember stuff like that.'

'It's not that hard to understand, is it?' And as she didn't understand it herself, Story sounded cross and snappy. Jude understood that process only too well.

'But what does it all mean?' he wondered aloud.

'Gaskell said that ghosts don't suffer.'

'So?'

'I was limping at first. But my limp has gone.'

Jude stopped abruptly. He stared at her. The full force of what she was getting at made him feel dizzy.

'When you found me, I couldn't remember anything at all,' Story continued slowly. 'But now my memories are starting to come back. Once I'm a real ghost, I'll remember everything, won't I?'

Jude nodded dumbly. Why hadn't he thought of that?

'Then I'll know how I died and where I came from.'

Jude swallowed. His throat was dry.

'So if I keep on remembering more stuff from the past,' Story continued, 'then that means I'm in the process of turning into a ghost.' She looked at him earnestly. 'You know what that means.' Her eyes filled with tears. 'It means that I'm dying.' She forced the words out. 'I'm slowly dying, and that's why my memories are coming back one by one.'

A wave of despair engulfed Jude. He tried with all his might to conquer it. They couldn't give up now, not when they'd come so far. It was imperative that he keep her going. 'We need to find your body as quickly as possible.'

'What then? Who knows whether anyone can help me, even if we find it?'

'Let's cross that bridge when we come to it,' Jude said firmly. 'It's not going to happen. Stories don't end like that.'

'Not ones with happy endings, anyway,' Story whispered.

'This is going to be one with a happy ending.' Jude had no idea where all this confidence had come from, but there it was: clear and firm and irrevocable.

'And what if it's a story with an unhappy ending? One of the ones that have you crying your eyes out by the time it finishes?' Story was trembling from head to toe. 'I want to live, Jude, really live again.'

He took a step towards her and touched her hand. She didn't move away. Her hand felt firm; cold, but firm. Jude knew that he could touch ghosts, and he knew that ghosts could touch objects in ordinary life. But there was something else too: the radiance that had surrounded Story ever since he'd first met her at Highgate Cemetery, the strange gold glow, had started gradually to diminish. Jude had already noticed it; he'd had the vague feeling that there was something different about Story when they entered Abney Park via the Egyptian gate. But now he suddenly realised what it was. And he found it deeply disturbing.

'Let's carry on,' he said quickly.

She nodded silently.

Hand in hand, they continued down the path that Miss Rathbone had told them about. She had told them that the statue of the Loveless One was behind the chapel, at a fork in the path.

'Be polite to her,' Miss Rathbone had drilled into them.

'And beware of the stone angels,' Gaskell had called after them as they set off.

'What's all the stuff about the stone angels?' Story asked as they walked on. 'What do you know about them?'

'They're mourning. You have to beware of them, because if they touch you, you turn to stone.' That's what the vixen had told him.

'Where do they live?' Story looked around anxiously.

'All graveyards have them. They're just there. Some of them roam around at night, looking for victims.' Just thinking about it gave Jude goose bumps. 'They're unpredictable.'

'Have you ever seen one?'

Jude shook his head. 'I hope I never do.'

They stopped, glanced around to see if any stone angels were lurking, and were relieved not to see any.

'That's the chapel ahead of us,' said Story.

Everywhere in the bushes and hedges to either side of the path were small animal sculptures that looked as if they had been turned in mid-motion to dark stone.

'They're foxes!' Story whispered.

'Stone foxes,' Jude replied.

Their mouths were open, revealing small, sharp teeth made of pale stone. Their ears were pricked with horror.

'What on earth happened to them?' But Jude could tell that Story already knew the answer to her own question.

'She turned them to stone,' he said softly. 'Like a stone angel would.'

The Loveless One.

'You mean they came here even though they knew and...'

'Yes.' He knelt on the earth close to one of the foxes. 'Maybe they didn't know the danger.' He touched the animal, feeling cold, hard stone instead of soft, warm fur.

'You mean the story's so old that it's been forgotten about?'

'It's possible.' Jude stood up again. He wiped his hand carefully on his trousers.

'Let's carry on,' said Story. 'This place gives me the creeps.'

Loveless Lovelace, Jude thought. *The Loveless One*. For the first time, he had an unpleasant feeling that coming here hadn't been such a good idea.

They reached the chapel. Jude listened. There was nothing to hear but the soft wind – and the traffic, as if from miles away. Nothing else.

Story said what he was thinking. 'Where are they?'

Jude looked around.

'Where are the ghosts?'

The place made Jude feel very uncomfortable. At first glance the graveyard didn't appear all that different from Highgate. And yet the brown leaves scuttering across the ground seemed more ragged, the flowers on the graves more wilted, and the candles were nothing but stumps.

'Shouldn't we already have met heaps of ghosts?' Story stopped. She had buried her hands in her jacket pockets. 'Why isn't anyone bothered that we're here?'

Jude sniffed the air. Even that smelled of danger. 'Yes. It's weird.'

The shadows stretched across the endless of rows of crosses in the twilight, as if they were greedily seeking sustenance.

'Let's see,' Jude suggested. And before Story could reply, he went over to one of the graves and tapped it cautiously. He waited. When there was no answer, he called softly, 'Hello?'

No reply.

He read the inscription. *Mary Hillum. 1803–1864.*

Never left her dwelling place.

'What?' Story asked nervously.

He looked at her uncertainly. 'Maybe it's just an empty grave.' He did of course know how improbable that was. 'Abney Park's just a normal graveyard.' He said the words as if they were a mantra. 'That's what Miss Rathbone said, anyway.'

'You think there's no ghost in there?'

'Could be.'

Jude walked down the row of graves, tapping on all the stones. Old, sooty candle stubs flickered in battered lanterns.

'Hello?' Jude called again and again.

Nothing.

Ghosts normally appeared when he called them. It was regarded as rude in the ghost world not to greet a visitor at the door. And, moreover, most of them relished a change of routine, for visitors brought new stories to the graveyard.

'What if they've all gone? Like...like in the story Miss Rathbone told us...' Story's voice faltered.

Jude didn't reply. They had reached a rather splendid vault. He rattled at the gate, which led down into a dark chasm. Loudly but politely he called the inhabitant (*James Braidwood, 1872–1924, merchant*). Again, though, there was no reply. 'There must be *someone* in this graveyard!' Jude ran his hands through his tousled hair.

'It looks as if there really aren't any ghosts here any more.'

'But where have they gone?'

'They've just gone.'

So it's a ghost town, thought Jude, not finding the idea in the slightest bit amusing.

'It's going to be dark soon,' Story said. 'What are we going to do now?'

'We'll go straight to Lady Lovelace and ask her,' Jude said, although the idea gave him the shivers. 'She'll help us. After all, she's the reason we came here. It'd be feeble to just go away again.'

'What if she's not in a mood to help us?'

'We need at least to try.'

They rounded the chapel, continued to the next fork in the path and finally reached the statue of Lady Lorena Lovelace, the Loveless One.

Story stopped as if rooted to the spot. The statue was standing on a high basalt plinth. Or, rather, her remains were.

'Is that supposed to be Lady Lovelace?' Jude too couldn't believe his eyes.

'Who did that to her?' Story asked quietly.

They both stared silently at the statue, their reason

for being there. Her stone countenance had been smashed. A deep crack ran across her face, separating her nose and mouth and obliterating an eye. On the ground around the plinth lay a heap of stone pieces.

'What on earth happened?' Story asked tonelessly.

A broken arm was lying in a nearby hedge. The fingers were pointing at a pond with autumn leaves floating in it, almost as if it were warning them that something might emerge from the water at any moment.

'What's going on?' Jude whispered.

He stared at the inscription on the plinth. *Loreena Lovelace. Lived and died.* That was it. No date; nothing. A stone snake was wrapped around the statue's feet.

'She's wearing boots,' Story blurted. A detail that Jude hadn't taken in.

Lady Lovelace was wearing an elegant dress with high-heeled boots. The statue looked the very image of a living woman who had suddenly been turned to stone. Her eyes were dreamy, as if she had seen distant lands without ever having travelled anywhere. A picture was embedded in the plinth, a drawing of a beautiful woman.

'So that's what she looked like.' Jude looked up at the remaining half of her stone face. It wasn't hard to imagine the Loveless One as a real live woman. He suddenly felt that the name given to her was mockery pure and simple, given the life that she must once have led.

Story stood immobile next to Jude. 'You look as sad as she does.'

'It *is* sad.' He looked at the rubble on the ground, the unmistakeable proof that someone had attacked Lady Lovelace. 'How's someone supposed to live when they've been turned to stone?' Jude ran his hand across the cold stone. 'And how can you kill someone made of stone?'

'And who'd do such a thing?' Story shook her head. She seemed positively distraught. 'Now nobody's going to help me.'

Jude was about to reply when a voice made him jump.

'Oi!'

Story whirled round too.

'That's all we need,' Jude muttered. A gardener was coming towards them. He was pushing a wheelbarrow.

'Oi!' he called again. 'What are you up to, lad?' He stopped a couple of metres away.

Jude raised his hand to greet him. He knew how hypersensitive graveyard gardeners were about their grounds. Very few of them liked teenagers hanging around on their patch. Especially not at this time of day, when there would need to be an extremely good reason to be there. Graveyards and teenagers were a bad mix in the eyes of most people.

'What are you doing here?' the gardener asked gruffly.

'He can't see me,' said Story.

The gardener was wearing a red checked shirt, blue overalls and dark green wellingtons. His round face was a mixture of suspicion and good nature. 'What do you want here? The graveyard's shutting soon.'

Aha, thought Jude. The man presumably thought he was a goth who'd come to the kind of secret graveyard party that took place in Highgate Cemetery too. They happened a fair bit, and they always ended up with a pile of litter and crushed beer cans which the graveyard gardener then had to get rid of.

'I wanted to find the statue,' Jude said. 'I was going to take a picture of it.' Let's hope he doesn't ask to see my camera, he thought. 'For a school project,' he quickly added. And before the gardener could ask to see the non-existent camera, Jude asked him a question in return. 'What happened to her?' He pointed to the statue's smashed face.

'Hooligans. Louts who come and smash up the graveyard at night.'

Jude nodded. 'When did it happen?'

'Night before last,' said the man.

Jude glanced at Story. He was wondering whether the date meant anything to her.

'Why do you want to know, lad?'

Story, who had been standing silently beside Jude, said, 'Let's see what you come up with now!'

'I need to do a presentation,' Jude lied without batting an eyelid, 'about the Magnificent Seven. I read a story with Lady Lovelace in it.' He paused. 'So I just wanted to see her.'

'Not bad.' Jude could hear that Story was smiling.

The gardener had turned away instinctively from Story, Jude now noticed. 'Hmm,' he murmured. 'There aren't many kids who write about graveyards.' He sighed. 'A presentation, eh?' He scrutinised Jude warily. 'And you're really not up to mischief?'

'No. I promise.'

A loud scream rang out across the graveyard, making Jude jump.

'What was that?' Story asked.

It had sounded like a lament, splitting the night asunder.

'Someone who's afraid,' Jude whispered.

The gardener gave him a suspicious look. 'Are you OK, mate?'

Jude nodded absently. It looked as if the gardener hadn't heard a thing. And if he hadn't heard a thing that could only mean that a ghost had let out that scream.

'Over there!' Story came closer to him. They looked around. Further down the hill a figure was tumbling out from between two gravestones. It was a small figure, probably a child. It stumbled, fell, picked itself up again and carried on running.

'A boy!' Story gasped.

Jude stared at the figure.

'What's up? Have you seen something?' Worried and alarmed, the gardener looked in the direction that Jude was staring in, but was evidently unable to see anything.

Jude had to get a grip. He knew that the gardener could neither see nor hear what he himself could see and hear – which meant that he couldn't mention the little boy.

But before he could say anything, Story said, 'He's a ghost.'

The boy was clearly younger than Jude. Or, rather, he had been younger when he died. Looking panic-stricken, he came running up the path. He was looking around wildly, for the long rows of graves offered endless hiding places. As he ran, he kept turning around.

'He's running away,' said Story.

'Yes. But from who?'

Or from what?

The boy was wearing flares, shoes with slight platform heels, and a blueish-yellow shirt with ruffles: classic 1970s garb. His hair was long and tousled, like Jude's. His face was pale, and even from a distance it was obvious that he was almost exhausted.

'He's seen us,' murmured Story.

And indeed the boy came running towards them. Just before he reached them, he braked abruptly. His eyes wide with terror, he stared at Jude and Story.

'Can you see me?' he called to them.

'Yes,' said Jude.

'Who are you talking to?' asked the gardener. Scarlet dots were standing out on his cheeks.

Jude ignored him.

The boy's face was dirty. 'But you're not a ghost.' He looked as if he'd been crying.

'No, I'm not a ghost,' said Jude.

The gardener shook his head. 'Of course you're not a ghost. What's all this nonsense about?' He seemed gradually to be wondering whether Jude had taken leave of his senses.

The young ghost cast another terrified glance behind him. 'They're after me.'

'Who's after you?' asked Story.

The boy had almost reached them. He seemed confused. 'Who are you? Where did you come from? All the others have gone.'

'Others? Who are the others?'

The gardener stared at Jude. 'For goodness' sake, lad. Who are you talking to?'

Jude wondered for one desperate moment how to act in this tricky situation. He couldn't possibly tell the gardener what was going on. In any case, he wouldn't understand it. And it would use up valuable time which they evidently didn't have. So he decided to carry on ignoring him. This boy was more important. He seemed to be in severe distress.

'The others who lived here,' said the boy.

'Why did they all go?' Story persisted.

'They're coming!' The boy suddenly froze. His frozen gaze was directed at something behind Jude. A rustling sound was coming from the bushes behind him. Jude almost didn't dare to turn round, but then he did so. And he saw the boy's pursuers.

The ghost's voice was like the crackle of dry leaves. 'Help me, please!' he begged.

Story, who also saw the two dark figures unpeeling themselves from the darkness, recoiled too.

'They got all the others,' shrieked the boy. 'And

now they're going to get me!' Then, without waiting for Jude or Story to respond, he ran off.

Jude would never forget the last look that the boy gave him. There was so much despair in it that it sliced his heart in two.

'The Faceless Ones,' gasped Story, so quietly that even Jude could hardly hear her.

Neither of them dared move a muscle. That, however, didn't bother the two Faceless Ones. They calmly strode past Jude and Story, hot on the heels of the fleeing boy. They were wearing elegant dark suits, like musicians or funeral-goers. Apart from that, though, they looked nothing like normal graveyard visitors. Mostly because they had no faces. Without appearing to notice Jude and Story or the gardener, they continued purposefully on their way; they were evidently interested only in the boy.

'It's all going on tonight,' the gardener said, looking in the same direction as Jude.

Jude turned to him, astonished. The gardener seemed to have seen the Faceless Ones. *But they must obviously have faces when he looks at them*, thought Jude, *or else he'd undoubtedly have behaved very differently when he saw them.*

'Good evening,' the gardener called to the men.

They were silent; or, at any rate, they didn't say

anything that Jude could hear. But their silence was like the coldness of a dream from which one awakens with a scream. And only now did he realise what the Faceless Ones were holding: something that looked like a lantern, only it was more alive. It sounded impossible, but the two lanterns seemed to have a heartbeat. As if they were strange, bodyless creatures with blood pulsing through their veins.

'What on earth's up with you, mate?' the gardener asked. He scrutinised Jude and shook his head helplessly.

The two men were following the boy, but were in no particular hurry. Neither did it seem to bother them that they were being watched. Jude suddenly understood why they were so calm: the boy couldn't run away. His body was lying in one of the graves in Abney Park, and his ghost wouldn't be able to go beyond the walls.

'We have to do something,' said Story. She too had presumably also worked out the horrific truth.

Jude thought feverishly.

'You really are odd, mate,' said the gardener, sighing deeply. He seemed to be wondering whether to call an ambulance.

Jude couldn't take his eyes off the Faceless Ones. The very sight of them made his throat tighten. He felt as if he were gazing into an abyss from which there was no escape.

'What are they doing now?' Story clapped a hand to her mouth. Further down the path, the boy stumbled and fell in front of one of the graves.

At that moment, another Faceless One emerged from the undergrowth right next to the grave. He too was carrying a lantern. It was black and glowed darkly, and when the boy saw it he held his hands in front of his face and started whimpering. Then his hands started to dissolve and crumble, as if they were made of dust. The little ghost was screaming his heart out, but only Jude and Story could hear him.

His two pursuers stopped. They were no longer bothered about the ghost-boy, but just left their companion to deal with him. Calmly they turned to look at another grave, as if they were just visiting the cemetery.

'What's he doing to him?' Story whispered.

Jude took a step forwards and clenched his fists. '*What are you doing?*' he yelled at the Faceless One who was bending over the boy.

'Oi!' Jude felt a heavy hand on his shoulder. 'Have you been taking drugs?'

Curses, Jude thought. He shook off the hand. 'No, I don't do drugs,' he said.

Unable to do anything, and as if paralysed, he and Story stood there watching the whole grisly performance that was taking place in the distance ahead of them. As the Faceless One held the lantern up in front of the ghost-boy, the boy's entire body now seemed to dissolve, his face seeming to wither, his pale skin cracking. He was literally disintegrating before their eyes.

'He's vanishing,' Story stammered.

The boy turned transparent; the lantern appeared to be sucking him up.

'There's nothing we can do.' Jude's voice failed him.

'Who for?' asked the gardener. 'There's no one there. Just those three men. But they're not doing anything.' He eyed Jude suspiciously. 'I think I'd better escort you back to the exit. The police can take you home.' He took a step towards Jude. 'I'm afraid I just don't buy this "I don't do drugs" line, mate.'

Jude looked at him. What on earth could he say?

So the gardener could see the Faceless Ones. But what did they look like to him? Normal visitors with faces, standing reverently at the graves and looking as if they were in mourning?

'There's nothing we can do. They're killing him,' Jude said to Story. Yes, they were killing the ghosts with their living lanterns – but he had no idea why they were doing it. Neither did he know what kind of creatures they were, or where they came from. But it looked as if the story that Miss Rathbone had told them in another graveyard just a couple of hours ago was turning into horrible reality. 'Hey, stop it!' he shouted. He grabbed a candle from the nearest grave and threw it with all his might at the Faceless One.

It missed him by millimetres.

It also aroused the attention of the two other Faceless Ones.

'Uh-oh,' Story murmured.

Too right, Jude thought. The Faceless Ones were now heading casually in his direction.

'What's going on?' the gardener asked again. But, again, he received no answer.

Jude knew, though, that silence from the Faceless Ones wouldn't make the gardener suspicious, since they appeared to ordinary humans to be just like them: quite normal people. They were the ultimate deceivers.

'Who are you?' Jude demanded angrily. They, of course, didn't reply.

'What on earth's up with you, lad? What have you got against these two blokes? They're not doing any harm.'

The two Faceless Ones were now barely a metre away from him. And suddenly the gardener's attitude changed. It seemed as if he suddenly realised how threatening they were. He took a couple of steps forward so that he was standing between Jude and the two Faceless Ones. He raised a hand and said, 'Easy does it, gents, easy does it.' He cleared his throat. 'What do you want with this lad here?'

Jude held his breath and drew back. Story grabbed his hand.

'Get out of here, the pair of you!' said the gardener.

These were his last words. One of the Faceless Ones pulled out a knife. It was long, and the blade gleamed, as if delighted to be put to use at last. Without betraying even the tiniest flicker of emotion, the man rammed the knife into the gardener's stomach.

The gardener stared at him in disbelief. His mouth opened and he let out a silent scream. The Faceless One withdrew the knife and slit the gardener's throat, as if as an afterthought. It all happened so quickly that Jude barely registered it. All he heard was a strange gurgling sound coming from the gardener's throat.

His body slumped and lay twitching on the ground. Jude and Story were rigid with horror. Hand in hand, they stood there watching as the ghost of the murdered gardener materialised next to his body. The ghost panted, sat down and regarded the body which had been his just seconds ago.

'He's dead.' Story wiped the tears from her face.

His eyes wide, the gardener's ghost stared at them. 'Who are you?' he asked.

But before Story could reply, the second Faceless One came over to the ghost. The black lantern he was carrying began to glow.

The gardener's ghost opened his eyes wide with terror, realising that death was coming to claim him again. The living lantern enveloped him in its dark glow, robbing him of all his dreams of the life that had been his.

The Faceless Ones stood impassively by. If they had had faces, they would undoubtedly have been smiling. Jude Finney, however, who knew that you couldn't waste time that you didn't have, squeezed Story's hand, not dreaming for a moment of letting her go.

'Run!' he yelled.

And that's what they did. They ran for their lives.

CHAPTER 5

Once dusk has fallen, old graveyards can seem like endless labyrinths. The tall trees and dense foliage, coupled with gravestones, crosses and pale statues, all meld together to become an inscrutable, baffling forest in which you quickly lose all sense of direction. The long shadows start to reach out for you, and whichever path you look at becomes an unfathomable runnel leading into the ever-increasing darkness.

'Are you sure this is right?'

'Yes.' Jude wasn't a good liar, but Story let it pass.

'It goes off to the right just there,' she said.

Jude couldn't object. It had turned even colder in the graveyard. The cold cut into his heart like a knife, and he still shuddered as he remembered the look on the gardener's face. Incomprehension and confusion coupled with extreme fear and desperate resignation at the moment of his death.

One thing was clear: the Faceless Ones took whatever they wanted from the living as well as from the dead. They were dangerous, and weren't afraid to commit murder.

The idea of Story's body falling into the hands of these monsters was deeply shocking.

'Are they following us?' Story was slightly ahead of him, almost pulling him along. Her stamina was astonishing; it was as if some invisible force were driving her on.

'One of them is.' Jude had looked over his shoulder and could see him following them down the broad gravel path that led away from the statue of the Loveless One. His silhouette stood out against the darkness like a baleful shadow.

'Just one?'

'Yes.' He could at any rate only make out one pursuer in the gloom of the impending night. Jude hoped desperately that there weren't any more of these creatures lurking in the undergrowth ahead of them. They had destroyed the Loveless One: he was quite sure of it. And he and Story had seen with their own eyes what else they were capable of.

'Thank God it's just one.' Story ran and ran, never getting out of breath. Her fluid movements were those of a girl who was used to doing lots of sport. She now looked over her shoulder too. 'The Faceless One's slow,' she said with satisfaction.

Jude's imagination, meanwhile, was conjuring up the craziest scenarios. In his head, new Faceless Ones were emerging from between every other gravestone and mausoleum. They were fixated on grabbing the two young people who had witnessed the gardener's murder – they had to do it to prevent Jude and Story from telling anyone what they'd seen.

Why? Good question: why? Who on earth could they tell? Nobody apart from a couple of ghosts would believe them anyway.

As he ran behind Story, panting and gasping for breath, Jude wondered who was orchestrating these weird goings-on. Who had ordered the Faceless Ones to capture the ghosts? And, more importantly, why?

He ventured to glance over his shoulder again. The Faceless One was still following them. But he was doing it so calmly and at such a leisurely pace that it seemed almost as if he weren't seriously trying to catch them. Maybe, Jude mused, the Faceless One thought it was in the bag: he must think Story was a ghost, and everyone knows that ghosts can't leave the graveyard. For her, there was no escape. The man's calm demeanour suddenly seemed all the more menacing to Jude.

'He thinks you can't leave the graveyard,' he heard himself saying softly.

'Because ghosts normally can't.'

'That's why he's taking all the time in the world. That's the way they hunt.'

'You reckon that nobody normally escapes from them because ghosts can't escape from here?'

Jude nodded.

'What should we do?'

'Run.' That was the only thing that came to mind. 'We've got an advantage: you can leave the graveyard. They don't know that.'

That might possibly be their salvation. If the Faceless One had known it, he might have quickened his pace. Calmly and at an even pace, he was following them down the main path, past the rows of clean stone crosses and well-tended hedges and park benches. On and on they went, until Jude and Story were finally able to make out the silhouette of the massive entrance gate. Fortunately it wasn't yet locked.

'Who on earth are they?' asked Story, who still didn't seem to be particularly out of breath.

'The Faceless Ones,' Jude gasped. 'The ones Miss Rathbone told us about. The ones who depopulated Lud-upon-Trent.'

Evil creatures who robbed graveyards of their ghosts... Jude recalled the ghost-boy's face. The way he had screamed for his life. Again, he thought about what would happen if the Faceless Ones appeared in Highgate. If they were already going about their vile business in one of the Magnificent Seven, what was going to stop them repeating the act in the other six? Could they just roam around London as they liked? Jude's lungs were burning and his mind was racing. He pictured Gaskell and the other quirky characters he'd come to know and love being sucked into those ghastly lanterns.

He gasped. He would do more sport in future, he promised himself. He looked back again and saw that their pursuer was still far behind them. But then something else happened. A strange, unfamilar smell hit his nostrils and long shadows fell across the path. Yes, there was something in the air. And an icy breeze that hadn't been there before.

'What's up?' Story asked anxiously, realising that there was something the matter with Jude.

Jude stopped abruptly. His fear of the Faceless One suddenly gave way to another fear. He was overwhelmed by a dark premonition. He looked over his shoulder once more, but there was nobody to be seen except for the Faceless One. Indeed, the distance between them seemed to be even greater now.

'Come on!' He set off again.

'Is it colder than it was?' Story asked.

So she could feel it too. 'Might be,' Jude replied evasively.

Story looked at him anxiously. But Jude carried on running, as if there were nobody there but their languid pursuer. *Something else is going on*, he thought. The very idea of it made his heart pound and drove him onwards.

Story suddenly slowed down. 'What's going to happen when we get outside?'

Jude shrugged. 'I hope he'll leave us alone. I think they only have any power in graveyards.' It was a glib answer. But if it wasn't true, then they had a serious problem.

'Yes, let's hope so.' Story didn't sound particularly confident. They were nearing the Egyptian columns and iron gate. 'You're a good runner,' she commented.

'I'm OK. Not as fit as you, though.' Jude suddenly stopped dead. A bitterly cold gust of winter air hit the side of his face. He felt as if his heart were about to freeze.

'Why've you stopped? That's the exit. Come on – we're nearly there.'

The gate was almost within touching distance. The Egyptian columns looked simultaneously imposing and threatening, but also out of place, as if they didn't belong there.

Any minute now, they would discover whether the Faceless One would be able to follow them outside Abney Park too.

'What's up?' Story asked again. 'Come on – let's go!'

But Jude just stood there motionless, his nerves as taut as the string of a bow. Something was stirring in the gloom. It was just a fleeting movement, so quick that it looked like a shadow. Jude had just glimpsed it from the corner of his eye.

From the corner of his eye.

Damn, damn, damn! He could feel his hands beginning to tremble. What had Miss Rathbone once advised him?

Beware of what you see from the corner of your eye.

Jude was breathing heavily. His pulse was racing. 'Curses,' he muttered. Not this on top of everything else. He gazed desperately in the direction of the half-seen movement.

'What?' asked Story.

'I thought I saw something.'

She looked around. The Faceless One was still a good way off, but was starting slowly to catch up with them now that they had stopped. He was holding something that flashed in the moonlight. A knife.

'Jude!'

The boy didn't move.

'We need to hurry!' Story urged him.

'There's something there.'

She couldn't see anything. 'Another one of them?'

Jude shook his head. 'No. Something else. Only visible out of the corner of my eye.'

Story looked him, baffled.

Beware of what you see from the corner of your eye.

How often Miss Rathbone and Gaskell had warned him about the mysterious creatures that lurked in the shadows of graveyards, taking advantage of people's natural inattentiveness. You had to avoid them at all costs.

You can't really see them.

'He's going to catch us up if we don't move.'

'There – can you see them?'

The stone angels were standing at the edge of the path, about fifty metres behind them.

Where you can't see them.

There were two of them. They were man-sized with wings tucked against their bodies. On their bare feet were roughly hewn sandals. They were wearing long, flowing robes. They stood there, apparently unmoving. They looked beautiful – but their beauty was deceptive. Pale marble, once white but stained by time, their noble faces stretched forwards so that moonlight flooded them like water.

Story drew in her breath sharply. 'Yes, I can see them. What about them?'

'They're hunting.'

Out of the corner of his eye, he could see that they were moving. Slowly but surely they were coming closer. Jude could hear the scrunch of gravel.

'We have to hold our breath,' he said.

'Why?'

'Anything that breathes lives. And we need to move slowly.'

Quick, sudden movements arouse their interest, Jude remembered the vixen warning him. Slowly, watching the stone angels out of the corner of their eye, Jude and Story moved towards the exit.

Never run from them.

It was damned difficult to go slowly when every fibre within you was telling you to run for your life. Jude turned his head slightly, just enough to look round. The Faceless One, still holding the knife, was closer now; he was following them relentlessly.

From the corner of his eye, he could still see the stone angels. They were staring back at him, their eyes narrowed, their mouths full of sharp teeth. They had stopped moving once Jude and Story had begun holding their breath.

The gate was near, yet seemed a million miles away. If they had been running, it would have been easy – but in slow motion, it was anything but. It was too far to manage without drawing breath.

The stone eyes were cold and lifeless.

'Jude!' gasped Story, pointing behind her.

The Faceless One seemed to have increased his speed, and was suddenly gaining on them.

'Damn!' muttered Jude, taking an involuntary gulp of air.

The stone angels immediately started to move.

Slowly, Jude and Story set off again. But it seemed as if the Faceless One had an inkling that something was afoot, as Jude and Story were heading so purposefully for the gate. The knife blade gleamed in the moonlight, and then Jude suddenly noticed something else. A lantern on his belt. Swaying with every movement. He went weak at the knees.

The Faceless One had reached the stone angels, but the latter made no response. They seemed not to notice him at all, and continued to follow Jude and Story with their narrow eyes.

He's not breathing, was all Jude could think. *The Faceless One's not breathing. What does that mean?*

Nothing good, that was for sure.

The stone angels didn't notice him because he wasn't alive. *OK, so the Faceless One wasn't alive. He was dead. Whatever. And he's following us. Oh my God.*

Jude suppressed a cough. His lungs felt as if they were on fire. Just before they reached the exit, he lost the battle. He let a deep breath out, took two gulps of air, then held his breath again.

This was enough to draw the stone angels' attention to them once more. With huge steps that looked more like bounds, they started pursuing them again. And now they had overtaken the knife-wielding Faceless One.

Jude's heart felt tight. He could feel Story's hand in his, and even though it felt light and almost unreal it made him feel better. They could hear the noise of the traffic beyond the gate, and Jude could see the endless lorries lumbering past. It somehow didn't fit together with what was going on in the graveyard.

Jude and Story increased their pace.

Will the stone angels follow us once we've left the graveyard? What will they do if they catch up with us? What's the knife-brandishing Faceless One going to do? Jude felt as if he were about to suffocate.

'Take one more breath,' he gasped, filling his lungs

with air. He could feel Story doing the same. 'Now run!' Without turning round, he raced off with Story at his side. He ran as fast as he could, drawing on every last ounce of energy, his gaze fixed on the columns ahead of him.

Nearly outside! Nearly outside! Stumbling, they reached the exit, ran out through the gates onto the pavement and stopped, panting and gasping for air.

Jude took several deep breaths and immediately noticed that the air out here was much warmer than inside the graveyard. The coldness hadn't followed them out. Cautiously he turned round. The stone angels were waiting silent and unmoving not far from the gate, their heads turned towards him. Nothing suggested that they had ever been alive.

Oh my God, thought Jude. 'Are you OK?' he asked Story.

'I'd never have thought I could hold my breath for that long,' replied Story. Her cheeks were red and her eyes had taken on a strange gleam. She looked back in disbelief. 'They're not following us.'

The Faceless One had also stopped before he reached the gate. He seemed unsure of his next move, but he finally turned and went back down the path just as smoothly and serenely as he had when pursuing them. He then disappeared into the grey darkness that had settled over Abney Park Cemetery.

'Wow, that was close.' Relief was etched across Story's face. Like Jude, she seemed almost not to believe that it was all over.

'I'm knackered,' Jude gasped, still out of breath. He stood there, his hands on his knees.

After a while, Story touched his shoulder. 'Come on, let's get out of here.'

Jude took one last look at the graveyard, which lay there in all its peaceful innocence. At that moment, a graveyard attendant came sloping up, pulled a key out of his pocket and locked the gate. They had been just in time.

'Yes, let's get out of here.'

Once they had gone a fair distance, they stopped to get their breath back.

'Good – they haven't followed us.'

'Yes, we're safe.' Jude had been on high alert for the past ten minutes. They had taken a circuitous route, zigzagging their way through numerous side streets, Jude constantly checking whether he could see anything out of the corner of his eye, and never feeling completely safe. He was horror-struck to the very core of his being; he still felt as if they were being chased.

But there was nothing there. It did genuinely look as if they had evaded their pursuers.

They walked along Stoke Newington High Street. There was nothing to suggest that the world could be any different from the way it looked now. The evening rush hour was starting to die away; the street lights were on; people were wending their way home or to the nearest pub. In short, it was a typical suburban scene: parked cars, hurrying people, an HSBC branch, Poundland, hairdressers, restaurants, trashy gift shops and pubs.

'What are we going to do?' asked Story. Now that the danger had passed, the disappointment was evident in her voice.

'We're going to come up with another plan,' said Jude. There was always more than one way to skin a cat. In any case, he was just happy to have escaped from the stone angels and the Faceless Ones. 'Give me a moment and I'll come up with something.'

'Fine.'

Jude, of course, had hoped that their visit to Abney Park would have had a rather different outcome. He'd at least reckoned on finding some clue as to Story's identity, a hint from the Loveless

One, or even some something that might lead them to Story's body. The sorts of things you might expect of an oracle.

But what had they achieved? Nothing. They'd seen a graveyard with no ghosts, witnessed a murder, and only just escaped from two stone angels. That was quite something, but it wasn't what they'd expected. Life seemed to be throwing huge boulders in their way. The thought of boulders reminded him of the two stone angels, and he almost laughed despite the gravity of their situation.

'You know what bugs me most of all?' Story said into the silence.

He gave her a sidelong glance, noticing her pert little nose in profile for the first time.

'It was these guys who abducted me. They know *who* I am and *where* I am. And I...' She sighed.

'You're still alive.'

'But for how long?' Her voice cracked. 'Jude, I'm so frightened. How much longer have I got? What if I really do turn into a ghost? We know nothing about anything, and your friend Miss Rathbone doesn't really have a clue either. People like me don't normally exist.' She swallowed back her fear as she said quietly, 'I shouldn't really exist, should I?'

Jude tried to look as unconcerned as possible. He

couldn't help thinking about some of the stories that Gaskell had told him. But this wasn't the moment to share them with Story. No: they'd only make her even more anxious.

'I've got an idea.' Once again, passers-by stared at him in surprise, then hurried on without a word. *Just another crazy teenager talking to himself*, they presumably thought.

Story sighed. 'Go on, then.'

'I'll call one of my friends. I'll ask him to look some stuff up on the internet for an essay' – she raised an eyebrow – 'and find out which school's doing *Social Media Networks: Blessing or Curse?*'

'Fancy you remembering that...'

He reached into his jacket pocket and pulled out an ancient mobile. It was rust-coloured and battered; the back cover was completely missing so that its battery and all its inner workings were visible.

'You're seriously going to call someone on that?'

'Course I am. Still works fine.' Jude liked his old monstrosity.

'It looks as if it's about to fall apart any minute.'

'What kind have you got?' he asked on the spur of the moment.

'It's red and—' She clapped her hand to her forehead. 'Damn! Another stupid memory that's no use to me. Anyway, it's red with a symbol on it...' She frowned, thinking hard. 'An ankh that I painted on at school with nail polish.' She twirled a strand of hair around her finger. 'Why can I suddenly remember that, then?'

Jude could guess why, just as Story could. But neither ventured to say it.

'I don't know which school I go to or which class I'm in, but I do know that I painted a hieroglyph on my mobile at school. That's completely ridiculous.'

Jude stopped at a crossroads. Yes, completely ridiculous. And, moreover, scary. He dialled a number and waited.

'What's your friend called?' Story asked.

'Benny Andrews,' he said. 'We jam together.' But the voicemail came on. 'No answer.' Jude dialled another number. 'I'll try Joolz instead,' he murmured.

Story gave him what felt like a slightly suspicious look.

Joolz answered and Jude quickly told her what it was about, looking at Story as he did so. Then he hung up. 'She's going to look,' he said. 'Might take a while – she's got to switch the computer on first. She's going to call back.'

'Who is she?'

'Joolz? A good friend.'

'Your girlfriend?'

He shook his head. 'No, just a friend. She doesn't go to my school, and neither does Benny. We get together for jamming sessions. Benny, Joolz and me. That's all.'

Story nodded.

That was that dealt with, for the time being. 'Come on, let's carry on,' he said.

'So where are you actually planning to go?'

He shrugged. 'To Miss Rathbone's. After all, you need to spend the night somewhere.'

They passed several restaurants, all of them full of diners sitting under warm air fans, enjoying the autumn evening. Beyond the windows, the world looked cosy.

It was strange, after everything they had been through, to walk down roads like this. Everything seemed so peaceful, so incredibly ordinary. It was a suburb of London like so many others, not much different from Jude's own. Smaller streets led off the main road, lined with rows of houses with front yards: narrow town houses with small steps up to the front door and a chimney pot on every roof.

The people they encountered had no idea about what had just been happening in their vicinity in Abney Park Cemetery. Maybe they would soon sense that there were no more ghosts there, that the dreams of the dead had disappeared for ever. Would the people who lived here feel as empty as the residents of Lud-upon-Trent did once upon a time? How would it affect life in the city?

Too many unanswerable questions. Jude really didn't want to think about what might happen if one of the stone angels ever managed to leave the graveyard.

'Jude?' He looked at Story. 'What's your life like?'

'My life?'

She rolled her eyes. 'You don't have to repeat everything.'

He nodded. 'I don't have to repeat everything?' He grinned broadly.

'Idiot.' She elbowed him in the ribs.

'Well, I've told you a bit. About my father, and about not having a mother. Otherwise, I like playing the guitar, I hang out in Highgate, grind my way through school. There isn't much else to say.'

'Don't you go out? To clubs?'

'No, but I like little pubs. With billiard tables and old-fashioned slot machines.'

'You play billiards?'

'Yes, but pretty badly.'

'What else?'

'River Raid, Star Raiders, Ghosts 'n' Goblins – all the usual stuff.'

She was evidently hoping to hear more. As he had to admit, it didn't exactly sound like the most spectacular life.

'Pretty boring, eh?'

She shrugged. 'What are you going to do when you leave school?'

'That's not until next year; I've not really thought about it yet,' he said evasively. The truth was that he didn't have the faintest idea what kind of job he wanted. He did want to do something with music. But he knew some people who lived that kind of bohemian existence, and he knew he didn't fancy that either.

Story was about to ask him something else when his phone rang. It was Joolz calling him back.

Jude listened, nodding every now and then. Then he thanked her and hung up.

'So?' Story asked.

'Joolz put out a Facebook request. There's a school in Finsbury.' He put his crumbling mobile back into his jacket pocket. 'Clerkenwell College. In Penton Rise.'

Story looked thoughtful, almost as if the name sounded somehow familiar to her. He looked at her expectantly, but she shook her head. 'Never heard of it.' Jude was about to respond when she raised her hand and said breathlessly, 'It's near King's Cross.' Story had evidently startled herself, as if the words had come tumbling out of their own accord.

Jude looked at her in surprise. 'So you do know the school after all?'

'No, I...' She looked despairing again. 'I just know it's in Penton Rise, close to King's Cross.' She rubbed her eyes. 'But that's all I know. My God, I don't even know what the school looks like. And...'

'It's fine.'

'I...'

'At any rate, they had a test on this topic the day before yesterday.'

'Two days ago?' she said thoughtfully.

'Do you remember it?'

She shook her head. 'I don't know.'

'Doesn't matter. We'll try to find out more.'

Story looked down at her shoes and laughed suddenly. 'Hey, I go to school. Amazing!' She looked up.

Jude was laughing too. 'Yeah, who'd have thought it?' Laughing felt good. It was liberating.

'What now?' said Story, turning serious once more.

'I'm going to go to Clerkenwell College

tomorrow...'

'If it's really my school.'

'We'll find out. At any rate, I'll go there tomorrow and have a scout around.'

Story was startled. 'How are you going to do that?'

Jude paused. Good question. 'I...' He didn't even know her name. If only he had a photo of her at the very least. How was he supposed to tell the other students who he was looking for? 'I can describe you.'

Story looked at him sceptically.

'Or I'll get someone to draw you,' he added. *Brilliant idea*, he thought to himself. 'Do you remember the artists in Hyde Park?'

She shook her head.

'Well, I know someone there. Or, rather, I did know an artist who always used to sit there. Hopefully he'll still be there. I'll go and see him and describe you, and he can draw you. I'm sure he's up to it.'

'Why don't *you* draw me?' she suggested.

'Me? No way. I can't draw.'

'Miss Rathbone?'

'She's a vixen. Vixens are good at loads of stuff, but not at drawing.'

'Fair enough.'

Jude's new idea had given him a new impetus. Yes: it would surely do the trick. His plan, like most good plans, was very straightforward. 'Most parks shut at seven in the evening,' he said. 'So we need to get a move on. The artist I'm thinking of was always by the Queen Mother's Gate. The one with the white rhino and the red lion.'

Story, as ever, was quickly infected by his enthusiasm. 'So what are we waiting for?' Even if her hopes were just a mirage, it was better than having no hopes at all.

'Who is this artist?' Story asked as they headed towards the Underground.

'His name's Bert Wayne. But he calls himself Van Dyck.'

'Sounds weird.'

'He *is* weird.'

'How do you know him?'

'This might sound a bit weird too, but we – that's Joolz, Benny and I – planned to start a band at some point. Not yet – we're still too young – but at some point in the future. And we play around town every now and then, just to get a bit of practice.'

She smiled. 'So you're a busker?'

'Yes.' Coming from her, it sounded quite charming.

'I'd like to see it sometime.'

He cleared his throat. 'Just looks like someone playing the guitar and singing.'

'You sing too?'

'Well, I try to.' He grinned. 'There are street performers all over the place – in Piccadilly Circus and by Embankment and in all the parks in summer. And last summer we sometimes played in Hyde Park. Nobody really notices us.' All the same, they had earned a bit. Not much, but not bad for extra pocket money.

They went down the steps to the Underground and, fortunately, a train immediately appeared.

'That,' Jude continued, 'is how I met Dyck. Van Dyck's such a mouthful that we just call him Dyck. He paints in Hyde Park, sometimes in central London too.'

'What kind of art does he do?'

'All sorts of stuff. Mostly chalk pictures on the pavement, portraits for tourists, caricatures, landscapes. Anything and everything.'

Story nodded, evidently mulling it all over. 'What things do you sing?'

'Justin Sullivan, the Pogues, that old stuff.'

'*That old stuff*?'

He nodded. 'Yes. That old stuff.' He found it

embarrassing to talk about his music.

She grinned. 'Right. I get it.'

'Dyck's bound to help us,' he said, trying to change the subject.

'Do you think he'll still be there?'

'We'll see. Worth a try.'

Story nodded. It was a done deal.

Less than half an hour later, they were getting out at Hyde Park Corner.

Hyde Park was already shut by the time they arrived. There were just a handful of teenagers hanging around outside, illuminated by the wan street lights, some of them locked in close embraces.

Dyck was kneeling undaunted on the pavement by the Queen Mother's Gate with its white rhinoceros and red lion. He was doing a chalk drawing of a green, hilly landscape in which there was a Victorian autumnal gathering complete with penguins. He seemed to be doing it entirely for his own enjoyment; his audience had gone home.

'There were still some children here when I started this picture,' he said when he looked up and saw Jude. He had short, jet-black hair and a round face with red cheeks that looked like apples and didn't go with his goatee beard. His cap sat crookedly on his head.

'Hi, Dyck.'

'The park shut half an hour ago.' He pointed at his picture. 'But I wanted to finish this before I go home.'

'Looks good.'

He looked up again. 'What are you doing here?' Dyck was wearing a battered leather jacket and jeans.

'I came to see you.'

'At this time of night?'

'Why are you finishing that picture if there's nobody around to see it?'

'Why don't you stop singing when everyone walks straight past you?'

'One–nil to him,' said Story.

'Because it's fun,' said Jude.

Dyck clicked his fingers. 'Got it in one, man!' With a hint of irritation, he looked in the direction in which Jude had turned to listen to Story. But as he couldn't see her, he turned back to his picture.

'I need your artistic skill,' said Jude. 'Your magic touch.' He knew that Dyck would need to be sweet-talked.

The artist looked up once more and made a performance of straightening his cap. Then he finished the drawing by adding a white bridge across the river that wound its way across the landscape. 'That's what it needed,' he said with satisfaction.

Dyck looked to be in his late twenties. He'd been at the Royal College of Art for a while, but had dropped out. 'You can't create real art if you've got no problems,' he had once told Jude. 'You need to devote your entire life to art.' If he meant living in a cheap dosshouse in Fleet Street, spending each day scraping together enough money to eat, and – most importantly, in his case – embarking on endless doomed love affairs, then he'd found what he was looking for. 'They have to leave you, man, or else you'll never understand what true love really is.'

Even though Jude couldn't entirely get his mind around Dyck's views on art, he liked the strange guy.

'Make sure you don't end up like me,' he always warned Jude, Benny and Joolz when they were busking.

'If we end up like you, won't that make us real artists?' they always retorted. That kind of riposte was right up Dyck's street.

'There's a party over there.' Dyck pointed to the green hill in the middle of the picture. 'You can't see it because it's behind the hill. But the bridge takes you there.' He looked at his picture. 'That's art, man. You can't see it, but you can still see it because you know it's there.'

Story smiled. 'I can hear the party,' she whispered dreamily.

'Me too,' Jude blurted.

Dyck stared at him. 'You what?'

'Nothing.'

'You said "me too".'

'I can see the party too,' Jude hastily replied.

Dyck shook the tin that stood next to his street picture. It was the indispensable tool of all London street artists, strategically placed to solicit alms, the few pence marking a show of appreciation.

'So. What brings you here?' asked Dyck. He rubbed his hands and blew on them. 'It's getting cold, and I'm about to go and find somewhere a bit warmer.'

'Could you draw a picture of someone for me?' Jude asked.

Dyck stared at him. 'Not you, I hope? I don't draw ugly things.'

'Thanks a lot.'

'Take it as a compliment between friends.' Dyck chortled to himself.

'No, seriously. It's...'

Dyck stared at him. 'You don't mean...'

'Yes, I do mean...a girl.'

Jude saw Story suppressing a grin. He was glad that Dyck *couldn't* see it.

'A girl? Where is she?'

'Um...she's not here.'

'Oh yeah?'

'Yes.'

'But I'm supposed to draw her.'

Jude nodded.

'So how's that going to work?'

'I'll describe her to you.'

Dyck whistled through his teeth. 'Chim Chim Cheree'. 'So you're going to describe her, right?'

'He's got the same tic as you – he repeats everything,' said Story.

This time, Jude ignored her.

A cold easterly wind had whipped up, and was blowing leaves across the chalk picture.

'Yes. I'll try to describe her as precisely as possible.'

Story, standing unseen next to Dyck, did a pirouette just for fun.

Dyck pondered for a moment. 'Have you got any cash? I mean, you're planning to pay me, aren't you?'

'No, but I'll do you a deal. Next time we're here, I'll sing a song just for you.'

'Can I choose one?'

Jude nodded. 'Yes.'

'Then I'll have the "Money" song.'

Jude sighed. 'Yeah, fine.'

Dyck scratched his goatee. 'Wouldn't it be better to go somewhere warmer? Warmer than here, at any rate. You could buy me a beer or two, then I'll draw whatever you like.'

'Sounds like a good deal,' said Jude. He helped Dyck gather up his things. They put his chalks into a long tin, folded up his stool and easel, rolled up a couple of sheets of paper and put them into a cardboard tube. Then they set off.

Story walked silently behind them, listening with amusement to the male conversation that could hardly have been described as intellectually stimulating.

After a short while they reached Ye Olde Yonghy-Bonghy-Bo pub in the centre of Marylebone. There couldn't have been a more fitting venue for what they had in mind. The walls were panelled in wood and covered with pictures of unknown artists. The chunky wooden tables were home to sticky cardboard drink coasters and candles in beer and wine bottles. Music by Ben Folds, the Avett Brothers and Mumford & Sons was blaring out of the loudspeakers into the smoky murmur of voices.

Together, they squeezed through the crowd and reached the bar.

'Wotcha having?' asked the barman. He was a short, beefy, bull-necked, red-nosed man who looked as if he could single-handedly take on an entire stadium of football fans.

'A shandy for me and a pint of lager for him, thanks,' said Jude.

He paid, and together they edged their way back through the throng until Dyck spotted a window seat overlooking the street. 'My favourite,' he said.

Jude sat down opposite him. As Story ghosted onto the window seat next to Dyck, the artist instinctively moved away with a faint look of horror on his face. So he too could feel her invisible presence, just like the pub-goers who had unconsciously stepped aside as she made her way through the pub.

'Right. Here we go.' Dyck rummaged around in his holdall and pulled out a sketch pad, a pencil and a rubber. He leant back and waited, his pencil poised.

Jude took a sip of his shandy.

'Where's mine?' Story demanded.

Jude only just managed to bite back a reply. Story sat bold upright and stared straight ahead of her, making a show of deliberately not speaking in order not to embarrass Jude.

'Before I start,' said Dyck, 'you tell me the whole story.'

'The whole story?'

'What's her name? Where did you meet her?'

'You know – the usual,' Jude lied. 'In a café.'

Dyck scrutinised him. 'You chatted up a girl in a café?'

'Starbucks in Gospel Oak.'

'Where else!'

'I didn't chat her up – I spilled my coffee. That was all.'

'And she was the lucky recipient of some of it.'

'Precisely.' Jude nodded vigorously. It didn't matter what he told Dyck. The main thing was to tell him something. 'We started chatting and...'

'What's her name?'

'Why do you need her name?'

'Names are important. You need them to get to the essence of the person you want to draw.'

'Really?' Jude avoided looking at Story. He knew that Dyck had unwittingly touched on a sensitive subject.

'Yeah, really. So what's her name?'

'She didn't tell me.'

'She found you so irresistible, man, that she walked off without telling you her name or where she lived.' Dyck grinned broadly. 'Seems to me that she was trying to tell you something.'

Jude sighed.

Story stared doggedly ahead of her. The fiction that Jude and Dyck were concocting conjured up a smile on her face.

'But I know which school she goes to.'

'Great. So you're going to start stalking her?'

'Of course not.'

'Then tell me why you need the picture.'

Jude took a deep breath. 'Look, Dyck, I've got a plan.'

Story leant forward, interested. She rested her head on her hands and gazed at Jude. Her reddish hair framed her face like autumn leaves.

'I'm going to wait for her at school and sing to her.'

Dyck looked at him sceptically. 'I wouldn't, if I were you.' He clapped Jude on the shoulder.

'Yeah, I'm going to write her a song and give her the picture.'

Story looked at him, her eyes wide.

'And you really think that she'll tell you her name in return?' Dyck emptied half of his glass in one long gulp.

Jude was about to reply, but Dyck raised his hand.

'It's fine, whatever. I've not got all night. So what does she look like?'

Jude glanced at Story. She was still looking at him, but more uncertainly now. She gave him a tiny wink. 'She's got hazel eyes,' Jude began. Hesitantly at first, then more boldly, his words wandered across her face. He described her hair, the dimple in her cheek when she smiled, the brightness of her eyes when she was amused. The hand that she used to twirl her hair nervously. Her unique nose. Her lips, sometimes pursed in mockery.

Dyck drew as he listened. He took the occasional sip of lager as he conveyed on paper what the mousy-grey boy dictated to him.

Every word that Jude said seemed to give more impetus to Dyck's pencil. His practised hand shaded the image, bringing out details here and there, and in no time at all a face appeared on the white sheet.

Story sat beside him regarding her portrait with fascination.

As Dyck continued drawing, Jude became bolder, and started correcting him. 'She scrumples up her nose differently when she laughs – look, just there.' Dyck immediately corrected it. 'And her neck's much more beautiful. Longer, more slender.' He described her earrings and everything else that he could remember. 'Her left ear sticks out a tiny bit.'

The whole time, Story sat there silently. Her eyes twinkled as she looked from Dyck's drawing to the garrulous Jude and back.

Finally, the artist held up the picture and scrutinised it. 'Well? Have I caught her?'

Jude, who had just returned from the bar with a third pint for Dyck, nodded. 'Yes, that's brilliant.'

'She's hot,' remarked Dyck.

Story couldn't help grinning.

Jude swallowed, then said oh-so-coolly, 'Yeah. What else did you think she'd be?' He deliberately tried to avoid looking at Story, though couldn't help glancing at her.

'She's out of your league.'

Story clapped her hand to her mouth.

'We'll see about that.' Jude intended to sound casual, but a slightly defiant tone came into his voice regardless.

'If I'd been you, I'd have got her name straight off. That's for sure.' Dyck whistled through his teeth. 'And, man, I wouldn't mind seeing her myself sometime.'

Story managed to smirk with her upturned mouth and her eyes.

When Dyck went to the toilet, Jude and Story sat

silently at the table. They were both looking at the picture which, despite being only a sketch, looked as wonderful and alive as the real-life girl who was searching for her story.

Dyck returned, and the magical moment between them passed. 'You owe me a song, man,' the artist said as he packed his things away.

'I bought you three pints!'

'And I gave you a picture.'

'Next time, OK?'

Dyck wagged his finger at him. 'I won't let you forget it – you can count on that,' he said, finishing his final pint. Outside, they went their separate ways. 'You go and find her, man,' Dyck said as they parted. 'And make sure you bowl her over.' He clapped Jude on the shoulder and disappeared into the night.

Story, standing next to Jude, acted as if she hadn't heard his final words. And Jude felt like a lonely knight who had lost his shining armour en route.

They stood uncertainly outside the Yonghy-Bonghy-Bo. Night had long since fallen. Jude had tried to call Miss Rathbone, but to no avail – she was presumably roaming around in the night, as foxes were wont to do. Either that or she had switched her mobile off. He hoped nothing had happened to her.

'What now?' asked Story. 'I'm completely knackered.'

'You can stay with me tonight.'

She looked at him. 'What about your father?'

'He won't be home till tomorrow evening.' In any case, he wouldn't be able to see her.

She didn't have to think for long. 'OK.'

Jude stared at her. *OK?* That was that? No objections, no discussion?

'Great, then let's go,' he said.

Three quarters of an hour later, they were standing outside 288, Twisden Road.

'So this is your house,' said Story.

It was just before midnight and the street was sleeping, save for a couple of windows where they could see the blue flicker of late-night TV. Jude unlocked the door and stepped over the post. The house was dark and silent. The floorboards creaked beneath his feet, but not beneath Story's. The narrow staircase led into the darkness upstairs. The house smelled of the sun, as if its rays had been caught in the curtains.

Jude switched the light on, then took Story into the kitchen.

'I like kitchens,' she said.

While Jude poured himself a glass of water, Story

toured the ground floor with its living room and hallway. She wandered around like a holidaymaker inspecting her accommodation. Jude knew that it was a completely normal house. There was nothing at all remarkable about it. But he liked it that way. He had no desire to live an extraordinary life; he just wanted to rumble along. That in itself was an achievement.

In the living room, Story sat in one of the armchairs. On the low coffee table were a couple of newspapers and two comics. Jude pulled the blinds and went across to the CD player. He switched it on and looked around for a suitable CD. But Story suddenly appeared beside him and switched it off again.

'You play me something,' she said. She picked up the guitar from beside the sofa and held it out to him.

Jude took it. 'Anything in particular?'

She shook her head and sat down on the sofa. 'Just play whatever you like best.'

He sat next to her on the sofa. His fingers touched the strings and the wood. Then he sought out the first note, and the second note followed as if of its own accord. He shut his eyes briefly and did what he otherwise only did when he was alone. He gave his fingers free rein and began to hum, quietly and dreamily. Then he gave himself over to the melody that had come into his head, and helped it to unfold. He could feel the song that had been sleeping within him, and in his thoughts – which were barely more than a vague feeling – he called it 'Storytime'. The melody was both simple and elegant; it began slowly like a smile and increased to become a dance to which you might invite a girl who is different from all the others. Jude's fingers stroked the strings, and the song that he had never heard before flew up into the overhead lights and rested there, even when it was long finished.

Story sat there silently, watching him as he played. At one point, she shut her eyes. When Jude had finished and the last note had ebbed away, she said, 'I'm kind of like that picture that Dyck drew.'

'What do you mean? That you really look like that?' He put the guitar down next to him.

'That too. But what I really mean is that I'm just a sketch. Nothing more than that.' She seemed sad again. 'Don't you remember what Dyck said? That you need names to get to the essence of a person. And that's precisely my point. Jude, I'm no more than a sketch.'

'No, you're much more than that.'

She sighed. 'Play me something else.'

Jude, who could already hear the next tune in his

CHAPTER 6

Jude slept badly. Somewhere between waking and sleeping, he was stuck in the stories that Gaskell had told him back in the days when he had first discovered Highgate Cemetery and a completely new world. It was barely six months ago, although it felt like an eternity.

'Have you ever heard of body-snatchers?'

Jude nodded. He'd seen several horror films featuring their peculiar practices. However, he also knew that films had very little do with reality, and that actors found words more quickly than people in real life.

'Life in London was grisly,' said Gaskell. 'Inhuman and humiliating.' He was talking about a time before he himself was born, but he made it sound as if he had experienced it first-hand. 'People were helpless victims of their fate.' Gaskell knew how to tell a good story. 'And we still don't know the half of it.'

‘Really?’ said Jude, just to keep him talking.

‘There were all sorts of diseases.’

Sickness was always breaking out in the city’s slums, and the living conditions – cramped, impoverished and filthy – meant that it spread like wildfire. Children played in alleys contaminated with flowing, stinking sewage. People were too poor to buy fruit and vegetables, and many of them suffered severe scurvy. Their teeth fell out; their inflamed joints and atrophied muscles caused unimaginable pain. The number of desperate day-labourers increased year upon year. Every day, a fresh army of job-seekers streamed to the harbour, to the docks in Rotherhithe and to the city, where they could at least collect horse manure from the streets.

‘Small children were sent up chimneys, and many of them never came back down again,’ Gaskell intoned, before putting in a pause for maximum effect.

‘The completely desperate ones became beggars. Others traded in the street in oddities such as preserved animal carcases or magic amulets; some resorted to theft. At that time, medical schools were undertaking completely new kinds of research, and were desperate for human specimens. And so a few clever entrepreneurs came up with the idea of stealing bodies from graveyards and mortuaries.’

All things considered, this was a pretty lucrative business, as the corpses could be sold on to the medical schools without difficulty.

'All on the quiet, of course.'

For body-snatching was a crime. The punishment was only mild, but one wouldn't want to be caught doing it.

'A practised body-snatcher would need less than thirty minutes to steal a corpse,' Gaskell explained.

The need for human specimens was constantly growing, and the body-snatchers committed themselves to providing new deliveries on time. It was therefore hardly surprising that they ultimately found other ways and means to get hold of new corpses quickly, by lying in wait for people in dark alleys and killing them on the spot.

'It spared them having to dig up the coffins,' Gaskell explained. 'Not to mention other unpleasant things.'

Demand grew inexorably. Initially, only anatomists had needed corpses. Now men in every possible line of business – from dentists to charlatans, merchants to wig-makers – claimed an interest in corpses. Even the clothes of the dead were washed and mended and sold in Field Lane.

'They sold the teeth to rich people.'

Jude looked disgusted.

'Corpses were a booming business,' Gaskell declared in a sinister tone.

Later, Jude often tried to imagine what city life might have been like in those days. He was familiar with some aspects of life in nineteenth-century London from Charles Dickens's novels, but he wished he knew more about it. He'd have loved to ask one of Dickens's relatives about it (though they mostly kept themselves to themselves and weren't particularly sociable, rather like the majority of the more prominent Highgate ghosts).

'You know what their disgraceful practices did to the ghosts?'

Jude didn't know. But Gaskell was going to tell him.

'Barely had the ghosts arrived at the graveyard than they were wrenched away from the community that had only just accepted them.'

Gaskell went into full detail about the vulnerability of a newly fledged ghost who realises what has happened to him; the loss of orientation he feels when he discovers that the graveyard is his new home; the tearful memory of his own burial and the faces of those left behind; the relief that comes when he realises that he's not alone; the sense of security he feels when he becomes part of a new community.

It was terrifying for ghosts to find themselves suddenly robbed of their bodies.

For they inhabited their bodies.

They had to watch helplessly as someone dug up their body, loaded it onto a rattling wagon, and carted it off down the gaslit streets and alleyways in order to deliver it to a customer.

'The ghosts had no choice but to watch it happen. And they had to follow their bodies whether they liked it or not.'

Jude felt desperately sorry for them in their helplessness.

'Lots of ghosts lost their lives in practical anatomy.' Or, as Gaskell told him, in cheap dosshouses where they had to watch some doctor or quack brutally dissecting their bodies with strange instruments. They were forced to look on as they were dissected, and then breathed their last in unconsecrated ground beside their mutilated bodies, disfigured beyond all recognition.

'It was a dark time,' Gaskell concluded. 'The remnants of the bodies were dumped in random holes in the ground.'

Some were simply thrown into the Thames and were carried away by the current. Others ended up in the sewers that began to be constructed in the mid-nineteenth century, a gigantic project that dramatically improved London's hygiene.

Miss Rathbone, for her part, told Jude shortly afterwards about the mass graves in London. About the mediaeval plague victims – the last plague epidemic was in 1665–1666 – who were buried deep in the earth; about the overcrowded graveyards and the pervasive stench of dead bodies. About the ghosts who wandered around aimlessly. Doomed to homelessness for all eternity.

'Many of them went mad,' Gaskell added. 'Ghosts need homes too.'

Then Jude understood for the first time what it meant to be a ghost. The dangers involved in being a ghost, and the torment they had to endure.

Sighing, he awoke from his dreams.

It was pitch black outside. He was at home in his living room, among his familiar things. Safe.

Gaskell and his damn stories! He shook his head. Then he thought about Story, wondering anxiously what might happen to her body once her remaining time ran out. The thought that Story – the real, genuine, proper Story – was lying in some hidden place somewhere in the city, possibly buried under the earth, might now at this very moment be dying, was so horrendous that he couldn't get it out of his mind.

He woke up several times that night, tossing and turning in the armchair, trying to find a comfortable position, glancing at the peacefully sleeping girl, then dropping off again.

What would happen if she died? Would she suddenly vanish? Would some force that he didn't know summon her ghost to be close to her body? He didn't have the faintest idea. He only knew that he was terrified. Not for himself, but for her.

On the other hand, the Faceless Ones hadn't killed her; they had just abducted her. There must be a reason for that. What were they up to?

'There's a reason for everything,' Miss Rathbone had once said.

At last, grey light was filtering through the gap in the curtains. The start of a new day.

The radio alarm clock clicked on, playing the usual morning jingles. The programme shifted into the news and Jude stiffened as he listened to a report about a dead body that had been found at Abney Park in the early hours of the morning. A witness had seen a teenager leaving the graveyard the previous evening, but they weren't able to identify or describe the boy in detail. The knot inside Jude's stomach eased slightly, and a strange thought crossed his mind: *I'm lucky, even now*. Somebody had seen him but nobody suspected him.

A breeze rustled the curtains and as the sun rose, Story woke up too. She stretched and sat up on the sofa.

'How did you sleep?' Jude asked.

She blinked, trying to get her bearings in the unfamiliar surroundings. 'Fine. Just like normal. Like a human, I imagine.' She looked through the gap in the curtains. It was still relatively dark in the room. 'How about you?'

'Badly.'

She didn't ask why.

'Do you want any breakfast?' he asked. As the words left his mouth, he was suddenly aware that he had never seen her eat anything.

'No thanks,' she replied.

'Stupid question.'

'No, Jude, I mean I never have breakfast.'

He registered what she said, though didn't really grasp its full significance. He knew that ghosts slept. And he'd thought they could eat...

Then he realised that she meant something

different. 'Ah. You're saying that you remember stuff.'

'Only that I never eat breakfast.'

The unspoken questions that this raised whirled around like particles of dust in the air.

'What are we going to do now?'

'My father will be back this evening. Then I won't be able to spend whole nights out.' Everything would become more complicated when George Finney returned.

'What's he like, your dad?'

'He's almost always away. He works away a lot.'

She nodded quietly. 'I get you.'

Jude suddenly remembered that he had to go to school. Whatever. There wasn't time. He'd find some excuse. Excuses seemed to have become his speciality in the past couple of days. He'd managed to completely suppress the conversation that Mr Ackroyd was intending to have with his father. *Thank goodness*, he thought. He stood up, stretched, shuffled off to the bathroom. After a cold shower, he returned refreshed and feeling relatively bright.

Story was already in the kitchen. She was playing dreamily with a saltcellar that she had found on the table. 'It's mostly cosiest in the kitchen,' she said, returning to her thoughts the previous night. *Another memory*, thought Jude.

Story watched as Jude had a quick breakfast of tea, toast and marmalade. 'Whatever Hurts You Through the Night' by Glasvegas was on the radio. Strangely apt.

'That song you sang yesterday...' Story suddenly said.

Jude looked at her expectantly.

'...it was lovely.'

He smiled, hoping that his smile didn't look too stupid or, worse, smug. He couldn't get the tune out of his head either; it drowned out the memories of the horrible dreams that had plagued him.

'Do you do this every morning?' Story asked. 'Eat breakfast? Listen to the radio?'

Jude understood why she was asking, and told her about all the things that normally belonged at breakfast: tea, cereal, toast, marmalade, boiled eggs and, of course, the radio, which was at its best before nine o'clock. He felt as if he were prattling on about sheer trivia, but the way she was listening to him suggested that there was magic for her in these apparently mundane details.

'You're crazy,' she said, and smiled.

'Maybe. Who isn't?'

She turned serious. 'Most people aren't.'

He knew what she meant.

Just before eight o'clock, he rang the school. At that time of day there was nobody in the office, so he got the answering machine. He gave his name and form teacher and said he was ill. A cold. He punctuated his message with subtle coughing for good effect.

'You're a good liar,' said Story, 'even if it doesn't come naturally.'

And she is a good audience, Jude thought.

Then they set off.

They took the underground to King's Cross, then walked the rest of the way to Penton Rise.

As Jude had noticed many times before, London awoke with a jerk. Hordes of kids were streaming out of the stations onto the pavements, all of them hurrying to school. Delivery lorries clogged up the roads outside shops; commuters sped to work. Even the beggars at the stations and on street corners were on their feet.

In the sky were a couple of sparse clouds which looked like deflated balls of cotton wool. The leaves fell from the trees, and were blown along the pavements. *Clues in the autumn leaves*, thought Jude, who was tired and psyched up at the same time. *That's what we're after.*

Neither Jude nor Story said much on the journey. Both were lost in their own thoughts. Jude was holding the cardboard tube containing Dyck's picture. He had brought his guitar too. He could carry it quite easily in an old case over his shoulder.

'That's it.' He stopped outside a building and pointed. Now they would see whether his plan would come to anything.

'Looks nice,' said Story.

Clerkenwell College was housed in a modern building surrounded by a wall. Through the shimmering windows, they could see the silhouettes of pupils hurrying towards their classrooms.

Like many schools, this one had a security system to keep an eye on who was coming and going. Here, a guard sat at the reception desk inside the main entrance. Jude looked through the glass panel and observed the man as he sat there with his tea or coffee, an open newspaper in front of him, watching the pupils wearily as they drifted in. Most of them said hello to him, and he greeted them in return. Otherwise he seemed not to be particularly interested in what was going on.

Jude looked around, disconcerted by the idea that

this could well be the place where Story had routinely come and gone, day in, day out. He was curiously relieved to see that Clerkenwell College was a normal school. Not some exclusive private school, which meant that Story was a normal girl – assuming that this really had been her school.

Anyway, Jude would have to ask around. That, after all, was why he was there.

'Do you really think it'll work?' Story had asked several times on the way there.

'Yes.'

'You're an optimist.'

'That's what Miss Rathbone always says.'

'She ought to know.'

'Precisely. She's a vixen, after all.'

But now that he was standing by the door, he wasn't so certain. He'd be bound to look suspicious once he started talking to people. But that seemed to him to be the only way to find anything out about Story. Even at best, he'd make a fool of himself, because the story he'd concocted was anything other than cool.

'Do you know your way around?' he asked Story quietly as pupils hurried past to either side of them.

'Yeah, vaguely. It's like a dream that I can't quite remember.'

'So you can't remember whether you go to this school.'

'It's possible, but I can't say for certain.' Ever since they had arrived at the school, she had seemed thoughtful, even slightly apprehensive.

'OK,' Jude murmured. He suddenly felt a thirst for action.

He made sure that the guard hadn't clocked him yet. Luckily enough, he seemed more interested in his newspaper than in the horde of pupils. Then Jude went over to the wall by the entrance, took out his guitar, put the bag down by his feet and carefully unrolled the portrait. He Sellotaped it to the guitar case to protect it from the autumn wind. Finally he took up station next to the gate and waited. If anyone asked him what he was up to, he'd come up with something.

Story, meanwhile, had climbed up onto the wall and was dangling her legs. 'You really think that someone who knows me is going to stop and tell you my name?'

'Yes, I do.' Jude suddenly felt quite convinced of it.

For half an hour, he stood outside the school with nothing happening. But then a boy stopped by the guitar case. He was taller than Jude and was wearing a biker-type leather jacket with studs and a shiny zip. An RAF rucksack hung from his shoulder.

'Hey,' said the boy. He fixed his narrow eyes on Jude, then looked down and stared at Story's portrait in surprise.

'Hey,' Jude replied equally non-committally.

'What are you doing here?'

'Waiting,' said Jude.

'Waiting. Right,' the boy repeated, a threatening undertone in his voice. 'I've never seen you here before.' He was wearing a red and green checked scarf. His hair was very short and his thin face was neither friendly nor unfriendly, but alert and curious: someone who would make trouble if anyone provoked him – Jude was sure of it.

'I don't go to this school.' Jude was tired to the core. He suddenly felt unsure and somehow out of place once more.

'What's that picture?' The boy sounded like someone who expected an answer on the spot. If need be, he'd help Jude along to make sure he got it.

'Do you know her?' Jude sounded slightly more cautious and, so he hoped, rather more friendly.

The boy wasn't fooled. 'What do you want with that girl?'

'I want to give her this picture.'

The boy hesitated, but only very briefly. 'Did you draw it?'

Jude nodded. 'Yes.'

Story, who was following the action from her safe perch on the wall, nodded towards a couple more pupils heading their way. 'Trouble on the way,' she warned Jude.

Jude had already noticed them. A boy and a girl had come running across the road arm in arm. They also stopped by the guitar case with the portrait.

'Jamie, Rose,' said the first boy.

'Dave!' Jamie and Dave exchanged a series of gangster-style handshakes. Cool, chilled.

'What's up?' asked the girl they had called Rose. She was wearing purple leggings, a denim skirt and a matching jacket.

'Look at that picture,' Dave said.

The girl looked at Story's portrait, then at Jude.

'Weird, eh?'

Rose nodded. She had a pierced nose, bleached blonde hair and ice-blue eyes like a husky.

Story remained calmly on the wall. She evidently didn't recognise the three teenagers. Tensely, she watched what was happening. Jude wondered how she was feeling.

'What do you want with Penny?' asked Jamie (long hair, hoodie, jeans, Converse).

Jude stared at him. The name felt like someone stabbing him in the heart. 'Penny?' he stammered.

Time seemed to stand still for a moment. His gaze slid across to Story, taking in her expression, the endless astonishment in her hazel eyes. And a flash of recognition, as if she'd seen her own reflection for the very first time.

Jude realised now that he had never really wondered what Story's real name might be. But now that he heard it, he knew instinctively that it was the right name for her.

Penny!

'Penny,' he heard Penny saying too, as if she were hoping to conjure up her entire identity by saying the name aloud.

All of a sudden, Story turned into Penny. From now on, she would always be Penny to him, as if the name had just been waiting to be said at last.

But Jude had no time to delight in this crucially important revelation. Before he knew it, Dave was pushing him roughly up against the wall and grabbing him by the collar. The guitar fell to the ground with a twang. Passing pupils turned to look at them.

'Listen, nutter,' Dave said menacingly. 'Save your

crap for someone else.' He shoved Jude against the wall again, still holding onto his collar. 'What do you want with Penny?'

Jude stared at him. He felt as if his heart had stopped. Penny, up on the wall, bent down. She made no attempt to help him. Why should she?

'Is that her name?' Jude stammered again.

The youth didn't let go. 'Do you know her?'

'I've only met her once and...'

'Dave, what does this guy actually want?' asked the girl called Rose.

'He's some weirdo who's waiting for Penny.'

Jude struggled free from Dave's grasp. 'Hey, I'm not a weirdo.' He coughed. 'What's so bad about waiting for someone?'

'You don't even know her name. Did Nick send you?'

'Nick?'

The girl with the pierced nose brushed him aside. 'Forget it.'

'Who's Nick?' Jude asked again.

'Nobody of any interest to you,' retorted Dave. He didn't take his eyes off Jude for a second.

'Come on, Dave, leave him alone,' said the girl.

The three of them – Dave, Rose and Jamie – seemed to be friends of Penny's, Jude thought. At any rate, they knew her. And they were concerned about her.

'I met her two days ago at a bus stop.' That wasn't entirely untrue.

'And?'

'We started chatting. I...'

Rose eyed him suspiciously. 'Where was this bus stop?'

Jude decided it was safest to stick relatively closely to the truth.

'Highgate.'

Jamie looked questioningly at Rose. 'So she did it.' Whatever it was, Rose seemed happy to hear it.

'Are you sure?'

'Maybe that's why she's not feeling too good now.'

'She hasn't answered her phone for two days,' said Dave.

'What has she done?' asked Jude.

'Hey, stranger,' said Dave, 'you've not even told us your name yet.' The mistrust which had vanished for several seconds now reappeared.

'Jude,' said Jude.

'*Hey Jude...*' Dave sang the opening words to the Beatles song, grinning ironically.

'She wanted to see him again, to explain it all,'

Rose said to her boyfriend.

'See who?'

'Who do you think? Nick, of course.'

Story looked puzzled. Nick? A friend? Her boyfriend? Her blank expression told Jude that she had no recollection of any Nick.

'So what's it got to do with you?' Dave asked Jude.

Jude sighed. It was time to tell them a story. 'I met her the night before last at the bus stop at the top of Swains Lane.' That was nearly true too: after all, Mr Monkford had said that that was where she'd come from. 'We were both standing at the bus stop, waiting for a bus, and we got chatting. That's the whole story.'

'And that's why you're here now?'

'Because you *got chatting*?' Jamie was mocking him. Jude didn't like it, but he could kind of see why. He was himself aware of how uncool his story sounded.

He shook his head. 'We got on the same bus. I got off first. Anyway, I asked if I could see her again.' It was a white lie, but Jude still felt as if he'd been caught red-handed. As if someone were sitting silently up on the wall, trying to piece together a picture of the situation – as he himself was – and could see precisely what was up with him. He avoided looking at Penny.

'Aha.'

'Mmm.'

'What about Penny? Did she want to see you again too?' Rose asked.

He cleared his throat. 'She said I should look for her. It was a kind of challenge, I think. *Find me*, she said. *If you can find me, you can see me again.*'

He could feel Penny's eyes gazing down at him.

'So that's why you're here?'

He nodded. 'I drew her.'

The three of them stared at the picture.

'You drew that from memory?' asked Rose.

He nodded again.

'So what's with the guitar? Are you planning to serenade her?'

'Yes...no.' Jude felt angry now. 'I just wanted to play a bit.' He bent down to check that the guitar was still in one piece. It sounded OK. 'To make her notice me.'

The others seemed slightly more forgiving now. 'That kind of sounds like Penny.' Rose grinned. 'She didn't tell you her name. Did she tell you anything at all about herself?'

'No.'

'Typical Penny,' Jamie added. 'I can just imagine

what was going on in her head: the next boy she gets involved with is going to have to make a real effort.'

'Wouldn't be hard to make more of an effort than Nick,' Rose remarked.

Before Jude could ask again who Nick was, Dave turned to him. 'So how come you're here?'

Once again, Jude decided to stick to the truth. 'We talked about school. She said she had to prepare for a presentation on *Social Media Networks: Blessing or Curse?*'

The three of them instantly rolled their eyes and pulled faces. *Bingo*, thought Jude. 'I asked around on Facebook, and found this school.' That made sense to them.

'Ooh, get Sherlock Holmes!' said Jamie patronisingly.

'She's called Penny Scott,' Dave added.

Jude looked up at Penny. *Penny Scott*. Her eyes were full of tears. The name had evidently summoned up memories of some sort. Her hands were clasped to her mouth. Jude wanted to say something to her, but of course couldn't.

'So you know her?' he said.

'We're in the same class,' said Jamie.

'Is she here today?'

Rose shook her head. 'She's been off for two days.'

Jude waited for her to continue.

'She's not answering her phone, and she's not calling anyone. She's not been on Facebook either. Doesn't reply to emails. Nothing.'

'Her mum rang yesterday and said she was ill. But that's all we know.' Dave shrugged. 'She's presumably in the dumps after all that crap.'

Jude deduced that he was talking about Nick.

'She'll get over it.'

Penny couldn't restrain herself any longer. 'I'm not ill, for God's sake. I was abducted.'

Jude tried hard not to respond in any way. He couldn't reply now. Instead, he had to try to find out more about her. Where she lived, for instance.

'We can tell her that you came, when she gets back in touch.'

That wasn't what he had in mind. 'The thing is, I wanted to give her the portrait.'

'It's a good likeness,' Dave commented.

'You really are a weird one,' Jamie grinned. 'You've not got a clue how to do this, have you?'

Jude gave him a quizzical look.

'Of course I'm not going to tell you where she lives.' Rose seemed a bit more sympathetic, though. 'I don't know you well enough for that. But I can tell you where you'll find her mum.'

Jude frowned.

'Then you can give her mum the picture to pass on to Penny,' Rose explained.

Penny clapped her hands. She made a gesture to confirm that Jude was on the right path. The clue in the autumn leaves: here it was, clear and unmistakable.

'Why are you helping me?' he asked Rose.

'Listen, Jude.' She looked at her watch, then again at the portrait. 'Penny was with a complete bastard called Nick.' She looked up. 'Don't worry, not for long.' She laughed. 'You look miles nicer. And it seems that she's dumped Nick.'

Was that was why she'd been in Highgate? To finish with her boyfriend? Jude didn't know whether to be glad (she's single again: hurray!) or sad (she was with a complete bastard: why?). He merely nodded.

'Penny's mum works for a tax consultancy firm.' Rose frowned, thinking. 'Morley and Someone, something like that. Somewhere in the City.' She grinned. 'But you'll find it. If you can find our school, you can find a tax consultant.'

A loud ringing came from within the building.

'Sorry – got to go,' said Rose.

'Us too,' said Dave and Jamie.

'Thanks,' Jude said.

The three friends nodded briefly at him, then

disappeared into the main entrance. Jude stared after them for a while. Then he packed his stuff up and set off. The girl who was now Penny Scott leapt off the wall full of elation and followed him.

He waited until they had rounded the first bend. Then he turned abruptly to his companion and said, simultaneously fascinated and excited, 'So you're Penny Scott.' The words were like magic.

'Yes,' she merely replied. 'I'm Penny Scott.'

'How do you know? I mean, how do you know that's right? They could have said some other name.'

'No, it's my name. I can sense it.' She smiled. 'Hey, Jude, I'm Penny Scott.'

Jude grinned.

She looked at him. 'So now we've met.'

'After two days.'

'And?'

He looked at her quizzically. 'What do you mean, *and*?'

'Do you like my name?'

'It suits you.'

She ran her hands thoughtfully through her hair. 'My God,' she stammered. 'They were presumably my friends, and I don't remember a thing about them.' She paced nervously up and down the pavement. 'I do remember Nick. No, I don't remember him. I remember that he hit me. Once.' She was talking more and more quickly. 'He said he was sorry, but I knew he'd do it again. He had a short fuse and broke into a car last week. He went joyriding and smashed it into a wall in Rotherhithe.' She seemed upset now. 'I was with him and...' She looked at Jude, stopped and gulped. 'Why on earth can I suddenly remember that?'

They both knew the answer. But neither wanted to say it.

'I even remember what the school toilets look like. I can tell you what colour my folder is.'

Jude swallowed. Time was starting to run out. Penny Scott was lying somewhere out there, and her state was worsening by the hour.

'What are we going to do now?' Penny questioned.

'Rose's idea wasn't bad,' Jude said. 'I could take the picture to your mum.'

Penny was sceptical. 'What would you say to her?'

'Um...that you...'

'That I'm a ghost?'

'No, I could tell her the same tale as I told that lot just now.' He stopped. 'But why did she ring and say you were ill?'

Penny sighed. 'No idea. I haven't got a clue what's going on.'

'I'm going to show her the picture,' said Jude. 'We don't have any choice.' It was at least a clue. His zest for action was renewed. 'But I need to call the vixen first.'

It was almost nine-thirty by the time he spoke to Miss Rathbone. He and Penny were still standing on the street corner which gave them a view of Clerkenwell College.

'Jude Finney, where on earth are you?' Miss Rathbone sounded both relieved and impatient.

Jude told her everything. He recounted the tale of their narrow escape at Abney Park Cemetery, before going on to explain how he and Penny came to be standing on a street corner in Clerkenwell. 'Oh yes, and her name's Penny Scott.'

'A lovely name,' said Miss Rathbone. 'She's lucky to have it.'

'I think she knows that.'

'Yes, it's not bad,' Penny commented.

'Names,' Miss Rathbone said again, 'are important.'

'I know,' replied Jude.

The vixen congratulated him on the sketch idea. Then she got back to business. 'I know who the

Faceless Ones are now,' she said.

'Who?'

'Or, rather: I know what they are.'

Oh, come on! 'OK, what are they?'

'All in good time. You have to keep away from them at all costs.' Typical of her! Always ducking and diving.

Penny rolled her eyes.

'What about the stone angels?' Jude asked.

'You need to avoid them too.'

'Oh yes?'

'Jude Finney.' Miss Rathbone lowered her voice. 'I've got bad news. Last night all the London kitsunes met over in Kensington Gardens.' She paused, presumably – Jude thought – for dramatic effect. 'The same thing happened at two other graveyards as happened at Abney Park Cemetery. There are no ghosts left at the Royal Hospital Cemetery in Greenwich or Chiswick Old Cemetery.'

That was bad news indeed.

'What now?'

Miss Rathbone pondered for a moment. 'You take the picture to Penny's mother. Then we'll see.'

Jude promised to return to Highgate afterwards.

'If anything happens,' Miss Rathbone said by way of farewell, 'then run away as quickly as possible.'

'Will do,' Jude replied. He hung up. He'd never have thought of that for himself, obviously...

There were only two bus stops between them and the nearest Internet café.

'Have you been there before?' Jude asked.

'Yes, I remember it. Maybe I skived off school to come here, I'm not sure.' Penny was distinctly hyper now.

They caught a bus heading south, and got off at Cambridge Circus. Greek Street was just round the corner. *The Doctorow Coffee Shop and Internet Station*, it said in garish neon lights above the entrance to a former cinema. The frontage was reminiscent of the theatres which had once shown Hallmark films, made during the war and in the years of austerity that followed. Jude had seen some of them with his father: old films were George Finney's only passion, apart from work.

An old revolving door led inside, and the smell of cigarettes, popcorn and sweets hit them in the face. The smell of the past. The walls were covered with posters from old films: *The Ladykillers*, *Blackmail*, *The 39 Steps*, *The Lady Vanishes*. Next to the former ticket-booth, a cardboard stand advertised the current event: *Déjà Vu*. There was a poster featuring images of Robert Donat and Madeleine Carroll. In between were digital images from modern films: *Tron Legacy*, *Little Brother* and *The Return of the Cyberking*.

'Weird place,' Jude remarked.

The café was in a renovated room which had once housed a cinema screen. The rows of seats had been largely retained. Round tables had been installed between the red plush chairs; on all of them were brightly lit computer screens. A test picture was playing on the big cinema screen, flickering endlessly and soundlessly and looking like interference.

Jude headed for a seat right in front of the big screen. They were the only people there.

He typed *Morley tax consultant London* into Google.

Bingo.

'That's it.'

'*Morley and Rodwell Ltd, 146 Cheapside.*' Penny read it aloud, as if it held some secret that she might uncover.

Jude typed the address into Google Maps, which instantly threw up the relevant part of London. 'Not all that far from here.' Morley's offices were somewhere between St Paul's Cathedral and the Bank of England. Right in the middle of the City.

A further click took them to the company's home page. It all looked very presentable: the soft yellow tones were evidently supposed to create the dignified atmosphere of a long-established tax consultancy. The proprietors of the firm were listed as Richard A. Morley and Peter Rodwell. The names of all the employees were listed too.

'There she is!' Penny said excitedly. 'Jacqueline Scott. Accounts.' She shook her head. 'She's in the Accounts department! But I don't remember her at all.'

'Maybe that's a good thing,' said Jude.

Penny knew exactly what he meant. 'Come on. Let's go,' she said.

Less than half an hour later they were standing by the entrance to the tax consultancy. They had no idea where the clue in the autumn leaves was going to lead them.

CHAPTER 7

It hadn't been difficult to find Cheapside.

Jude and Penny had taken the Underground to St Paul's, and had walked the rest of the way. Just as in the days of the British Empire, this central area was the beating heart of a huge economic powerhouse. Here were the banks, insurance offices, business headquarters, chambers, agencies and management consultancies, all housed in prestigious buildings with columns and imposing façades made of gleaming stone. Even the most clueless observer would have no trouble realising that this was where all the money was.

In times past, St Paul's Cathedral with its dome and lantern-topped towers had dominated the city, but it had been dethroned by the skyscrapers in the finance district. Further to the east were the silhouettes of Canary Wharf's huge skyscrapers. And not far away was the so-called Gherkin, a steel, concrete and glass monstrosity, one of the most recent landmarks on the London skyline.

People clad in their armour of designer suits and expensive dresses hurried past, serious expressions on their faces, as if they couldn't get back to work fast enough in order to become even richer than they evidently were already. In the background, the cathedral looked like a relic of times past, something that nobody believed in any longer.

Jude wondered whether there were still ghosts in the crypt at St Paul's, but had no time to take a detour to find out. Gaskell had once told him about a whistling ghost who was rumoured to be Admiral Lord Nelson. His ghost apparently lived in one of the side aisles of the cathedral (where he, as Miss Rathbone had added rather peevishly, rarely entertained kitsunes). The cathedral crypt was only sparsely populated. Nobody was entirely certain how many of the venerable ghosts still lived there (they had been distinctly solitary and reserved even when they were still alive).

'You're quiet,' said Penny as they walked down the road.

'I don't like this area.' Jude was looking at the numbers on the huge buildings. 'Too many fat cats,' he added by way of explanation. He was tense for another reason too, but kept that to himself. He was worried because Penny's memories were now starting to return with alarming speed.

'This is it.' He stopped.

Number 146 was an old, dignified-looking building with high windows. It was obviously home to a whole host of agencies and offices. A gleaming gold plate on the wall declared:

MORLEY & RODWELL LTD. FINANCIAL AND TAX CONSULTANTS

'Looks pretty grand,' Jude observed.

'So that's where my mother works,' Penny said, lost in thought.

For a while they both stared at the plate. A new world awaited them behind the door: that much was clear. The world of dry numbers.

'What are we waiting for?' said Jude, finally screwing up his courage. Then he opened the door and strode inside.

In the entrance hall was a signing-in desk. Jude said he urgently needed to speak to his mother, who worked in the tax office. The security guard seemed satisfied with this explanation. Who'd have thought there was anything to fear from an ordinary schoolboy like Jude?

Jude went across to the lift with Penny in tow.

Morley & Rodwell was on the third floor. The lift doors opened and Jude got in. Once the doors had shut again, he took a deep breath.

'You can do it,' said Penny.

'Yep.'

'We won't be able to talk once we're in the office.'

'I'll think of something,' he replied. 'Trust me.' One look into her hazel eyes was enough to convince him that he really was telling the truth.

The lift doors opened and Jude stepped out with Penny close by his side. A large reception desk stood in front of them. A secretary leant enquiringly towards them. The corners of her mouth looked as if they very rarely turned up; her eyes behind their spectacles looked as if they never laughed.

'Can I help you?' she asked.

'Good morning,' said Jude. 'I just wanted to drop something off.' He gesticulated to the cardboard tube. 'Is Mrs Scott in?'

The foyer was elegant and imposing. Impressionist art hung on the pale wood-panelled walls. On the window ledges were strange sculptures, too modern for Jude's liking.

'Looks very sterile,' Penny said. Jude wisely made no reply.

'Mrs Scott from Accounts?' The secretary

scrutinised him carefully. There was a nameplate on her desk: Angela Surridge. 'No, I'm sorry, she's not here yet,' she said. 'And I don't know whether she'll be coming in at all today or not; she was off sick yesterday. I've not heard from her yet.' She then seemed to wonder what a boy of Jude's age was doing in the office at that time of day. 'May I ask who you are?'

'Jonathan Smithfield.' Jude had come up with the name in advance. It somehow seemed advisable not to give his real name. He could get into serious trouble at school if word got out that he was skiving off to go hanging around the City. In any case, it was better to be on the safe side.

'As I said, Mrs Scott isn't in the office.' Ms Surridge turned to the PC on the desk behind the counter, and her fingers flew across the keyboard as she spoke to Jude. 'Would you like me to give her a message?'

'Show time,' he heard Penny saying.

Jude cleared his throat. Then he told her the same story that he'd told Penny's three school friends.

He told her about meeting the girl at the bus stop and about the portrait that he'd drawn as a present for her. He even told her about his trip to Penny's school, and that he'd gone to no end of trouble to find out the office where Penny's mother worked. 'Mrs Scott's daughter is ill, you see, and I don't know where she lives. That's why I'm here.'

The secretary's expression instantly softened. 'Oh, that's so sweet,' she breathed. Even her smile looked genuine now. 'You're very welcome to leave the picture here if you like.'

'I'd rather give it to Mrs Scott myself.'

Ms Surridge nodded. 'But I don't know when she'll be here.'

'That's fine. I'd like to wait for her.'

One of the office doors opened and a man in a dark suit emerged. Tall and thin, with spectacles and hair flecked with grey, he looked every inch the English gentleman. He went over to his secretary's desk and placed a folder on it. Then he noticed Jude.

'Aren't you slightly young to be needing tax advice?' he asked.

'No, I...' Jude stammered.

'This boy wants to see Mrs Scott.'

The man nodded. He looked as if he were a regular at a gym.

'I wanted to give her something. For her daughter.'

'Isn't Mrs Scott here yet?'

Jude had the feeling that he had inadvertently dropped Penny's mother in it.

'No,' said the secretary. 'She hasn't been in touch yet. It's not at all like her.'

The man nodded again. 'I'm Richard Morley.' His eyes were narrow and clear, bright blue. He put his head slightly to one side as he regarded Jude. Then he smiled pleasantly and held out his hand.

'Hello,' Jude said awkwardly, shaking hands.

'Is Mr McGuinn here yet?' Mr Morley asked his secretary.

'He should be here any minute now.'

'He and I have got a meeting,' Mr Morley explained to Jude. 'Would you like a drink? You're very welcome to wait here for Mrs Scott, if you like.'

'Thanks – that's very kind,' said Jude.

Penny, standing next to him, was silent. She had moved closer to Jude, as if being close to him would protect her from the lurking dangers of life. Jude could see that she had no recollection of ever having been there before.

'Shouldn't you be at school?' Mr Morley suddenly asked. He was still smiling, but he fixed Jude with a look that Jude recognised very well: the same look that his father and Mr Ackroyd gave him. The look of adults who have caught you telling a lie, but who derive entertainment from playing along with it for a while longer.

Jude felt uncomfortable. 'I...'

'You took a day off.' Mr Morley grinned. 'That's what a boy sometimes has to do if he's trying to impress a girl, isn't it?'

Jude stared at him. Why shouldn't he admit it? 'Yes,' he said. 'I'd be grateful if you—'

'Don't worry – I won't snitch on you. Everyone's skived off school at some point.'

Jude smiled gratefully.

'Which school do you go to?'

Jude gave him the name of a different school, and Mr Morley seemed satisfied.

'Where's the McGuinn file?' The secretary pulled a folder from her filing cabinet and handed it to him. Mr Morley fished an iPhone from his jacket pocket, held it up and looked at the display. Then he turned back to the secretary. 'McGuinn texted. He'll be here in five minutes.' The iPhone disappeared back into his pocket. 'Right.' He clapped his hands. 'Then let's get back to work.' With these words, Mr Morley vanished back into his office, the McGuinn file under his arm, without bothering to look at Jude again.

Ms Surridge gestured to Jude to sit down, then returned to her PC.

Jude wandered across to the chairs by the window and sat down. He flicked listlessly through one of the magazines that were filed neatly on the low table. They were mostly economics-related: *The Economist* and several trade publications to do with tax; nothing of any interest to him.

Penny, who knew that nobody could see her, wandered up and down the lobby, looking around with interest. She finally stopped by the bookcase behind the secretary's desk and started reading the spines of the files, which bore the names of several clients.

Ms Surridge was shuffling uncomfortably around in her revolving chair. She could evidently feel the invisible presence of the ghost-girl. She suddenly stood up, ran across to the shelves on the other side of the room and pulled out a file. Then she made herself an espresso from the hi-tech coffee machine, as if she had to fortify herself before venturing back to her work station. Jude watched her strange behaviour; she herself was presumably unaware of its oddness.

Ten minutes passed, then the boss's door opened once more. Mr Morley in turn helped himself to an espresso from the machine, savouring every tiny mouthful. 'Is she still not here?' he asked with interest. It was hard to say how old he was – he might well have been older than he looked – but Jude guessed he was about the same age as his father.

'No,' said Jude.

Mr Morley emptied the espresso cup. It looked far too small in his long, slender fingers. When the secretary stood up and went into a nearby room, the tax advisor smiled agreeably. 'I can see your girlfriend,' he said, winking at Jude. He nodded at Penny and gave her a smile that made him look like a wolf baring its teeth.

Jude was petrified. He felt as cold as ice and he didn't dare move. Penny, who was half bending over the files, stood, horrified, by the bookcase.

'You'll soon have company.' This time Mr Morley was looking at Penny.

Had he misheard? Jude stared at the man in disbelief.

The secretary returned, instinctively giving Penny a wide berth, then returned to her work as if nothing had happened. She picked up the phone, made some notes and checked her emails.

'Perhaps I'd better come back tomorrow,' Jude gasped, once he finally found his voice again. 'Anyway, I really ought to go to school. Otherwise I'll miss the second lesson too.' He wanted only one thing: to get away from there as soon as humanly possible. He had the horrible feeling that he'd fallen into a trap.

'Yes,' said Mr Morley. 'Perhaps you should.' He was still standing there, holding his empty espresso cup and scrutinising Jude.

The lift doors opened and a man emerged.

'Charles – how *are* you?' Mr Morley greeted the newcomer like an old friend. 'Could you bring Mr McGuinn a cup of tea, please?' he asked the secretary politely. He seemed to have lost interest in Jude and Penny, who were both still standing there as if rooted to the spot, as he opened his office door and ushered his client inside.

Before following Mr McGuinn in though, Mr Morley turned back to his young visitors. 'Never fear imminent death,' he whispered, looking Penny straight in the eye. There was no trace of friendliness in his voice now; he sounded cold and malicious. He winked again, and disappeared into his office.

'Is everything OK?' the secretary asked.

Jude felt completely befuddled. 'Yes, it's just a bit stuffy in here,' he stammered. He felt even greyer and more mousy than ever; every word was an effort.

'Ah, yes, the central heating,' said the secretary. 'It can get a bit much.'

Jude stumbled dizzily into the lift. He only dared breathe again once the doors had shut behind him and the lift was moving downwards. Neither he nor Penny spoke. They both stared at the door. When it opened and there was nobody lying in wait for them, Jude breathed with relief.

'Damn it!' he said.

'Who *is* that guy?' asked Penny. 'I had a feeling right from the start that he could see me.'

'I haven't the faintest idea.' Jude ran past the security guard and out onto the street.

He was amazed that they had been able to get away so easily. He had increasingly come to feel that they had become involved in something that was too big for them.

Never fear imminent death.

Penny was agitated. 'He knows who I am,' she said as she trotted alongside Jude, struggling to keep up with him. 'Do you think we're being followed?'

Jude looked around but he couldn't see anyone obvious – just ordinary passers-by, who paid no attention to him: bank employees, people in suits, a handful of tourists on their way to St Paul's. His heart was pounding. 'Let's get out of here. Quickly!'

You'll soon have company.

He suddenly saw a Land Rover braking sharply on the other side of the road. Two men got out. One was holding a smartphone and was reading something on the screen. Jude stopped abruptly, his mind whirling. If Morley knew who Penny was and could see her ghost – or whatever it was – then did he have something to do with her disappearance? He felt dizzy.

The two men on the other side of the road looked anything other than pleasant and Jude thought back to what had happened in the building. Morley had gone into his office before this Mr McGuinn had appeared. How long had he been in there? Ten minutes? More? Enough time, at any rate, to contact someone.

He rang someone. That much was clear. Then Jude remembered that Morley had had a text on his iPhone. *Christ*, he thought. *He held it up and took a picture of me*. It didn't take much imagination to work out that the two men across the road were now studying that photo on their smartphone. They were looking for him. Of course: Morley had summoned them. Jude cursed silently. How could he have been so stupid?

'Come on!' he said to Penny, ducking quickly into a doorway.

Never fear imminent death.

He knew that Penny didn't have much time left, and this knowledge was like a dagger in his heart. He looked across the road. The two men were wearing suits, black shirts and black ties, coupled with secret agent-style mirrored sunglasses.

'Those guys look just like something from a gangster film,' Jude whispered.

'Smith and Jones,' said Penny.

Jude allowed himself a fleeting grin. But the two gangsters were looking around now. One of them stopped short, his gaze fixed on the doorway. Damn: he'd spotted them.

'Come on – let's go!'

Penny and Jude ran along the street, heading for St Mary-le-Bow church. 'Into the church!' Jude hoped that someone there might help them. He grabbed Penny's hand and together they raced towards the entrance and rattled the handle – but the door was locked.

'To the underground!' Jude panted.

Penny stood stock-still. 'They're there!'

'Where?'

'Over there.'

She was right: Smith and Jones were on their heels. Penny and Jude raced down Bow Lane, heading towards Mansion House. When Jude looked back, he saw that the car was following them too. So there must be three men.

Here, where the pavements were less busy, the

two gangsters could move faster. They were catching up, though it occurred to Jude that they could only see him, not Penny. He could feel his guitar banging against his back. He was still holding the cardboard tube containing the picture.

The other passers-by paid no attention to him. For them, Jude was just some kid rushing along, late for school.

Then, finally, they reached the Underground. It was the best place to shake off their pursuers, especially during the rush hour. Better, at any rate, than out there on the streets where those guys had a car at their disposal as well. The Underground was a crush of people; there were countless corridors and escalators and you could easily lose sight of someone, though the besuited men didn't look the types to lose sight of anyone in a hurry – they seemed quite accustomed to hunting people down.

Jude and Penny ran down the escalator, ignored the ticket machines, leapt over barriers. It flashed through Jude's mind that it was rather handy for ghosts, being able to travel by Tube for free. Then he remembered that ghosts didn't normally get to wander around taking advantage of the perks of ghostdom, and that Penny was very much an exception.

He risked glancing back. The two men were now

on the escalator too. But the distance between them had increased. The two gangsters seemed to want to come across as normal passengers in a hurry, so as not to attract attention.

Come on! Don't stop! Jude jostled past the stationary commuters and descended the final flight of steps with one bound. Then he ran onto the platform. He could already smell the fuggy air from the fans sweeping along the tunnel. He was panting heavily; Penny, for her part, was breathing almost inaudibly. The posters on the tiled walls flew by and he could hear the clickety-clack of an oncoming train in the distance. It was the Circle Line, going towards Westminster.

'Thank God,' Jude croaked.

The wind from the oncoming train blew into their faces as he made his way along the platform. He looked over his shoulder once more. The two men had just reached the bottom of the escalator.

'Stay where you are, boy! We won't harm you!' one of them called to him. The man sounded quite calm. He wasn't even out of breath.

He really can't see Penny, Jude thought. *Whoever he is, he's a normal man. A normal gangster, that is. Oh, great.*

The train stopped with a squeal, and disgorged a stream of people.

'This won't work,' Penny suddenly said.

'And now you tell me?'

'Listen. If we get on this train, then they'll tell someone who'll get on at the next stop.'

Penny was right. Jude ran further down the platform, making a path through all the people coming and going, thinking madly. Should they go back outside and try to dodge their pursuers out on the streets? How? Bus? Taxi?

The two men – Smith and Jones – were coming menacingly closer. Without any regard for the bystanders, they were making their way towards Jude.

'We need to get rid of them,' Jude gasped. 'Somewhere down here.' Up on the street, the men were at an advantage. They were obviously also much fitter than Jude. Then he suddenly had an idea. 'Penny, nobody can see you but they all avoid you,' he burst out. 'You need to go and start interfering with people. You can, can't you? I mean, they'll avoid you even if they only start to feel your presence.' She could after all touch objects – and him.

Smith and Jones had almost caught up with them; Jude could already see their faces coming up close behind him. One of them had twisted his lips into a nasty grin.

'I'll try.' No sooner said than done, Penny threw herself into the crowd, barging into anyone who crossed her path. Most of them looked round indignantly, evidently suspecting other passengers but unable to work out exactly who it was. Several of them cried out. Nobody had a clue who or what had clattered into them so roughly.

Movement started to swell within the crowd. Out of nothing, a subliminal sense of panic started to drive everyone to the exits. Nobody knew what had caused the panic, but they all let themselves be infected by it, and were carried along by the current.

'Duck!' Penny cried over her shoulder.

It was as if she were ploughing a furrow for him. Jude disappeared into the crowd, letting himself be swept along towards the exit opposite. Someone banged into him hard, and he heard the sound of splintering wood.

'Damn!' he cursed. His guitar. 'Can you see them?' he called to Penny.

She shook her head. The two secret-agent types had lost the trail and disappeared into the crowd.

Jude and Penny were now on the upwards escalator at the other end of the platform. Jude took a deep breath as he saw daylight. They had almost done it. He joined the throng heading for the exit. Finally out on the street once more, he took several deep breaths of fresh air.

'That way!'

They ran toward the Thames. As they left the Underground behind them, the streets became emptier. After a while, Jude dared to glance over his shoulder. Nobody was following them.

They didn't stop until they reached the edge of the Thames. Jude leant against a post box, panting. He was starting to get a stitch.

'I know where I live,' Penny said suddenly.

'What do you mean?' Jude gasped.

'I can remember.'

'You mean...'

'Gerridge Street, Southwark. Near St George's Circus.' She stammered out the address. 'But I don't remember anything else.' As if she were trying to reassure herself.

It bore in on Jude again that time was running out like fine sand through their fingers. Once Penny Scott had all her memories back, she would be dead. Then she would dissolve and disappear to wherever her body was. They had to find her as quickly as possible.

'Then let's go there.'

She nodded. 'It's not far,' she said.

Jude reached out and touched her shoulder. 'We can do it.'

'Yes we can.'

Although neither of them knew where this would take them, they both suddenly felt a deep inner confidence; they breathed it into their hearts, completely without foundation, like hope, and it refused to be blown away with the autumn leaves.

Less than twenty minutes later they were standing outside a flat in Gerridge Street in Southwark. They'd had no problem getting into the building. Jude had rung several doorbells; there had been a buzzing sound and the door had opened. The Scotts' flat number was written alongside their name next to their bell.

Newspapers lay on the floor of the bare, cold hallway. Flyers and letters were spewing out of the overstuffed letter boxes on the wall. There was a lift – but it looked so rickety that Jude decided to use the stairs.

'This is where I live,' Penny murmured. She was playing nervously with a strand of hair, apparently taking in every tiny detail of the hallway.

The flat was on the third floor. The lock had been forced, and the door was ajar. Part of the frame had been smashed. Penny looked anxiously at Jude, asking countless silent questions that he – as so often in the past couple of days – couldn't begin to answer.

Cautiously he pushed open the door. He could feel the hairs on the back of his neck standing on end as he went into the hallway. When he saw the chaos that awaited them, he let out a low whistle.

Penny was very pale. This presumably wasn't how she had imagined her homecoming. 'What's happened?' she whispered.

The flat was a total mess. Clothes and furniture were strewn across the floor. Books had been swept off the shelves; all the crockery in the kitchen had been smashed. The floor was covered in instant coffee; food had been hurled around. The fridge door was open, and water was plopping onto the vinyl, where it swirled together with the coffee granules to make a dark lake.

Jude stopped in the living room. 'Do you recognise anything?'

'It's weird,' she said. 'The living room's like an echo that I can't quite hear.'

Silently he looked at the photos, which lay on the ground in shattered frames. They were of a woman and a girl. Penny. There was no man in any of the pictures. No father? Pieces of paper and letters were scattered around and Jude bent down and picked up one sheet: an electricity bill.

'Jacqueline Scott,' he said. That was the name of Penny's mother.

Penny sighed. 'Jackie,' she said. Another memory arriving unannounced. 'People always call her Jackie. My mum.'

'What about her face?' Jude asked. 'Do you remember that?'

She shook her head. 'Not really.' She rubbed her temples. 'No, I don't recognise her.'

Jude wondered how it felt to see all these once-familiar possessions and not to remember them.

The flat wasn't particularly spacious. A typical town flat, big enough for two people. A flat for people who didn't lack anything, but didn't live in luxury either.

'This is my room,' said Penny. She had gone out into the hallway and was standing outside one of the two bedrooms.

Jude went and stood next to her. On the walls were posters of Scouting for Girls and Richard Ashcroft along with a film poster of *The League of Extraordinary Gentlemen* and, above the untidy desk, one of *The Decoy Bride*. On the desk was a pile of A-level textbooks that Jude recognised.

A smashed record player was lying among all the

junk on the floor and Jude couldn't help looking at the records that had likewise been swept onto the ground. 'You collect vinyl?'

She shrugged. 'Looks like it.'

He knelt down and flicked through them. The Who. Sigue Sigue Sputnik. The Rolling Stones. The Good, the Bad and the Queen. New Model Army. The Black Eyed Peas. Gary Barlow.

'You like Gary Barlow?'

She rubbed her eyes. 'I might do.' Confused and uncertain, she paced around her own room. Every now and then, she touched something. Her bed was rumpled; a stuffed monkey was tangled up in the covers. She picked it up and held it briefly, uncertainly, as if she wasn't sure what to do with it. Then she glanced into her wardrobe and looked at her things as if they belonged to a stranger.

'Someone's been here and has trashed the place,' she murmured. 'But why?' The intruder had obviously been looking for something in particular. For what? 'We've not got anything valuable,' she added thoughtfully. 'We've got nothing worth stealing – as you can see.'

Jude was wondering how Mr Morley, the vanished ghosts in the graveyards, the appearance of the Faceless Ones and Penny's abduction all fitted together. He couldn't make head nor tail of it.

'And where's my mother?'

Jude shrugged. 'I don't think she's on her way to work.' The flat didn't look as if anyone had been in it for the past couple of days – apart from the intruder. The fridge had largely defrosted; it had presumably been open for quite some time. 'She hasn't been here for a while,' he said.

'But why?'

'Because she's hiding. I can't think of any other explanation.'

'Who would she be hiding from?' Penny sat on her bed and clutched the stuffed monkey. Then she started to cry quietly.

Jude put his guitar case on the floor and sat down next to her. He felt as if he had suddenly been catapulted right into the middle of her life and here, in this unfamiliar flat, he suddenly saw Penny in a completely different light. His head was flooded by images: Penny Scott waking up, drinking coffee, doing her homework. She reached out her hand and he held it. He bent down to open his guitar case. The body of the guitar had been spoilt by a large diagonal crack.

'I'm so sorry,' she said.

Jude stroked the guitar. 'I'll leave it here, in your room.'

'Why?'

'Because it gives me a reason to come back. Once this is all over...'

Penny also stroked the guitar, gently and somehow intimately. Then they went silently downstairs.

'Oi – you!' Jude jumped. In the hallway, someone had suddenly grabbed his wrist. He whirled round and looked into the exhausted face of a woman who looked like Penny, only older. Jude immediately recognised her from the photos in the living room.

No doubt about it: she was Jackie Scott, Penny's mother. Jude stared at her. He hadn't noticed her; she had presumably been lying in wait by the bin cupboard.

'What are you doing here? Who are you?'

He knew that the explanation he was about to give her was going to be tricky to say the least.

Jackie Scott looked like someone who had been in hiding for several days. She was glancing around nervously with the same hazel eyes as Penny and, although life had left its mark on her, it was clear that she had once been just as attractive as her daughter. 'Did Mr Morley send you?'

'No.'

'So what were you doing in my flat?' She was wearing jeans, a suede jacket and a floral scarf. 'Well? Has the cat got your tongue?'

Jude didn't know what to say.

Penny was standing beside her mother, looking just as surprised as Jude was. She reached out her hand and quickly withdrew it, seeming not to dare to touch her mother. She looked beseechingly at Jude.

He shook his head. 'I know your daughter. I met her two days ago.'

'You met Penny?' Jackie Scott was taken aback. 'Where?' She noticed the cardboard tube in Jude's hands. 'What's in that thing?'

'A drawing,' Jude said. 'Of Penny.'

Penny's mother was visibly surprised.

He held the tube out to her. 'Here – look at it. I just wanted to give Penny this picture.'

'What's all this nonsense about?'

Penny came up close to him. 'Just tell her.'

Jude stared at her.

'What? What are you looking at?' Jackie Scott followed his gaze but, of course, couldn't see anyone.

'I...'

'Tell her what's going on.'

'Are you sure?'

‘Who are you talking to?’ Jackie Scott asked suspiciously.

‘Tell her, and give me the tube,’ Penny suggested.

‘Out with it, boy.’

Jude swallowed hard. ‘OK. You won’t believe me, but I’ll tell you anyway: I can see ghosts.’

‘You can do what?’

‘See ghosts.’

Now Penny’s mother was lost for words.

‘I don’t know why,’ he said, ‘but it’s true. I met Penny two days ago in Highgate. She isn’t a ghost, but is kind of halfway there. She was abducted by two men. We think she’s still alive...I mean, the real Penny, the physical one’ – he was getting muddled now, to his irritation – ‘but she’s unconscious. We need to find her quickly because... I mean, Penny’s ghost, or whatever she is...is remembering more and more stuff about her life, and that’s bad because it means she’s in the process of turning into a proper ghost, which in turn means that her body is dying...’ He stopped for breath, then finally said despondently, ‘I know it all sounds pretty crazy.’

‘Are you on drugs?’ asked Jackie Scott. She was frowning.

Jude looked at her in despair. ‘No, I...’

‘Why—’ Jackie Scott began, but then broke off.

She stared wordlessly away from Jude, at the place just next to him.

Penny was holding the cardboard tube. Jude knew that Jackie Scott couldn't see her daughter, but she could see the cardboard tube floating about a metre above the ground. Penny opened the tube and pulled out the rolled-up picture. She slowly unrolled it and held it up to her mother.

'How are you doing that?' Jackie Scott stammered. She let go of his wrist which she had been clinging onto the whole time, as if afraid that he might escape.

'I'm not doing anything. It's Penny. You just can't see her,' said Jude.

'What's going on?'

'Penny's here with us,' said Jude. 'I mean, her ghost' – he cleared his throat – 'or whatever she is.'

Jackie Scott reached out and touched her daughter's portrait. 'Yes, that's my Penny,' she said. Her voice quavered and she tottered slightly. 'I think I'm going to faint.'

'Oh no, please don't,' said Jude.

Rather against her will, Jackie Scott smiled. Penny, meanwhile, touched her mother's hand briefly. Shocked, Jackie pulled away. 'What was that?'

'Tell her I touched her.'

'Penny touched you.'

Jackie was breathing heavily and her face was as white as a sheet. 'What did we have for tea? Last Saturday?'

Jude stared at her. 'What's that got to do with anything?'

'That's what they always ask in films like *Ghost*. If Penny's really there, she can tell me what we had for our last tea.'

Jude looked at Penny, who shrugged. 'No idea.'

'She can't remember.'

Jackie Scott's expression immediately became mistrustful again.

'I said it was complicated,' said Jude impatiently. Then he took a deep breath and told her as much of the story of how he had found Penny as he could, and what had happened since. Once he'd finished, Jackie Scott still didn't seem convinced; his story was just too outlandish. But she had at least listened to him without interrupting.

For a moment, she seemed to be trying to work out how to react. Then she apparently made her decision. 'Come on. We need to get away from here. They could well be watching the house.' Without waiting for a reply, she led the way, just as Penny would have done too.

She led them to a bright red Mini parked under a

tree in the road around the corner. Penny squeezed herself onto the back seat and Jude sat in the front with his legs jammed in and his head touching the roof.

Jackie Scott switched the ignition on and accelerated away. Her pink Playboy bunny key ring dangled to and fro. 'There's one thing I do know,' she said. 'They'll be after you too. It was a bad idea, going to see Morley.' She seemed extremely nervous, and her driving was correspondingly erratic. She accelerated, braked, speeded up again, had to brake sharply again.

'What's been happening?' Jude asked.

'They abducted Penny,' said her mother, 'and now they're blackmailing me.'

She looked tensely ahead of her, constantly glancing in her rear-view mirror without apparently seeing anything suspicious. Accompanied by the hoots of other drivers, she kept switching lanes abruptly, as if trying to shake off an invisible pursuer. In less than fifteen minutes – Jude felt as if they'd circled half of London – she stopped.

'We're here.' They were in Blackfriars Road – not actually far from her flat, Jude realised. Jackie parked outside a pub. 'We can talk undisturbed here,' she said as she got out. 'I know the owner; I've been staying here since the day before yesterday.' She pointed upwards, to where a window was ajar. 'The pub and the B & B above it belong to Shane Busiek. He's a good friend of mine.'

Jude read the name on the sign. *Chez Shane*.

Jackie Scott, who noticed him looking, said, 'He once had a French girlfriend, and he's been into French stuff ever since. But he's a nice guy.'

Jude wondered whether the two things were mutually exclusive, but kept that to himself.

She opened the door and they went inside. The pub was empty. The chairs were up on the tables, and dim light fell through the narrow windows.

'He doesn't open till late afternoon,' Jackie said. She went across to one of the tables by a back window and put the chairs on the ground. 'I don't know if Penny wants a seat,' she said. It was clear that she still couldn't get her mind round her daughter's strange presence. However, she appeared to be trying her best to come to terms with this bizarre situation.

Jude sat down and Penny sat next to him. 'Do you think I look like her?' she asked as she sat down.

Jude looked at her, baffled. He didn't have much experience of girls, but he did know that whatever he said would be wrong. He therefore pretended that he hadn't heard.

'I just mean because she talks so much.'

Jude couldn't help smiling.

'Did she say something?' asked Jackie.

'No.'

'She's full of curiosity,' said Penny.

'Like you,' Jude blurted out.

Jackie moved round to where Jude was sitting. 'Is she there?'

He nodded.

Jackie reached out her hand, then immediately withdrew it. She sighed. 'Right. I'll fill you in on what's happened. I've worked in the accounts department at Morley and Rodwell for years. I've always thought that Mr Morley was a perfectly nice bloke and a good boss. In the last couple of years, he's been away a lot, on holiday or on leave. But when he was here, it was nice working for him. Nobody ever complained—'

'So why's he blackmailing you now?' Jude interrupted impatiently. 'And how's he blackmailing you? What for?'

'That's a complicated story.' Penny's mother folded her hands to try to calm herself, to little avail. 'I came across something weird in the accounts,' she said. Her hands were trembling. 'A week ago. The figures didn't add up and there had been some unexplained business – probably concerning drugs.'

Jude and Penny exchanged worried glances.

'Anyway, Morley was definitely involved in illegal business,' Jackie Scott continued. 'There were large amounts of money – some entries were getting on for almost a quarter of a million pounds. But someone had been cooking the books. Clients' accounts were involved, and the amounts were all mixed up with turnover and expenditure. Whatever the case, I realised that something funny was going on.'

'And word presumably got out,' Jude said.

Jackie Scott nodded. 'Mr Morley worked out that I'd been in the system. Three cheers for data protection. Every time you log in, it's recorded in the office.'

'So he knew that you'd seen something you shouldn't have seen.'

'Sharp, aren't you? Yes, that's it.'

'So then he abducted Penny?'

'He confronted me and threatened me first. That was two days ago.' She swallowed. 'He looked at me like...you should have seen his eyes. They're normally sky-blue, but they were suddenly...different.' She was searching for the right words. 'They had gone a really weird colour.' She shuddered at the memory. 'There was something about him that terrified me. I'd never seen him like that. And then I did something really stupid. I...I threatened *him*.'

'You what?'

Penny rolled her eyes. 'I told him that I'd copied the files.'

Jude stared at her. 'You blackmailed him?'

'Hey, I watch thrillers every now and then. It was a gamble. "If you do anything to me," I said, "then the USB stick with all the account files will be sent to the police. It's all sorted, just in case anything happens to me."'

'I don't believe it,' Penny groaned.

'What did he do?' asked Jude.

She sighed. 'He kept his cool. He thanked me for telling him, and then let me go.'

'And that was that?'

'I pushed off straight away. He didn't make any concrete threat, but I knew full well that I'd regret it if I crossed his path. I saw the anger in his eyes.'

'What then?'

'I was in a terrible state. I was running around town like a headless chicken. I had no idea what to do.' She stared at her hands, which were nervously shredding a paper napkin. 'I was on the way home when I got a text: *Do you know where your daughter is at the moment?*' She looked ashen. 'It came from

Penny's mobile.' Jackie was fighting back the tears now. 'When I got home, the place had been turned upside down. You two saw it yourselves. The phone rang. It was Mr Morley.' She swallowed. 'He said that if I wanted to see Penny alive again, I wasn't to tell anyone about the account files.'

Jude shook his head incredulously, while Penny sat open-mouthed.

'I was in a terrible panic. Someone had searched our flat for that blasted memory stick, which didn't even exist. Those heavies obviously meant business.'

Jude remembered his own narrow escape from Smith and Jones.

'They're evil,' Jackie Scott said quietly. 'They will stop at nothing.'

Penny briefly touched her mother's hand. Jackie looked up, as if she had felt a breath of wind. Defiantly, she quickly wiped away a tear. 'I got straight out of there,' she said, 'and came over to Shane's. I'm pretty sure that nobody followed me, but you never know.'

'What does Mr Morley want from you now?' Jude asked.

'He wants the USB stick. That's why he abducted Penny.' She rubbed her eyes, exhausted. It was obvious that she had barely slept for the past couple of days. 'He wants me to ring him, on my daughter's mobile.' Her voice faltered. 'I know I can get him on Penny's phone.'

'Why didn't you go to the police?'

'I'm frightened. About Penny. She's my entire world. Her father buggered off when she was ten. The bastard. I couldn't bear it if anything happened to Penny. I rang school to say she was ill, so that people didn't wonder why she wasn't there. What else could I have done?' She fumbled around in her jacket pocket and pulled out a packet of cigarettes. She lit one with trembling hands and took a couple of hasty drags on it. 'I even hung around the office, lying in wait. I thought that Morley might lead me to her.'

'You were going to shadow him?'

She nodded.

'That was incredibly stupid,' Penny whispered – although Jude could tell by her face that she was secretly full of admiration for her mother's courage.

'And he didn't spot you?'

'I don't think so. In any case, he only went from his office to his house, so far as I could tell.'

Jude coughed. He hated the smell of cigarette smoke. 'What should we do now?'

She shrugged.

'Give him a memory stick?' It was the best idea that Jude could come up with.

'But there isn't a memory stick.'

'Any old stick. We need to do something. Penny's running out of time.'

Jackie Scott looked uncertain. Then she nodded firmly and stubbed out her cigarette. 'You're right,' she said. 'We need to trick him.'

'And if we follow her when she hands it over,' said Penny excitedly, 'then we'll find out where my body is.'

Jude pondered. There were just too many unknowns here. What did Mr Morley have to do with the Faceless Ones? And, if it came to that, exactly what kind of creature was Mr Morley himself? He could see the spirits of the dead, just like Jude. And he was a man who lived a normal life in London.

For one brief moment, he wondered whether he ought to tell Penny's mother about the Faceless Ones, but decided against it. It would sound just too unbelievable. He only had to imagine how he would have reacted a year ago if someone had spun him such a crazy yarn.

'I've got friends who can help us,' said Jude.

'You mean you're going to talk to them beforehand?' said Penny. 'To Gaskell and the vixen?'

'We *have* to talk to them.'

'Do you think he knows the answers?' Penny had come to know him well enough to know who he had in mind.

Jude nodded. 'Maybe not the answers we need, but he might give us one that helps us, all the same.'

It was time to ask several questions.

'What kinds of friends?' asked Jackie Scott, who had listened silently to the one-sided conversation.

Jude sighed. 'Do you trust me?'

Jackie Scott shrugged. 'What choice do I have? There's no one else I can trust.'

Jude pulled a face. 'So that's a yes.'

'Yes, I trust you,' said Jackie.

Penny frowned and dreamily twirled her red hair around her fingers. Jude had come to know what this meant. She was remembering something else connected with her real life.

'Arrange a meeting with him,' said Jude. 'A handover. The stick in return for Penny. He needs to tell you where to meet.' He was instinctively assuming that it would be a graveyard, possibly even one of the Magnificent Seven. But he kept this to himself. 'Penny and I will come with you. Secretly, of course.'

'Are you going to get advice first from your friends – whoever they may be?'

'Yes. But they won't come to the handover,' said Jude.

'Have you got a mobile?' asked Jackie.

He nodded.

'Give me your number, and I'll send you a text.'

Jude gave Jackie his number, and she keyed it into her phone. Moments later, his mobile vibrated.

They sat there without speaking for a while. Penny suddenly broke the silence. 'I remember my childhood,' she said quietly. Her memories were starting to flood back now.

She's dying, Jude thought. His throat felt tight with panic. *She's lying somewhere in this cursed city, dying, and I'm sitting around twiddling my thumbs.*

Never fear imminent death, Mr Morley had said.

But Jude did fear imminent death. He could have screamed with fear. Then he remembered something else that he wanted to ask, and was glad that he hadn't forgotten it. 'Is Mr Morley the tax advisor for a funeral director called Lightwood & Son?'

Jackie sat up. 'How did you know that?'

'It was just a hunch,' said Jude.

The threads were slowly pulling together, even though they still didn't make any sense. Mr Morley could see ghosts. Just like Jude. What did that mean? He looked at his watch and groaned.

'What's the matter?' asked Penny.

Instead of answering, Jude sent off a text. Then he stared at his mobile. When the reply came a minute later, he sighed deeply and looked at Penny. 'I've just checked, and my father's going to be home in an hour.' George Finney's return from his business trip suddenly reminded Jude how there had been a life before Penny Scott: a life that now seemed drab and unrewarding. 'I have to go.' He stood up. 'But I'll be back soon.'

It was time to ask some questions. And he was strangely certain that the answers – if he found them – would help Penny as well as him. For one brief moment, he felt like the courageous hero of one of his own stories. But outside on the street, he remembered how grey and cold the autumn could be when night fell slowly but surely over the city and its graveyards.

CHAPTER 8

'You're afraid of him.'

'I wouldn't say I was afraid,' Jude replied. 'He's just picked the worst possible time to come home.'

They were approaching Jude's house in Twisden Road. His father's old green Land Rover Defender was parked in the road. George Finney was back. He had presumably had a shower with his loud music on, then would have settled himself on the sofa to watch TV. He was bound to be tired after the journey, and Jude wondered exactly how long it took to get from Manchester to London, which was weird, as he'd never bothered to wonder before. When his father was tired, he tended to be grumpy too. And when he was grumpy, he was best avoided.

'I can wait outside,' said Penny. 'If you'd rather talk to him on your own.'

Jude shook his head.

'I'll quite understand.'

'No,' he said. 'It's fine.' He stood for a moment by

the front door, looking at the house. Home again. But was this what it felt like to come home?

Penny touched his shoulder.

'In we go,' Jude said firmly.

Every step was difficult. His courage had long since evaporated. However, he was still determined not to be fobbed off with excuses about his background. He could only help Penny if he knew who Mr Morley was, and what was driving him. And if he and Mr Morley were similar, then Jude had to find out why he could see ghosts. There was no turning back; he needed answers. He could sense that everything fitted together. All the same, he felt desperate rather than brave, and he wondered whether every hero didn't feel like that at some point. Jude had always known that this day would come. But now that it had arrived, it seemed strangely unreal.

He took a deep breath. Then he opened the front door. The noise it made was too loud and too penetrating. He would rather have slipped silently up to his room.

'Jude?'

Even Penny jumped.

'Where've you been, Jude?' The voice came from the kitchen.

Penny pulled a face.

Yes, Jude indicated, *that's what my dad's like*.

There was a song on the radio that Jude had never heard before.

Whatever.

He went into the kitchen. His father was sitting at the table with *The Times* spread out in front of him.

'Hi, Dad,' said Jude.

There was barely any resemblance between George Finney and his son. Jude had inherited only his father's hands.

'You look tired,' his father said. 'Too many late nights, I imagine.'

'I've had a tiring day.'

George Finney groaned with irritation. 'Right. My son's had a tiring day. School, food, sleep, listening to music, more sleep.' He sighed. 'Just you wait 'til you get a job, then you'll know about tiring days.'

'You asked how I was.'

'Oh. Right.' George Finney turned back to his newspaper.

'And I replied,' said Jude.

George Finney looked up from his paper. Jude knew what was coming: a lecture on life being grim and earnest. A lecture on why Jude wasn't to be a wimp, and on how his father was preparing him for real life.

But before his father could launch into his lecture, Jude came straight out with it. 'I need to know who she was.'

George Finney was startled. He stared at his son. 'Jude! Not that stuff again. I've only just got home, and I'm tired. Let's talk about it some other time.'

'Dad, you have to tell me. Now!'

Penny stood beside Jude with bated breath. She seemed as tense as he was.

'You know everything. There's nothing more to tell you.' George Finney looked his son straight in the eye. 'In any case, there's something else I need to talk to you about. I've had an email from your English teacher. Mr Ackroyd.'

Jude sighed. He'd completely forgotten about Mr Ackroyd.

'You weren't at school today, and you handed in a practically empty sheet of paper in your last test.'

'Dad, please. This matters to me. Something's happened.'

'Nothing is so important that it can't wait. School is important, Jude. We've talked about this over and over again.' There it was again: the tone of voice that Jude most hated his father using. The teacher-like tone, with its overtones of 'I only want what's best for you'.

Penny glanced at him. *Keep calm*, she seemed to be saying. Jude was trying. 'I need to know who she was,' he said again. 'It's really important, Dad.'

George Finney stood up and went over to the cupboard to find something to eat. He found some cornflakes and shook them into a bowl. Then he fetched the milk from the fridge, poured it onto the cornflakes, noticed that he had splashed a bit on the work surface, calmly put the milk bottle back in the fridge, tore off a sheet of kitchen roll and wiped up the spilt milk. He scrutinised the work surface carefully, as if it were the most important thing in the world.

He went deliberately across to the bin and threw the kitchen roll away. 'You're better off not knowing anything about your mother, believe me.' He turned the radio up and sat back down at the table with his bowl of cereal.

That was the final straw. Jude felt all the anger of the past seventeen years rising up in him. All the questions that had never been answered came bursting to the surface. Without really being aware of what he was doing, he grabbed the jam pot and hurled it at the radio. The radio clattered to the ground and was silent.

'Good throw,' Penny remarked.

Shocked, George Finney sprang up. 'What on earth do you think you're doing?' he yelled. But then he looked into Jude's eyes. They had an unfamiliar expression. He stopped.

'I need to know. Now.' Jude was calm but firm.

Silence fell in the kitchen. Jude could feel that something had changed.

George Finney could feel it too. He stared silently at his dripping spoon. Ignoring the little pool of milk that was forming on the floor, he put the spoon back down on the table. 'Why now?' he asked, his voice cracking.

'I can see ghosts.' Jude met his father's astonished gaze calmly. 'I don't know why, but I can. I've been able to do it for the past six months. And now something's happened. Someone's in danger and I absolutely have to do something. There isn't enough time to tell you the whole story but I need answers, and fast. Something terrible's going on. There's this man – a truly evil man – and he's like me. He can see ghosts too. That's why I have to know who I am. Do you see? I have to know who I am so I can understand who he is.'

George Finney looked like someone who had finally lost a lifelong battle. He sank back onto his chair. 'I knew this would happen. She said it would.'

'Mum?'

'Yes.'

'What did she say?'

'When you're a child,' said Jude's father, 'you think that adults are completely sorted. But they're not. They make mistakes and then reach the end of the line and see them, but can't do anything about them.'

Jude frowned. 'We haven't reached the end of the line, and people can make up for their mistakes.'

George Finney nodded. He didn't look convinced. 'I met your mother in India,' he said.

'You've never told me her name.'

'She never told me her real name.'

'But who was she?'

George Finney took a deep breath. 'I was one of a team of British scientists employed by the government to advise on a building project in Haryana – a way to contain the floods. One evening I went down and sat by the banks of the Yamuna.' He seemed to be lost in his memories now. His eyes were soft and gentle in a way that Jude had never seen before. 'India is a strange country. It's colourful and dangerous and magical... it's so...' He searched for the right words. 'There's no other country in the world quite like it.' His eyes flashed with the glow of a far distant sun. 'Anyway,' he continued, 'that day, I saw a young woman swimming in the river. When she saw me, she dived underwater and I didn't know whether she'd really been there or whether my eyes had played a trick on me.'

'And that was that?' Jude had hoped for more from this story. It had sounded so promising to start with.

'If that had been that,' his father said, 'you wouldn't be here.'

'Oh, yeah,' Jude murmured, looking at the radio which lay smashed on the ground.

'The next day, she came looking for me at our base. We'd pitched our tents beside the river. We spent all day analysing soil samples and the river flora and the pollutants in the water.'

Jude had never been particularly interested in his father's job. He was always analysing things and could never just enjoy what was there in front of him. Or that's how it had always seemed to Jude.

'She was fabulously beautiful, like something from a fairy tale. She said I should call her Yamuna.'

'Like the river?'

'She said she and the river were twins.'

'What did she mean?'

George Finney shrugged. 'She never told me. She was very mysterious, you know.'

Jude tried to imagine this beautiful creature who had been his mother, but failed.

'We spent two weeks together,' said George Finney. 'Then, one evening, she said she couldn't stay. She looked sad – but she also seemed restless, as if her mind were already in some distant place. She kept looking longingly at the river.'

Jude could tell that there was going to be another unexpected twist to the story – a twist that was also the reason why Jude's father seemed so unfazed by Jude's claim to see ghosts.

'She said she was a *jalpari*.'

'A jalpari?'

'A creature of the river, a kind of water-nymph. She was born in the Himalayas, at the source of the Yamuna, home of the Yamunotri shrine. She said it was her fate to follow the course of the river, first the Yamuna, then the Ganges which, with the Yamuna, forms the Padma. She would, she said, die as an old woman in the Indian Ocean. That's the fate of all jalpari, according to her.'

Jude stared at his father. He couldn't believe that this same father had once been together with such a mysterious woman. The whole story was so far removed from the man he knew.

'What happened then?' he urged.

'One day she had simply vanished.'

'You never saw her again?'

George Finney shook his head. His eyes had lost their sparkle; he suddenly looked infinitely old and tired. 'I was there for another fortnight, and I spent every single day hoping she'd come back. But she didn't. I never saw her again. When I finally returned to England, I wanted to forget her as quickly as possible.' Jude's father looked at his son. His eyes were sad and empty. 'It was very painful, you know. I thought if I could erase her from my memory it would hurt less.'

Penny looked equally sad.

'Then, one day, I found the holdall on the doorstep.'

'You,' said Penny.

'Why would she have done that?'

George Finney laughed bitterly. 'I don't even know how she did it. How she got to this country. Your mother was a complete mystery to me. And I never understood what had got into me. Me, of all people: a scientist!' Another bitter laugh. 'In any event, she couldn't keep you. How could a water-nymph have coped with a human baby? That was my explanation for what happened. And so she brought you to me. So that I could take care of you.'

'Do you think that's why I can see ghosts?'

'I don't know. When we were together, she was a normal, flesh and blood woman. There was nothing to suggest that she was a magical creature. No: she couldn't have been more real...' Once again, George Finney gazed dreamily into a distant past that only he could see.

Jude's mind was struggling to process all this. His brain was whirling. His mother was a jalpari, a spirit from India. Surely there couldn't be any more surprises in store today? 'Tell me more about her,' he said.

'She was lively. She liked laughing and dancing.'

Jude nodded.

'But there was something else.'

'Something it said in the note?' Jude instinctively knew he was right.

'Yes.'

'What?'

'She asked me to tell you a story. When you were old enough and wanted to know more about your mother.'

'I've asked about her loads of times, and you've never told me anything about her. Just lies.'

George Finney chose not to hear the reproach. He seemed to be speaking from far away. '*When you're mature enough for the story*, she wrote. When you ask as insistently as you asked this evening.' He stared at the milk bottle on the table. 'She told me so many stories. About mighty tigers and men, tricksters and elephant-headed deities. Tales of lost and forgotten temples, and tales of temples dedicated to the past.'

'So what kind of story did she want you to tell me?'

Penny, her eyes wide, was hanging on George Finney's every word as he began his tale.

'Once upon a time there was a powerful maharajah in Punjab. The maharajah was famed across the empire for his laugh. He loved to laugh; he held fabulous parties and was well liked by his subjects. He was a cheerful person, perhaps because there had never been a war during his reign.

'More than anything, he longed for a child. And when his wife – the maharani – gave birth to a son, his happiness was complete.

'But as time passed, he started to notice that people avoided the child. The boy was cold and inert. He never laughed. So the maharajah sought out all the country's sages and asked for their advice, but none of them was able to help him. On his long, arduous travels, he finally met a priest who lived in the Deccan uplands. The priest had renounced sleep. He revealed to the maharajah the nature of the child's illness: he couldn't dream, and anyone who can't dream isn't properly alive.

'That was why the boy was so cold and inert; that was why other people avoided him. The maharajah returned to his palace. He was devastated. He had found the answer to his question, but the answer only made him even more desperate.

'He did know that his son slept a dreamless sleep and, far worse, led a dreamless life. But he couldn't help him. And so he set off on his travels again, cloaked in rags like a beggar. He had long since stopped living the life of a maharajah. He finally came across a strange woman. She was a trickster, a shape-shifter, and had lain in wait for him in the jungle.

'She handed him a lantern.'

Jude and Penny both pricked up their ears. 'A lantern?'

George Finney nodded. 'A magic lantern.'

'What did the lantern have to do with all of this?'

'Let me finish, and you'll find out,' replied his father. 'The trickster, who had taken on the guise of a tiger, offered him a swap. The lantern, she said, wasn't just any old lantern. It was alive. "Give it to your son," she said. "Its light will give him strength and let him dream again."

'As she spoke, she smiled a horrible smile – but desperation had clouded the maharajah's vision, and he didn't notice. And so he agreed to the exchange. "And what do you want in return for the lantern?" he asked.

'"Your smile," said the trickster, "and all the joy that lives within you."

'And the maharajah, who cared more for his son's happiness than for his own smile, agreed. And that was the start of all the misery,' said George Finney.

'What misery?'

'Patience, Jude. You're always so impatient.' Jude's father paused briefly before carrying on with his story. 'Back in the palace, the maharajah gave the living lantern to his son. "You look sad, Father," the boy said. But the maharajah, who could no longer laugh or smile, remained embittered and solemn and silent. And so life itself made him wither away, because only people who can laugh gain smiles in return. His soul starved to death because he had become as cold and dreamless as his son had once been.

'One beautiful day, the maharajah died.'

Jude bit back the question as to what had happened

to the maharani. She had presumably died of grief.

'His body was ritually burned and in the jungle a magnificent tomb containing his ashes was built in his honour.'

'What happened to the boy?' Jude asked.

'One night,' George Finney replied, 'he crept secretly into the tomb. He was carrying the lantern and was looking for a piece of jewellery that had once belonged to his mother. He wanted to give it to a beautiful girl from the palace.'

'Typical boy,' Penny said, rolling her eyes.

'Then, suddenly, in the middle of the dark tomb, the young prince found himself staring at his dead father. It was the ghost of the maharajah who was speaking to him. "Why can I see you, Father?" the boy asked. "You're a vetala," was the maharajah's mysterious reply.

'Then the light from the living lantern reached for the ghost of the maharajah and devoured him.

'The boy, however, greedily breathed in the sweet, beguiling aroma that streamed from the lantern. That night, the boy dreamed a dream that was more beautiful than life itself. He wanted to hold onto it, but it flew away in the daylight.

'He went to a graveyard to try to find peace and comfort. He spoke to the dead, whom he could now see, and lived off the harvest that the lantern brought home. For he had learnt at his father's tomb that the magic lantern needed to be fed if you wanted it to carry on giving you dreams.'

'So he killed the ghosts?' said Jude.

'Something along those lines, I reckon.'

Jude felt dizzy. Was it possible that his mother had known what would one day happen to her son?

'Do you want to know how the story turned out, or not?'

'Of course I do.'

'Then listen.'

'Yes,' agreed Penny. 'Just listen.'

'The boy who was now the new maharajah was constantly drunk on new dreams. The people, however, sensed that all the ghosts were disappearing. They could see it in the colour of the trees and could hear it in the rustling of the grass. Even tigers went nowhere near the settlements any longer, for they too sensed that something had changed. And eventually the new maharajah's subjects found out what he had done and drove him away.' George Finney leant back.

'And?'

'That's it,' he said. 'The palace fell to rack and ruin, and nobody knows now where it ever was.'

Penny looked just as baffled as Jude.

'So why did my mother want you to tell me this story?' Jude asked.

'I don't know. I just did as she asked.' George Finney ran his hands tiredly through his hair. 'I can still remember the evening we sat by the river and she told me the story.'

Jude's mobile vibrated. It was Jackie. He took the call, listening intently. Then he hung up. 'Dad, I've got to go.'

'You can't just—' his father began to protest.

But Jude interrupted him. 'Yes, Dad. I have to.' Then he did something that he hadn't done for a long time. He went over to his father and kissed his cheek. 'Wish me luck!' Smiling, he handed his father the cardboard tube containing the drawing. 'I'll tell you everything later.'

George Finney made no attempt to stop his son. He possibly realised that Jude had no choice: that he had been set some task that he had to fulfil.

Followed closely by Penny, Jude left the house in Twisden Road and went out into the gathering dusk. He was secretly hoping that things might still turn out well after all.

* * *

'Was that my mum who rang just then?' Penny asked.

'Yes. Morley wants to meet her tonight, at nine.'

'Where?'

'Kensington Cemetery.'

'What should we do now?'

'We'll discuss that with Miss Rathbone and Gaskell.'

Together they headed for Highgate Cemetery, following the route that Jude had come to know so well.

'Your father's strange,' said Penny. 'Completely different from you.'

'Yeah, and even if I now know who my mother was, she's still a mystery to me.' Jude sighed. 'Looks as if some questions are never really answered.'

'You don't necessarily need answers.' The ghost-girl smiled mischievously. It made her look even prettier than ever, Jude thought.

They reached Swains Lane and made for the gap in the lower section of the graveyard wall. Jude held the brambles aside for Penny. He was glad to be back here. Everything looked familiar: the rows of graves, the crosses, the statues, the paths.

En route to Egyptian Avenue, they met Mr Winterbottom (1813–1856). He was playing golf by the little pond with the water lilies, and waved at them. Then they bumped into Mr and Mrs Bradlough, who were walking their dog (who was buried alongside them, also in 1891).

Yes, Jude felt more at home here than outside in the loud, chaotic city.

He didn't want to remember that all of this could change. Moreover, he couldn't stop thinking about the story that his father had told him. It was as if his mother had foreseen all the dark events that Jude had been drawn into over the past few days. But was there any way that she could have known? What on earth *were* jalparis capable of? How was it possible that he – a completely ordinary boy – had a magical creature for a mother?

'You're thinking about her, aren't you?'

They were walking along the rose path, but the roses had been over for weeks now. A couple of withered buds adorned the thorny brambles which, robbed of their glorious array of flowers, looked cantankerous and fickle.

'I still haven't got a clue who I am.' Jude kicked a stone off the path.

'You're Jude,' said Penny, 'and you're living your own life. That's a pretty good start.'

He smiled.

'Look – we're here!' said Penny. They had almost

reached Gaskell's grave. 'I'm getting to know my way around this place.'

Jude was curiously proud that Penny felt as much as home in Highgate as he did. Quentin Gaskell was sitting on the grey stone. He had been waiting for them.

'Ayelet's down below, studying the books.' He clapped Jude on the shoulder. 'She's made a discovery of not inconsiderable significance.' A cunning smile ghosted across the old rock star's face. 'You look as if a ghoul's been weaving a net in your hair.' He often said things that Jude still found completely baffling.

They had to duck in order to go down into the tomb. Miss Rathbone was curled up in the armchair, and was just noisily shutting a fat tome when Jude and Penny appeared. 'Jude, Penny!' she cried. She jumped up in delight, then she went across to Penny, took her hands, looked her in the eyes and said, 'Penny, Penny, Penny.' She seemed to like the name. 'Penny Scott. How marvellous.' She let go of Penny's hands and grabbed the glass of wine that was standing on the shut coffin. 'Didn't I tell you that we'd find your story?'

Penny smiled. 'It's still a bit strange. But I keep remembering more and more.'

'That,' Gaskell declared, 'is why we have no time to lose.'

The cold grave felt suddenly colder to all of them.

'So, what's been going on?' asked Miss Rathbone.

'Lots of things.' Jude told her what they had been up to. He told her about the encounter with Mr Morley the tax advisor and about Jackie, Penny's mother – not to mention the story of his own mother, the jalpari.

'Do you think Mr Morley is the boy from the story?' Jude asked.

Miss Rathbone and Gaskell looked at one another and shrugged simultaneously.

'Could be,' said Miss Rathbone.

'Or he might just be very similar to the boy in the story,' Gaskell added.

Miss Rathbone took a sip of red wine. 'I think your mother might well remain a mystery, Jude.'

Jude had already worked that one out. 'We need to go to Kensington Cemetery,' he said.

'Is that where they're doing the handover?'

Jude and Penny nodded.

'You're surely not planning to take Jackie Scott with you?' Gaskell pressed them. He straightened his spectacles and adopted a teacher-like expression.

'Yes, we are,' Jude and Penny replied in unison,

but both sounded hesitant and uncertain.

'You're putting her in danger,' said Miss Rathbone.

'She won't be able to *see* whatever danger she might be in,' Gaskell warned them.

'So what are we supposed to do?' Despair and fear of her impending death were etched across Penny's face.

'This is what you need to do...' Miss Rathbone lowered her voice conspiratorially as she outlined her plan. She sipped her wine, talked, took another sip, talked some more. Gaskell filled in the pauses, trying to be amusing, even though nobody felt like laughing. In the end, they were both talking wildly over the top of one another, though Jude still understood what they meant.

'So that's the plan?' he said.

Gaskell and Miss Rathbone nodded eagerly and looked at him expectantly.

Jude didn't have to look far for weak spots in their plan; they were blindingly obvious. But he remembered what Quentin Gaskell always said: 'great gigs don't always need a sound check.'

Miss Rathbone rolled her eyes. 'You just need to get hold of a USB stick.'

That shouldn't be a problem, Jude thought. He knew of several shops that would still be open at that time of day. He glanced at his watch. They had just under two hours. Then he remembered something else. 'Gaskell said you'd found out something.'

Miss Rathbone nodded slowly. She tapped on the fat tome which was now lying on the ground. 'That's right. There are creatures called Sluagh.'

'*Sewer?*' said Penny.

She shook her head. 'No – it's nothing to do with sewers,' she said. She repeated the word, slowly this time. 'Sluagh.'

'Sounds like someone being sick,' said Jude. Penny laughed. *It's good to hear her laugh*, he thought.

Miss Rathbone ignored them. 'The Sluagh are the spirits of the restless dead. The spirits of criminals, good-for-nothings, miscreants, murderers. They live nowhere, because they lived nowhere when they were alive, and died that way too. They live off the will of whoever breathes life into them.'

'You mean someone steers them, like puppets?'

'That kind of thing.'

'It was said that John Dee even had his own Sluagh as a servant,' said Gaskell, fiddling with his spectacles. 'Have you heard of Dr Dee?'

Jude and Penny nodded.

'Good.'

'And it looks as if the Sluagh are the Faceless Ones,' said Miss Rathbone. 'John Dee mentioned in one of his occult writings that the restless ones had no faces.'

Jude nodded slowly. A new piece was finding its way into the massive puzzle of the strange events of the past few days. Yet he couldn't do anything with it. He thought again about the plan that the vixen had outlined to him and which he would be putting into action at Kensington Cemetery. He imagined Kensington to be like Abney Park Cemetery. Gloomy and cold, like the hissing voices that answered you when you whispered in a cave.

'We ought to get going straight away,' he said. They still had to call Jackie Scott. And he also had to get hold of a USB stick somewhere in Kensington. Regardless of who or what the Faceless Ones were, number one on the list was saving Penny. Miss Rathbone and Gaskell nodded in agreement.

They left Gaskell's grave and went back up to the surface.

'We'll come with you as far as the wall,' said Miss Rathbone, going ahead with Penny. Jude and Gaskell trotted behind. Golden autumn light was falling through the branches and even the distant noises were shadowy.

'I've got to do this on my own, haven't I?' said Jude.

Gaskell nodded. 'You're doing it for the most honourable reason imaginable.'

'For the ghost community of Highgate?'

Gaskell cleared his throat, then laughed uproariously. 'What are you talking about? No – to impress a girl, of course.'

Jude turned red.

'Oh, go on then, to save a girl.' Gaskell straightened his spectacles. 'That's an even more noble reason, if you ask me.'

Jude turned even redder.

'Whatever the case, you're smitten, and you want to win her,' Gaskell continued. 'That's all that matters. That's why I was a musician. That's what rock 'n' roll's all about.'

Jude didn't reply.

'Did you leave your guitar at her place?'

He nodded.

'Q.E.D!' Gaskell grinned knowingly.

'That doesn't mean anything.'

'That, Jude Finney, means *everything*.'

Jude secretly knew that it meant *everything*, but he didn't want to admit it just then.

'In any case, you're nearly an adult. The time

comes for everyone when they have to leave home.'

'Do you mean the graveyard?'

'Isn't Twisden Road your home?'

Jude shrugged.

'You've got to do your heroic deed alone.'

'What if I fail?'

Gaskell threw back his thin hair dramatically. 'If you fail, then do so in the only proper way.' He winked at Jude. 'In style.' His hands went up in the air and played a riff on an invisible guitar. 'But you won't fail, Jude Finney. You've got guts, and you're clever.' Gaskell stopped. 'And you're in love.'

'Don't say it so loudly.'

'No?'

'Please!' Jude begged.

Miss Rathbone and Penny had already reached the graveyard wall.

'Before gigs, we always planned to set fire to the guitars on stage, and explode the drum kit. Let them rock 'til they drop, that's what we said.' Gaskell elbowed Jude in the side. 'That's what it's all about.'

Jude knew what he meant. And his friend's way of expressing himself so clearly was one of the things he liked best about him.

Gaskell, though, suddenly turned serious. 'Listen, Jude. When I was alive, I thought everyone worshipped me.' He drew himself up to his full height. 'I was the lead singer in a rock band and if there are still gods around nowadays, they're the lead singers in rock bands.' He made a victorious gesture that he presumably had also made on stage. 'I felt like a god. My female fans were completely crazy about me.' He was smiling, but suddenly looked troubled. 'But then I died. Just like that. No warning.' He pointed back toward his grave. 'You know who came to my funeral? Just a handful of people. A couple of friends, my most dedicated fans. But not the thousands I'd imagined.' He sighed, theatrical once more. 'Unfortunately, ghosts are often forced to watch their miserable funerals. Even though I had grown older, I thought my grave would be surrounded by hot, leggy young girls in miniskirts, all crying their eyes out.' He scratched his ear thoughtfully. 'The kind of sexy creatures you see on record sleeves.' His pretence of cheerfulness vanished. 'And who was crying? My cleaning lady; Jack, an old roadie: people who I'd not bothered with in years because I was so damn famous.'

'That's sad.'

'It's piss awful,' replied Gaskell.

Leaves were whirling through the air like confetti.

'You need to grab life by the scruff of the neck

when it crosses your path. It's over faster than you think.'

Jude nodded. 'Thanks,' he said.

'What are you doing?' called Penny.

'We're here,' said Jude, catching up with her. 'What were you talking about?'

Penny shrugged. 'Just stuff.'

'Gentle sepulchral melodies.' The vixen was half-hidden. But she had something in her hand that was glittering in the light of the sinking sun. It was a small, narrow bottle with a filigree pattern.

'What's that?' Jude asked.

'Everyone who knows you and who cares about you has contributed to it.'

'But what's in it?'

'That,' said the vixen with a mysterious smile, 'is a secret.'

Jude knew that the graveyard was full of secrets. 'Will it help?'

'That depends. If you don't want it, don't take it.'

'I do want it,' Jude said quickly. 'I'm taking it.'

Miss Rathbone smiled again, smugly this time. 'Then I'd say that it will help.'

Jude nodded. You should never question magic. If you did, it could lose its effectiveness. 'What am I supposed to do with it?'

'Give it to her to drink,' said Gaskell. 'Whatever poison Penny's been given, this is the antidote.'

'Drink it once, and it will make you ill – as ill as if you were dying,' Miss Rathbone added.

'They presumably knocked me out and then gave me something like that,' said Penny.

Jude resisted the temptation to ask again what was in the bottle. Instead, he took it and thanked them.

'Take a second drink,' said Miss Rathbone, 'and you'll immediately get better again.'

That was easy enough. 'OK,' Jude said.

Miss Rathbone had one final warning for him. 'Never drink it for a third time. If you do that, you've had it.' She hugged him like a mother, and Gaskell clapped him on the shoulder like a father.

'And now, Jude Finney,' said Gaskell, 'off you go!' He grinned. 'And save the girl,' he whispered so quietly that Penny couldn't hear. Then he hugged Penny like he would a daughter.

And so Penny and Jude left Highgate and went out in the world where the sun would rise the following day regardless of what happened now.

Kensington and Chelsea Cemetery and Hanwell Cemetery – two graveyards in West London – were founded in 1850. Kensington Cemetery was originally a little churchyard belonging to the parish of St Mary Abbots, but over the years it had grown to become a grand graveyard.

'Mum's not very happy about this,' Penny said again.

'It's for the best.'

They both knew that Penny's mother would otherwise only have ended up in unnecessary danger and so, after vigorous protestations, Jackie Scott had finally capitulated and was now holed up – or so they hoped – in her room at *Chez Shane*.

'So here we are then,' said Penny. It sounded as if she were trying to talk herself into feeling brave.

Jude checked for the hundredth time that he had the memory stick in his pocket. He had bought it in a junk shop in Tothill Street.

The entrance to the graveyard was a neogothic archway dating back to Victorian times. Once inside, they found themselves in the shadow of countless tall holly and yew bushes. Their path meandered between rows of overgrown, neglected graves. They passed a huge cross; its broad base was covered with little mosaic stones, and it was surrounded by cast-iron railings. Here lay Mr Wheeler, a building contractor (dates illegible). The neighbouring grave, which looked like a stone shell, belonged to one Edgar Smith, formerly chronicler of the British Museum (dates covered with weeds and moss). Neither of them was at home, and Jude assumed that they would never come back.

He avoided calling for anyone, as he knew that there were no ghosts there. He could sense it by the fact that this place felt exactly like Abney Park.

'What's with all the heads?' asked Penny.

Jude looked around. Kensington Cemetery was indeed a sea of statues with strange heads on mostly damaged torsos. Some gravestones even had heads embedded in them with gazes fixed up at the sky and expressions simultaneously mysterious and full of suffering. The ones who smiled had their eyes shut, and the ones who looked sad had their eyes open.

He sighed silently. It would be difficult to make out the stone angels among all these statues. 'That way.' He pointed to a path that branched off one of the main ones.

Mr Morley had given Jackie Scott a particular grave as a meeting place. It was in the northern part of the graveyard, among a collection of graves that peeped out of the earth like crooked doors and stood in the shadow of tall willows. Here too ivy had taken hold of the paths and railings. Roots twisted and trailed their way across the earth, giving homes to wild animals.

'How kind of you to come.' Barely more than a silhouette, Mr Morley was standing by the tomb. He was looking around. 'Where's Mrs Scott?' He was wearing a long black coat, gloves and elegant shoes which looked more suitable for the city pavements than the sandy paths of a graveyard.

'I've got what you're after.' Jude was holding the memory stick.

Penny was close by his side, her nerves taut. Although Jude couldn't see her, he could sense that she doubted that the plan would work. He himself suddenly felt uneasy. In Highgate in the sunshine, the whole thing had sounded like a pretty good idea. Now, though, in the darkness of this unfamiliar graveyard, it all looked very different.

They both knew what they had to watch out for.

Beware of what appears in the corner of your eye, Jude remembered.

Mr Morley was leaning casually against the entrance to the tomb. 'Absolem Rodwell, my dear partner,' he merely said.

Jude read the inscription: *1921–1958*.

'Where's Penny?'

Mr Morley smiled, and his teeth flashed in the

moonlight. He stared at the stick that Jude was holding.

'I'm in the tomb,' Penny said.

Mr Morley nodded approvingly. 'She can sense it.' He emerged from the shadow of the tomb so that Jude and Penny could see him properly. 'So? Are you going to give me the stick? Or am I going to have to make you?'

Jude's fingers tightened around the little object. 'I want to see her first.'

'The girl?'

'Who else?'

'And why should I oblige you?' Mr Morley asked.

Two Sluagh unpeeled themselves from the darkness. Two faceless men in dark suits. One of them was holding a lantern. It was swaying gently in the wind.

Jude swallowed. Penny clutched him, trembling. All the animals had either flown or crept away from the graveyard so there was barely a sound to be heard. Only now did Jude realise how noisy the night normally was.

The Sluagh didn't do anything. They just stood there. Evidently waiting for their orders.

'Before we do this,' said Jude, 'could you answer one question for me?'

'One and only one.'

'Why are you doing this?'

Mr Morley laughed out loud. 'You haven't worked it out?' He took a step towards them and stopped. 'That does surprise me.'

Jude didn't reply.

Mr Morley folded his hands. 'There's only one thing that really matters in life. Haven't you worked that out yet?' Like a big, black bird he spread out his hands in their smooth, black leather gloves. 'It's business, my boy.'

'You're killing all the ghosts. Why?'

'We call them our harvest.'

A shiver ran down Jude's spine. Penny moved even closer to him. Jude could feel her nervousness as if it were his own.

'You're murdering them.' He thought about Highgate, about the life that pulsated there, and what would happen if the Sluagh and their living lanterns carried out their vile business there. 'Why are you doing that?'

'To make money.' Mr Morley strolled towards them. 'A ghost is nothing more than a dream that carries on living once the person is dead. This city is full of ghosts.' He spread out his arms. 'London, a gigantic city full of dreams.' He chuckled. 'Nobody sees these dreams. People don't see the ghosts, even if they're sharing an Underground carriage with them. What could be more valuable than the dream of a dead person about life?' He laughed with amusement – though it was a laugh that felt to Jude like a punch in the stomach: cold, evil, and heartless. 'What do I do? That's quite simple. We harvest all the dreams, then sell them.'

'Who to?'

Penny had turned pale. She was rubbing her eyes. 'You trade in ghosts?'

'It's a dream job,' said Mr Morley. 'And so very lucrative. You've got no idea how high the demand is. Drugs have got nothing on other people's dreams.'

Jude was flabbergasted. 'You're depopulating the graveyards to make money?'

'Can you think of any better reason?'

Jude suddenly understood. Hence the office. Morley's tax consultancy enabled him to use all the tricks of the trade to hide his earnings. To launder the money and make the cash flows appear legal.

'You're a filthy drug dealer,' said Penny. Her eyes blazed.

Mr Morley gave her a tired smile. 'Jackie Scott, your mother, accidentally came across accounts that she shouldn't have seen. An unfortunate coincidence.'

Jude too was now so angry that he had clenched his fists and was struggling not to go for Morley's throat. 'You're killing the ghosts and selling them as *dreams*?' he repeated.

'You can't imagine,' said Mr Morley, smiling again, 'how many people out there don't dream any more.' He gave an evil laugh. 'They have enough money to buy whatever their hearts desire.'

'But they don't dream...' Jude whispered. He was wondering whether the customers knew what they were buying.

'That's right,' said Mr Morley. Jude could tell from his expression what was going to happen if someone didn't put a stop to it: abandoned graveyards, humans confused and rootless with no idea why. A city without dreams, devoid of magic, in which everything would have withered and become a cheap commodity.

'You'll pay a heavy price for this,' said Jude.

'Are *you* going to make me?' Mr Morley still seemed to find it all very amusing.

The Sluagh were still not moving. But at that moment Jude saw a movement out of the corner of his eye. He had almost missed it: a gigantic creature rising from its hiding place by the statues near the tombs. A stone angel, coming closer.

'The contents of your little bottle will attract them,' Miss Rathbone had told them. 'And once they're there, everything else is up to you.'

He winked at Penny. Yes, she had understood.

'But you two didn't come here to chat to me in the moonlight.' Mr Morley seemed not to have noticed the stone angel. 'You wanted to see the girl.' He looked at Penny. 'You're running out of time, aren't you?'

Without waiting for an answer, he gestured to them to follow him. Jude wondered what he had in mind. Was it possible that he was going to keep to the bargain after all?

That was the tricky thing. For the memory stick had nothing on it. Sooner or later, Mr Morley would realise that he'd been deceived, and then...what would happen then?

'My memories,' Penny whispered. 'I've got a feeling that they're all suddenly coming back.'

That was not good news. Not good news at all. Jude grabbed her hand, which was colder than usual. Soon Penny would have turned completely into a ghost.

No. It couldn't come to that. He hastened after Mr Morley, who was handed a lantern by one of the Sluagh. There was still no light in the lantern. Close up, it didn't look the slightest bit dangerous, just somehow alive, as if it were in a restless sleep.

Immobile and silent, the two Sluagh guarded the entrance while Penny and Jude disappeared into the tomb with Mr Morley. Jude could tell that Penny was as worried as he was. How on earth were they ever going to get out again? The way into the tomb was a dead end. They went down steps that ended in a spacious chamber. Jude watched his footing, as the steps were crooked and crumbling as well as wet and mossy. Statues of Indian deities lined the walls, watching over nothing but silence between the huge columns.

Mr Morley opened an old, stained wooden door that was fixed to the stone wall with heavy hinges. A creaking sound broke the silence. Insects or creatures of some kind – Jude couldn't tell what they were in the darkness – scurried across the floor, and he felt spiders' webs tickling his face; he brushed them away.

He kept glancing quickly behind him, keeping the steps in sight from the corner of his eye. A small patch of moonlight hung over the entrance to the grave. Suddenly, though, a clear silhouette rose up from the night. A stone angel with folded wings swooped down towards the darkness, like a bird of prey in the gloom.

'Here we are,' declared Mr Morley.

As Jude stepped forward, he saw the girl lying in an old coffin. She had been covered with a filthy blanket. Her arms were lying across her body. She was motionless, silent. For the first time, he could see Penny in bodily form. And for the first time, Penny herself looked alive.

'That's me,' she moaned.

Jude wondered how it must feel. She looked exactly like her ghost. They were wearing the same clothes and had the same hairstyle. Only the real Penny's eyes were shut. Her breathing was calm and rhythmic.

'The poison's doing its stuff,' said Mr Morley. 'Tick-tock, tick-tock.' He held out his hand to Jude. 'The stick,' he said. 'You've seen her now.'

'Help her!' Jude said angrily.

'Help her?'

'Yes – make her wake up!'

'First the stick.'

Penny was standing next to herself by the coffin. As if paralysed, she stared down at her body – already in a coffin, but not yet a corpse.

Suddenly Mr Morley grabbed the girl. Penny yelled and struggled in his arms, but he held onto her tightly. 'You know what's going to happen when I light these lanterns?' he asked.

Jude had no idea how he was planning to light the lanterns, but he knew for sure what would happen to Penny once the lantern was lit.

Beware of what appears in the corner of your eye.

He started. The stone angel was now standing near the door, one foot already in the chamber. Its talons were long and curved, its eyes open.

'I can see it too,' said Mr Morley.

Jude cursed silently.

'What a cunning young man you are,' said Mr Morley. 'You thought you could lure the stone angel into the grave, then let it attack me. Tell me: how long can you hold your breath?' Mr Morley took a deep breath and stopped breathing.

This took his mind off Penny for a few moments, and she seized the opportunity to wrench herself out of his grasp and race to the exit, where the stone angel was waiting.

Mr Morley, lithe as a tiger, leapt after her, lighting the lantern as he did so. A glowing red light filled the tomb and blinded Jude. It all happened so quickly that he hadn't even seen exactly what Mr Morley had done – the lantern seemed to have lit itself.

Penny screamed as Morley grabbed hold of her again. He was holding the lantern up high; its red light was aiming straight for the struggling girl.

The stone angel was still standing there motionless as Jude raced across to the coffin, pulled the little bottle from his trouser pocket and held it to the sleeping girl's lips, wetting them with a couple of drops. *Drink, please, just drink. The first time it poisoned you; now it will cure you.* That's what Miss Rathbone had said. *You just have to drink.* He raised her head slightly, hoping that the liquid would trickle down her throat.

Over by the entrance to the tomb, Mr Morley was grinning in the fiery red glow of the lantern which, living and hungry, was lusting after Penny's ghost. She screamed in panic as the flame touched her skin. It looked as if the fire were about to suck her into itself and Jude let go of Penny's body and dashed to help her ghost – but suddenly she had gone.

The flame blazed up for a second time, then went out. Jude felt a burning sensation in his chest. He was coughing, gasping for air.

Mr Morley turned to him. 'Now give me that memory stick.'

Jude staggered over to the coffin. He touched the girl, but she didn't move.

'Your pretty girl,' said Mr Morley, 'is going to give me sweet dreams, don't you think?'

The stone angel was approaching now. *I mustn't*

breathe, Jude thought madly. *If I breathe, it'll see me.* The stone angel stopped again.

He could feel tears burning his eyes, hot and bitter. He suddenly realised how stupid and hopeless their plan had been. How on earth could he have imagined that he was a match for someone as dastardly as Mr Morley? He had lost Penny, for good this time. Not all stories had happy endings.

Steaming with rage, he hurled the memory stick at the wall.

Mr Morley was instantly by his side. 'Did you really think I believed you?'

Jude stared at him. The man's eyes were glowing yellow like fire as he pulled out a knife. Jude could see the stone angel's reflection in the blade.

And Jude remembered Gaskell's words. '*In the olden days, they always sent out a sacrifice. Before an alchemist ventured out into a graveyard, he sent a sacrificial victim as prey for the stone angels. Once the stone angels were busy devouring their victim, he could carry out his business undisturbed.*'

The evil yellow eyes were glittering expectantly. Morley was completely confident: all he had to do was let the stone angel do its work. Jude could sense it with every fibre of his being. *Penny is dead*, a voice inside him was screaming. *She's dead and she's never coming back. She's dead, and you're soon going to be dead too.*

His world fell apart with a deafening crash.

Mr Morley made a grab for him. Jude felt as if his lungs were on fire. He was still clutching the little bottle. He wouldn't be able to hold his breath for much longer. The stone angel was still waiting silently for its victim to show himself again. It had all the time in the world. Just a couple more seconds, then Jude gasped for air. He felt a blow to his stomach, gasped, and at the same moment was shoved away by Mr Morley, straight into the path of the stone angel. The angel had stretched out its talons towards Jude and its expression was the vicious grimace of a predatory animal.

With his last remaining bit of strength, Jude put the bottle to his lips and sipped the cold liquid. He coughed, then fell headlong to the ground.

'What the hell...?' he heard Mr Morley saying.

I'm almost dead, Jude thought as he saw himself lying on the ground at the other end of the tomb chamber. *Almost dead, but not quite. Just like Penny, when she was Story.*

His body lay there. Lifeless, barely breathing.

For a moment or two, Jude still knew who he was.

Penny was dead!

There was a girl in the coffin, and he felt as if he knew her, but he didn't know her name. She was dead.

And who was he?

Who am I?

Jude (who didn't know that he was Jude) looked at his hands. He saw the body of a boy lying on the ground.

On the other side of the tomb was a man. He was wearing a long black coat and gloves made of smooth leather. He was looking across at him, and the mousy-grey boy knew that the man was evil.

The evil man turned his head sideways. 'You miserable wretch!' he shouted, and the mousy-grey boy, who knew neither who he was nor how he had come to be in the tomb, realised that the man was aiming his words at him.

What have I done and, more importantly, why?

He felt empty and lifeless.

The evil man with the black coat and the leather gloves, who was now suspended in mid-air, was screaming his guts out.

Something – some kind of silhouette – seemed to be gnawing away at him. The mousy-grey boy had no idea what was going on, but he could tell that there was something there in the darkness, something that he couldn't see.

Something that was eating the man alive – the evil man with the black coat and the leather gloves. Crumbs of some kind trickled to the floor. It looked like stone, black and granular.

What on earth was it?

Then, just as quickly as it had started, it was over. The evil man had vanished. All that was left were his black coat and smooth leather gloves. With a whispered weeping sound, the Sluagh vanished into the dust. There was a chilling breeze and the boy realised that this was the dead returning to their graves. They were free now, he knew that for sure.

Silence reigned.

The mousy-grey boy pitied all the harvested souls from the other cemeteries, whom nobody would ever be able to save. Some things were just not meant to change.

He sighed. Then he took a cautious step forward. He looked at the boy on the ground. He was barely breathing. A glittering bottle lay in the corner, not far from him.

The mousy-grey boy knelt down on the ground by the other boy.

Is that me? He was in turmoil.

He's wearing my things. How can he be?

Dazed, he stood up, and happening to glance

sideways he became aware that there was a large statue of an angel in the corner of his vision. It was standing by the entrance to the tomb, smiling.

The mousy-grey boy started. He jumped up and stumbled towards the coffin. *She's fabulously beautiful*, he thought, as he looked at the girl. *So beautiful that she can't be dead.* He began to sob silently, although he had no idea who she was.

I don't understand, he thought. His sadness was a flood that he couldn't contain.

'You're crying.'

The mousy-grey boy jumped. The girl had opened her eyes and was looking at him.

'Who are you?' he asked.

She frowned and reached out her hand. 'You're not cold like the others,' she said, then clambered carefully out of the coffin, still a bit giddy. As she tried to stand up, her legs gave way and Jude instinctively caught her.

She's not dead.

The girl looked at the boy lying on the ground. Then she spotted the bottle. 'You drank from it,' she said.

'Yes,' he said, because he thought he needed to say something. 'Is that me lying on the ground?' he asked.

The girl didn't know whether to laugh or cry.

'You're crazy,' she said. Then she stumbled across to the little bottle, picked it up, and dropped a couple of drops onto the lips of the boy on the ground. With her other hand, she stroked his hair. 'Jude,' she whispered.

He opened his eyes and looked into hers. 'You're alive,' were his first words.

'Of course I am, and so are you,' she replied. Only then did she realise what she had said. 'I'm alive,' she stammered, completely overwhelmed.

'Penny Scott,' he whispered as she put her arms round him. 'I think it's all over now.'

CHAPTER 9

They celebrated the whole of the following night. Jude and Penny, completely exhausted, slept for the entire day as if they were vampires making their way from Scotland to London in order to go shopping in Bloomsbury and forget the miserable daily grind of a castle life. As the following night fell, though, Jude and Penny returned to Highgate Cemetery. Jackie Scott and George Finney thought that their offspring were out with friends, which wasn't unreasonable. In fact, nothing could have been closer to the truth.

'Penny Scott.' He had whispered her name in that distant tomb. 'I think it's all over now.'

'Yes,' she had replied, though she still wasn't entirely convinced.

The stone angel had remained in the tomb, silent and sated. The Sluagh who had been guarding the entrance to the tomb had disappeared. All that was left of Mr Morley in the tomb itself was his black coat and smooth leather gloves.

'Where's the lantern?' Penny had asked.

They had looked everywhere. 'It's gone,' said Jude.

'Thank goodness,' said Penny.

Up in the graveyard, not far from the tomb, Miss Rathbone had been waiting for them. The night had been a deep shade of grey. 'I thought I'd drop by, just in case anything went wrong,' she said, then smiled knowingly. 'Come to Highgate tomorrow night, and we'll have a party.' She disappeared into the undergrowth as nimbly as a fox.

Now they were all gathered in Gaskell's tomb. He had strung up garlands and paper lanterns with brightly coloured Indian motifs, which cast a colourful glow onto the walls of the grave.

'Why can I still see you all?' Penny asked.

'There are many mysterious things about the graveyard,' said Miss Rathbone. 'And if we don't question them, they are just as real as everything else around us.'

Penny was satisfied with that answer. She was there, and it was like the day that she had first appeared. None of them could believe that it was only four days since she'd been sitting on that bench in the moonlight; none of them could remember what life was like before she'd arrived. They played their music so loudly that even living people outside the walls could have heard it (which, fortunately, they didn't): 'Hang on Sloopy' (The McCoys), 'Friday on my Mind' (Easybeats), 'Through a Long and Sleepless Night' (Scott Walker) and 'Everybody Knows' and 'The Tower of Song' (Leonard Cohen). Everyone who had been there on the day that Gaskell died had gathered together once more: Sir Harvey Humblethwaite, Tilda Murray, Nettie Palliser, Albert Lament and several others.

It was a memorable night, and they were all delighted to be there and nowhere else.

'I can see ghosts,' said Penny. 'Wow – I can really see them.'

Jude handed her a glass of home-made elderflower juice generously donated by Nettie Palliser, whose grave was next to an elderflower bush, and helped himself to some too.

They danced and laughed and celebrated life itself, which never seemed further away than in a graveyard.

Gaskell had even gone so far as to hang an old disco ball inside his grave. To mark the occasion, he couldn't resist singing 'My Perfect Little Daylight', first with backing from the radio, and then, standing on the coffin with his head raised, unaccompanied.

Jude felt happy and distinctly grown-up. But there was just one thing...

As daylight started to break and the party was still in full swing, a girl and a boy stole off and headed for the north gate. Back to where it had all begun.

The ground was shrouded in mist, as soft as the promises that nobody could ignore on nights like these. Swept along by the breeze, autumn leaves went scurrying across their path like dormice.

'You still need to collect your guitar.'

Jude could hear the music resounding over the graves. 'Heart of Gold' by Neil Young. Perfect for that time of day. He could sense the ghosts' characteristic merriment; the joie de vivre that many of them had only found in death.

'They're only dead,' Miss Rathbone had once said. 'That's no reason to be miserable.'

They were standing on the path, looking at the park bench which stood right next to the high black-painted iron gate.

'There's always a goodbye at the end,' Penny whispered, looking across at a gravestone shaded by an ivy-clad willow. She gave him a sidelong look so that her nose was tickled by the light of the rising sun. 'So is this goodbye?'

Jude didn't have to think for long. 'No, no

goodbyes.'

Something fluttered through the quickly vanishing night.

'*Hey Jude*,' said Penny.

He looked at her, and saw something wonderful, something whose full value had only just dawned on him. And if ever a kiss were more than bright autumn leaves swirling around two people's feet, then it was this one; a kiss that was by no means the end of their story, but its real, true and everlasting beginning.

A COMPELLING **URBAN** FAIRY TALE WHERE **LOVE, DEATH** AND THE **STARS COLLIDE...**

READ ON FOR AN EXTRACT FROM CHRISTOPH MARZI'S CRITICALLY-ACCLAIMED NOVEL,

HEAVEN.

The night that Heaven lost her heart was cold and moonless. But the blade that sliced it out was warm with her dark blood. Forlorn, bewildered and throbbing fearfully, the heart was mirrored in the curved, silvery knife. Fingers encased in gloves made of shiny black leather held the heart up before a face that wore an expression of the utmost satisfaction.

This wasn't the first heart the man had stolen. And he wasn't alone. Lurking in the shadows was a second man, a raggedy tramp of a figure who limped over when motioned to do so.

They were all on a roof. A keen wind blew around them, and wisps of smoke from the chimneys hung in the air like living creatures. This particular dark-tiled roof belonged to number 16 Phillimore Place, which lay between Holland Park and Kensington Gardens. It offered a splendid view of the city, but neither of the figures on the roof was interested in the view.

Instead, they were staring at the body that lay motionless at their feet.

The girl was young, and her jet-black hair was wet from the puddles on the roof. Her dark skin shimmered in the night; tears glistened on her cheeks.

The tall man, who was known by different names in different parts of London, had that evening set off to find a heart in Chelsea. He had first spotted the girl in Wilton Crescent, and had followed her for the next two hours. His raggedy companion, who looked like a mangy dog in his shabby old clothes, had picked up the scent in Sloane Square – and there was no escape then. The girl – a young woman, in fact, who would once upon a time undoubtedly have been referred to as 'Miss' in Hampstead – had been wandering the streets alone, heading for nowhere obvious. She had walked down Brompton Road, looked in the window of Harrods, and then had a snack in the Bunch of Grapes. Then she'd headed northwards towards Kensington Gardens, but instead of entering the park, she'd set off in the direction of Notting Hill. Outside High Street Kensington station, she had run into a group of teenagers who seemed to know her. They'd exchanged a few words (words that didn't seem to interest the girl much) and one of them, a young man whose tiepin bore the crest of some posh private school, had called the girl by name: Heaven.

Her nocturnal pursuer, who had sharp eyes and ears, thought that Heaven was an odd name for a young girl, but it wasn't his job to worry about things like names. Names were but sound and smoke. He just wanted her heart.

The girl had stopped outside 16 Phillimore Place and looked up at the roof. Then she'd fiddled around with the lock. She was clearly trying to get into a house that was nothing to do with her. Then she'd darted through the door.

The raggedy man and Mr Drood, as the tall man called himself when he was out and about in Kensington, had watched the whole thing. They followed her like beasts of prey in the night. Through the door, into the house, up the stairs, and onto the roof.

She had taken a long object out of the rucksack that she'd been carrying. It was a telescope, which she hurriedly set up on the roof of the house. She stood there looking at the stars. At least there were stars here.

Then Mr Drood and the raggedy man had suddenly appeared. She hadn't heard them coming. Nobody ever did. Mr Drood and the raggedy man were like cats in the night, their boots like velvet paws.

If someone needed a secret service, they rang Mr Drood or one of the many other names that he went by. They whispered their problem to him, and he did their bidding. That included stealing hearts.

Mr Drood was cunning. He always worked with someone who was able to scent a trail. This particular raggedy man would soon disintegrate; he'd have to find another one then.

Whatever. The graveyards were full of them.

Life, mused Mr Drood, could be so easy. Funny that nobody else realised it.

He allowed his thin lips to twist themselves into a smile, and looked at the heart in his hands. It looked just like all the others he'd stolen. He took pleasure in slicing them from their bodies. As a child, he had sold cat skins to the traders in Whitechapel: he'd used just the same knife as he used now. His client would be pleased. All his clients were pleased with his work.

He'd already got hold of several hearts. The girl was his latest victim. Mr Drood knew that his client wouldn't be satisfied with any old heart. Even just selecting the right heart took patience. Hence the raggedy man. It had to be a healthy heart, one that wasn't unhappy. The dead quickly sense when living hearts are happy. Presumably because they are dead and long for a warm, beating heart.

This dead man had done Mr Drood's bidding. They had found the heart; Mr Drood had drawn the blade, had made a long incision, and had taken it out. It was quite straightforward, and the more often one did it, the easier it became.

Heaven's heart was no exception.

But then something happened that didn't normally happen. Something that couldn't, in fact, happen.

The young woman, who had seconds ago been lying there motionless and dying (yes, dying: Mr Drood was quite sure of it); that young woman with the odd name of Heaven and the even odder habit of clambering up onto strange roofs to look at the stars; his victim – who was no different from any of his other victims – suddenly jumped up and began to run away.

Mr Drood stood stock still. This was a completely new experience. Nobody ran off when they had had their heart cut out.

But Heaven did.

She ran for her life.

Baffled, but quite calm, Mr Drood watched her go. There was no point following her. He had got what he came for.

As for the raggedy man: he could follow a scent, but he was no hunter. He'd been dead for far too long to be able to chase the girl.

Anyway, thought Mr Drood, girls running away after they've lost their hearts isn't normally part of the deal. Just to be sure he wasn't imagining things, he looked again at the heart in his hands. Then he shook his head and put it into the big leather pouch that he'd had specially made for the purpose by a furrier in Soho.

The raggedy man emitted a noise that sounded like a dry cough.

'We've got what we need,' said Mr Drood.

The raggedy man, whose clothes had dry earth clinging to them, made no reply. They both watched the girl as she ran off into the distance, and as her silhouette vanished in the darkness they set off on their own way. For the night was still young – and Mr Drood and the raggedy man had not yet entirely carried out the task that had brought them to Kensington.